GHOST BULLY

Brian Corley

ISBN (e-book edition): 978-0-692-04842-9
ISBN (Paperback edition): 978-0-692-04841-2

Library of Congress Control Number 2017918555

All of the characters in this book are fictitious. Any similarity to real persons, living or dead, is coincidental and not intended by the author.

Cover images from istockphoto.com
Cover and Interior design by Jessica Reed

Printed and bound in the USA
First printing 2018

Independently published by Brian Corley
PO Box 42203
Austin, TX 78704

www.brian-corley.com

Chapter 1

The sun was shining, the birds were chirping, and the spring flowers were blooming in the yard.

Hold on … those are weeds.

The weeds were blooming in the front yard of my first house, but the pink and purple blooms felt more like a warm greeting than an invasive species.

It was easy for me to see past the tangle of lawn and year of neglect. My new home, an older bungalow on the south side of Austin, had potential. Built on a budget and maintained through good intentions, it had two bedrooms, two bathrooms, and all the air-conditioning I could handle. The red front door and mossy-green exterior seemed to smile to me from the street. "Welcome home, I've been waiting for you," it would say if it could.

"Hello," a voice rang out. I turned to locate its source (it wasn't the house) and saw a solid woman, probably in her early sixties, walking toward me with a smile that was just as big as her hair. "I just wanted to say 'hi' and 'welcome to the neighborhood.' I'm Tess Keller, and I live right over here." She pointed to the house next door.

"Jonah Preston," I said, wiping my hand on my pant leg before offering it to shake. "Sorry, hand's a little dirty from the move. Nice to meet you, Ms. Keller."

"Nice to meet you too, Jonah. It does my heart good to see someone back in that house. Such a shame about the young man that lived there before."

"What's that now? What happened to the guy that lived here before?"

Her eyes bugged a little as she gasped, and her face struggled to choose an emotion between empathy and delight. "You mean no one told you? No, that can't be possible. Not even your Realtor?"

"Told me what?"

It appeared as though empathy was losing the battle, but it did its best to hang on. "Now I'm not one to gossip …"

Doubtful.

She leaned in conspiratorially. "And you didn't hear this from me—especially if Ms. Viola asks—but the previous owner died in that house."

I looked at the house again. Suddenly, "Welcome home, I've been waiting for you" took on a more sinister tone, and I imagined the tops of the windows bowing like angry eyebrows. I shook it off; it was just a house.

"Well, I suppose there are better things I could hear on moving day, but there are certainly worse. At least he wasn't some broken soul that decided to end it all by his own hand."

Her face dropped, and she turned to gaze at an old pecan tree standing between our houses. It was probably easier to look at than I was at the moment.

"OK, like I said, I just wanted to come over to say 'hi.' Nice to meet you, Jonah."

"Nice to meet you, Ms. Keller."

"Jeez, kid, ever hear of Google?" she mumbled to herself as she walked away.

I pulled my phone out and walked up the crumbling flag-stone walkway as I retreated inside. It was time to have a chat with my Realtor.

"This is Allison," she said.

"Hi, Allison, it's Jonah."

"Hey, Jonah. How much are you *loving* the place?"

"I'd say a little less than I did an hour ago."

"Oh no, what happened?"

"I just met one of my new neighbors, and she said the guy that lived here before me died ... in the house."

There was a palpable silence at the other end of the line.

"Hello?"

"Yeah, sorry Jonah, I'm here."

"Did you know about this?"

"Uh ... yes."

"Don't you think that's something you should have told me before now?"

"Technically the seller doesn't have to disclose suicides in the state of Texas."

"Suicide? What? Allison, you're not the seller—"

"You didn't see the stories when you Googled the house?"

"No, I must have missed them," I said, hoping she wouldn't catch on to the fact that I didn't do a simple Internet search on the most important decision I'd made in my entire life.

"Welp," she said, "he hung himself in his bedroom, and no one noticed for days until, eventually, the smell alerted one of the neighbors. She found his suicide note on the front door—which he left unlocked—and she walked in on the grisly scene. His body was all gassy and exploded right around the time she found it."

"That's disgusting," I said.

"Relax, Jonah. You got an amazing deal on a foreclosure property in an incredibly hot market. People forget about this stuff quickly. It probably won't even come up in a couple years."

"Hmm," I said, "you think so?"

"Yeah, sure," she said. "Sorry, have another call coming in, gotta run. Enjoy the house! Bye, Jonah!"

"Bye," I said to an already disconnected line.

I'd wandered into my room during the conversation and had a sudden flash. *Which room was his? Did the house smell bad and I just missed it?* I breathed in deeply through my nose but didn't detect any malodor, just polish from the refinished floors—floor. My room was the only one with a refinished floor. I racked my brain for a way to convince myself that there was another reason for it. *Wait . . . was Ms. Keller the neighbor that discovered him? That poor lady.*

I heard the front door open and walked into the living room. My best friend and roommate, Maxim Alvarez, was back from returning the rented moving truck. He and I met in line while registering for classes on the first day of college and bonded over our love for almost all things '80s, board games, and horror films. We'd been roommates ever since.

Max was built like a fireplug and was a visual offset to my skinny, six-foot frame. He had a doting mother and a hard-ass older sister named Nicole that was a cop here in town. Nic thought Max was underachieving and that I was a bad influence. I'm not sure why—Max was the one who always dragged me out on weeknights.

I filled Max in on the conversation I'd had with our new

neighbor and the Realtor. He looked a little freaked out.

"I'm calling Nic," he said.

"Ugh. Why?" I asked.

"Because she can tell us more stuff."

"I already know enough."

"Come on, don't you want to know? I've never lived in a haunted house before."

He was being sarcastic, but I didn't even like the thought.

"Max, the house isn't haunted."

"You don't know that."

"Nic doesn't either."

"Eh. Still calling her."

Max put his phone on speaker and called his sister, who was on the scene at one of Austin's finest haute hippie boutiques on South Lamar. It was apparent that Nic didn't have much time to talk and didn't appreciate her little brother calling while she was on the job. Max was relentless though, and after some back and forth, he relayed the news of the previous owner's death. That was enough to pique Nic's interest, and she said she'd get back to us with more information.

We were exhausted, and even though we'd planned to go out that night, the move had taken its toll, so we decided to stay in, order a pizza, and watch a movie. We went off to our respective bathrooms to shower up and wash off as much of the day as possible.

I returned to find Max on the couch with a movie cued up and ready to go. He had a strange look of pride on his face as he revealed his laptop screen. Tense chords of music erupted from the speakers as the title Ghost flashed across the screen.

"You think you're funny," I said.

"I know I'm funny," he replied.

"How do you even know about this movie?"

"I watched it once with my family when I was a kid."

"Same. How did the pottery wheel scene go over?"

"Awkward. You should have seen Nic. She was humiliated watching it in front of our parents. She always left the room for stuff like that."

"Yeah, I know the feeling. Hey, did you order the pizza?"

"Sure did. They said it takes longer to deliver this far south."

We watched the movie for a while until the doorbell rang. I jogged to my room to grab my wallet, but couldn't find it. *Strange, I could have sworn I left it on my dresser.*

"Hey man," I said to Max. "I can't find my wallet. Do you mind grabbing this one?"

"Sure. You know, I like to keep mine in my pocket—you should try it some time," Max said and made a show of producing his wallet on his way to answer the door.

Instead of the pizza guy, it was Nic, holding a stylishly rustic, brown-handled paper bag. She was a little taller than Max and lean. Nic lucked out and inherited her mom's genes.

"Hey, Maxim," she said and gave Max a big hug.

"Hey, Nic," I said.

"Hello Jonah," she said like she was talking down to a plate of cold, day-old noodles. "How many friendship bracelets have you two made for each other today?"

"Not as many as we'd like obviously," Max replied. "We need to make a run to the craft store, but they're closed for the night."

"OK," she said with what passed as a smile for her, "I like the house."

Oh my god, a compliment.

"Thanks," I said, "still have a lot to unpack, but I kind of love it. It feels weird to own a house."

"Speaking of weird," Max said, "what did you find out about the dead guy?"

"Not much yet. The guy was a local accountant named Willard Hensch, no sign of foul play. I'll look into it a little further on Monday when I get into work."

"What's in the bag?" Max asked.

"Oh, yeah, some girl in flowy robes and expensive boots overheard our conversation while I was investigating a shoplifter at that store and said I should get this for you as a housewarming present. Sage stick or something," Nic said and handed me the package.

I pulled the gift from the bag—a bundle of dried sage sprigs bound with bright pink and orange twine at both ends. Turning it over in my hands, I knew I'd heard of something like this before, although I wasn't sure why. Probably read about it somewhere on the Internet.

"It's a smudge," Max said.

"Yeah," Nic said, "how do you know?"

"It's supposed to help get rid of ghosts, like a spirit cleanse," Max said.

"You're weird," Nic said.

"I don't know if you knew this," I said, "but Max is giving a lecture on spiritual healing this weekend at the New Age Community Center if you want to go."

"Yeah, yeah, I learned things. Eff me, right? Also, Nic, I found this great spa. Check out my nail beds—they look amazing."

"I hate this conversation," Nic said. "I just wanted to come by and check on you. Have you talked to Mom lately?"

"What counts for lately?" Max asked.

"Max, call her. She's worried about you."

"Why?"

"You know she's superstitious."

"What did you tell her?"

"Same thing I told you."

"God, Nic, stop stirring shit up. You just don't want me living here."

"Well, that's true. You need to get serious about your career, Max. You're settling at that job, and moving in here with Jonah isn't helping. Come on, I had to tell her."

"Hey—" I said.

"No, you didn't," Max shot back. "You didn't have to tell her, Nic."

The doorbell rang, and it was the pizza guy this time. He looked a little uncomfortable—probably heard the yelling from outside. Max paid for it while I searched around the house for my wallet. I looked underneath the couch, the table, and the TV stand. Couldn't find it. Finally, I gave up and made my way to the kitchen before all the pizza was gone. I was sure it would turn up.

"Jamumafuhyawalla?" Max asked, more pizza than words.

"Did I find my wallet?" I guessed. "No."

Max pointed to a spot on the kitchen floor where a breakfast table should be but wasn't because … well, because new house, new job, no money, and no immediate need for a breakfast table for my roommate and me. Anyway, he pointed to my wallet on the floor.

"Of course," I said, "I should have thought of that. I *normally* leave my wallet on the coffee table, my dresser, or on the floor in the kitchen."

"Oh," Nic said through a mouthful of pizza, "so your wallet mysteriously went missing right before it was time to pay for dinner. How convenient."

"Fuck off, Nic. What if it was the ghost of the guy that died here?" Max asked.

She shook her head and punched her little brother in the arm a little harder than he anticipated. We stood and ate in the '50s-inspired kitchen until we finished off the pizza, which didn't take long because Max and I hadn't anticipated sharing it with Nic.

"You want to light that thing up?" Max asked, chewing his last mouthful of crust and nodding his head toward the sage stick I'd left in the living room.

"Sure, why not," I replied.

I rummaged through one of the unpacked boxes in the kitchen until I found a pack of matches. The smell wasn't so bad once we got a good burn going—notes of strange, new, pleasant fragrances mixed with something familiar, but I couldn't quite put my finger on it. I didn't want to be like that one guy in college that thinks everything smells like weed, so I let it go.

We took turns waving the smoking bundle of yard clip-pings around the house, humming the theme to Ghostbusters like Gregorian monks. I say "we." Max and I did; Nic just walked around like she was embarrassed to be there.

"Think that's enough to ward off the evil spirits?" I asked.

"I think someone died in here, so let's stop just short of setting off the smoke alarm," Max replied then stopped in his tracks, appearing to rethink his previous statement. "Actu-ally, let's go until we set off the smoke alarm—better safe than sorry."

He handed me the bundle once we arrived at the entrance to my room. It was cold—at least it was colder than the rest of the house. I wondered if there was something wrong with the A/C and cursed the home inspector under my breath for missing it. I was sure whatever the fix, it was going to be expensive.

The smoke billowed thick as I stood still. I felt weird … a little light-headed. It was getting dark, so I turned on the light to get a better look at my room. I don't know if it was the fog of the smudge or my eyes playing tricks on me as they adjusted to the light, but I could have sworn I saw the outline of someone in front of me.

Chapter 2

A floating humanlike form with just the slightest hint of a face and a look of surprise that probably matched my own expression stood before us in the smoky room. I jumped, and the shape darted away from me.

Boom, crack!

I looked over to my window and saw a spider web of split glass.

We all stood there in place, dumbfounded, as time seemed to move slower than usual. I blinked as though in slow motion while I processed what I just saw.

"Jumping Jesus Christ!" Max said.

Time sped back up.

"What the hell was that?!" Nic asked.

"What was what, that noise?" I asked, trying to play it off. I wasn't convincing.

"Come on, Max," Nic said, grabbing Max by the shoulder and pulling him away and toward the front door. "You're sleeping at my house tonight. We'll move the rest of your stuff tomorrow."

This can't be happening. Today is supposed to be one of the greatest days of my life.

"Get off me! What are you doing?" Max said.

"Max," Nic said, "you're not staying here. Did you see that thing?"

"Pull yourself together, Humpty. I spiked the smudge with a little something extra before we started. Jeez, aren't you a cop?"

Nic released Max and gave him a shove. "Dumbass, I thought I smelled something off. Still, that doesn't explain the broken window."

"Maybe it was a bird … or kids," Max said.

"I'll check it out … either of you have a flashlight?"

We searched a couple of boxes without any luck before she went to grab her police-issued version out of her car. She did a thorough sweep of the back yard, but didn't turn up anything incriminating. Max and I weren't much help and spent most of the time making jokes and trading landscaping ideas.

She finally gave up, checked her phone, and jumped into action. "I gotta go. They need me downtown. You guys have any eye drops?"

Max shook his head. "No, but good luck."

"Dammit, OK, I'll stop and get some on the way. They better not smell this on me, Max. Idiot."

"Love you."

Nic hurried out the door and took the tension in the room with her. Thank god the vision we saw was chemically induced. Max laughed to himself as he absentmindedly picked up around the house.

"You guys have any eye drops? I'm Nic. I'm an investigator.' My sister is a cop and doesn't know what weed smells like."

"What kind of weed did you put in there, and how did you

do it without either of us noticing?" I asked.

"This new stuff called Monster's Ink. The guy said it was a heady high, but Christ on a bike, that shit is strong."

"Yeah, but seriously, how did you get it in the smudge?"

"I have my ways."

"Fine, you're smooth. Got any more?"

He did. It was really good stuff. We unpacked a couple more boxes and turned in early; it had been a long day.

If what I'd read in books and seen in movies had anything to say about it, that Saturday was a sign of bad things to come. Of course, if books and movies had more say in my life, I'd probably come home to my sexy vampire girlfriend every night instead of Max.

We ended up regretting unpacking while high, and had a hell of a time finding anything from the night before, but other than that, we didn't really see or hear anything unusual for the rest of the weekend. I spent most of Sunday whipping the yard into shape, and we somehow convinced the cable company to come by and activate the line. Monday morning came around like an old friend for once, but it was still hard to get up and face the day.

"What time did you get to sleep last night?" Max asked, pouring me some coffee as we leaned against the cabinets in the kitchen.

"I don't know. I nodded off pretty quickly after I got into bed. Why?" I said, half-growling, taking the mug from Max and downing my first sip of the day.

I tried to let the caffeine do its work to lift my mood. I was not a morning person, but my job and work ethic required me to be an early riser.

"Thought I heard you moving stuff around until pretty late," Max said.

"Huh, I thought that was you," I said.

"Maybe it was one of the neighbors, and just sounded like it was in our house."

"Maybe," I said, "and maybe it was the restless spirit of a broken man inside the house." The joke was enough to get an early morning laugh out of my roommate. "We need more information. I'll put that on the to-do list."

I wandered over to the far side of the kitchen, rummaged through an open box, and produced a small white board, complete with dry-erase pen, that we had stuck to our refrigerator all through college. I slapped it on our new fridge.

"Why do you still have that?" Max asked, pouring himself what was likely his third cup of coffee for the morning.

"For times such as these," I said, making two squares on the board with the aforementioned pen. I wrote CREATE CHECKLIST next to the first square and then checked it as completed. Slightly below that: INVESTIGATE.

I went back to my room to grab my stuff for work. Even though it was still dark, it was time to start the day. I searched for my keys, but couldn't find them where I normally left them on the bedside table. *Damn you Monster's Ink.*

"Hey, have you seen my keys?" I yelled.

"What?" Max yelled back.

"My keys, I can't find my keys."

"Have you checked the middle of the kitchen floor? I know how you like to leave things there."

"Thanks, I'll give it a look," I replied sarcastically, but I did actually check the kitchen.

Sure enough, there they were, in the exact same spot where I found my wallet. It was plausible that I somehow dropped them earlier and didn't notice, but for some reason, it still struck me as strange.

"Max, are you fucking with me?"

"What?"

"Nothing."

He would have already been in the kitchen laughing if he did it. I chalked it up to his strong weed and my bad decisions, gripped the keys, and hurried out the door for work.

I pulled up to the office in my eight-year-old green F-150, grabbed my work badge from the console, and put it on while walking up to the front door.

The office was a converted warehouse among a park of similar beige warehouses. I worked as an analyst for a medium-sized, esoteric testing lab on the southeast side of town. It was more of a job than a career, but a job paid the mortgage for now. I could always find my calling later.

Austin was the corporate home where decisions were made, meetings were held, and bills were processed. I walked with purpose to the break room to fill my mug with some palatable free coffee, then on through a maze of dividers to my desk within what could be described as a cube farm. One could easily get lost in such a labyrinth, but after a couple months on the job, I knew enough to get to my cube from the

19

break room.

Arriving at my desk, I set my coffee down and started my morning routine. My little area was spartan, just a Travis Lou-ie print on the wall to my right, a D20 die for critical decisions left to fate, and an infinity top that I liked to spin during conference calls.

I had two managers who sat next to each other in an office with actual walls and a door. It was almost soundproof, but faint bits of crying still leaked out of the occasional perfor-mance review. I've heard it said that no one can serve two mas-ters, but I guess our executive staff decided to give it a try.

As an analyst, my day started off by booting up the com-puter and engaging in small talk with my neighbors while consuming as much caffeine as possible. After that, I'd look at spreadsheets and bend data to my will for the rest of the day with a break for lunch and a couple trips to the break room here and there. I was good at my job, and productivity was up significantly for the entire team since I started.

I was staring at my screen, distracted by everything that went down over the weekend, when Hank leaned against the entrance to my cube. Hank was the type of guy whose clothes looked like they were pulled from the hamper right before work, having passed a "clean enough" sniff test. He was funny though, and had worked at the company for years.

"How's the new house?" he asked.

"Yeah Jonah, how's the house?" Debra asked as she walked over to join Hank. Debra was a sweet lady in her forties who let me know she was a Wiccan and natural gardener within about thirty seconds of meeting her. She always dressed well but made a point of buying her clothes secondhand as a strike against consumerism while doing her part to reduce waste and save the environment.

I filled Hank and Debra in on the weekend and thought it would be fun to start with the mundane and build to the spectacular ghost sighting and cracking of glass.

Hank looked entertained, but Debra seemed concerned.

"Wait," Hank said, "how could you not know someone died in the house. Wouldn't it come up in any type of query? You Googled it, right?"

"Yeah, I just didn't find anything on it," I lied.

Hank grabbed his phone, unlocked it, and pulled up a search. Jeez, Hank, let it go.

Debra fidgeted with her fingernails and, after a few false starts, said, "I'm afraid you may have stirred up the spirit rather than moving him on this weekend. What kind of ceremony did you use?"

Ceremony? No one said anything about a ceremony.

"Uh, we used this technique we found online," I lied again.

"Oh good," she said, "most people just half-ass it and wave around the smoking bundle like idiots. You have to clean *and* bless. Never can be too careful."

"Oh my god, look at this," Hank said and motioned us over to share his handheld screen.

It was outtake video of a local news team interviewing Ms. Keller shortly after the discovery of the body. *So it was her.* I thought back to Allison's description of the scene—the smell, the state of the corpse. You could tell Ms. Keller was excited to be on TV; however, after a few moments of recounting the details, the focus changed to a cop rushing out from inside the house and retching into the flower bed. One of his compatriots calmly walked over to console him only to have his shoes covered in another volley of sick. That officer's face turned a shade of green right before he shared his breakfast with the world.

A crime-scene investigator emerged from the house and casually pulled a protein bar from her jacket to snack on while she observed the incident unfolding in front of her.

"Ew, right on his shoes," Hank said as he slid the toggle back and replayed the moment. "Look, look! Right there, you can see when he realizes what's about to happen, but he can't move in time. How did you not see this, Jonah? It's like the top twenty hits for the search. Look how many news outlets picked it up."

"Did you notice the one lady eating?" I said and laughed, trying to shift the focus away from my poor research instincts.

Our bosses appeared from behind their closed office door. "Alright, you three, we're not paying you to joke around and look at each other's phones. Get back to work."

The door shut as quickly as it opened. Hank turned on his heel and marched back to his desk.

"Congratulations on the house, Jonah," Debra said. "Things will probably settle down, but let me know if they don't. Seriously, I mean it."

She pulled her hair behind her ear as she walked back to her desk.

"OK, will do … thanks," I replied.

I spun back around and stared blankly at my screen for a while until the ping of a new message came across a few minutes later. I clicked on my inbox; it was from Max. The title read FW: WILLARD HENSCH. Nic was able to dig up a few things on our guy and sent them along to her brother. She included a few links, the first of which was to the interview we saw. The second was to the obituary from the Austin paper, which provided some details from Willard's life.

Another link pulled up a search related to social media posts: one of him complaining about kids on his lawn, another about how loud the cars were a few streets away, and a few other posts about loud kids again. Apparently, the guy liked himself some quiet, and not much else.

Nicole summarized everything she found in a brief commentary: only child, survived by his parents, lived alone, and was an accountant. He lost his job, couldn't keep up with the payments on his house, and decided to end it all. Sad stuff.

The last link was from an image search and pulled up a cache of pictures that perfectly matched my mind's eye of someone who would go by the name Willard.

I know that's not exactly fair. People can't help what they're named, and you should never judge a book by its cover—but this time the mental shortcut applied. Willard was in his late twenties or early thirties. Narrow-faced, slight of frame, and looked to be someone who maintained a well-regulated army of cats. Thankfully for Max and me, the last part wasn't true as we were both allergic. One picture featured Willard sitting in an antique chair at an angle, but looking straight into the camera, perfect posture, hair cemented in place with a healthy dose of gel. A feebly regal look of a fragile but proud young man looking to present his best side to the world. A motivational poster hung behind him emblazoned with an Einstein quote: "I have no special talent, I am only passionately curious."

I turned my focus back to work, pulling up a spreadsheet and downloading raw data from the night before. I didn't entirely hate this type of work, but it wasn't all that interesting. I summoned my inner statistician Conan and went to battle with numbers, popping in my earbuds and focusing on the screen before me. An '80s greatest hits channel motivated my spreadsheet manipulation.

It wasn't too long before I received another notification from Max. I pulled up his email to reveal a Photoshopped picture of Willard. Instead of sitting in an antique chair, he was sitting on top of a pyramid of wallets and keys, and the motivational poster now said, "IF YOU'RE CURIOUS ABOUT WHERE YOUR WALLET AND KEYS ARE, I HAS THEM. IS MY TALENT. MY PASSION. MY PRECIOUS."

I breathed out a quiet laugh and replied to Max's note: "Good one, but why does Edgar Allan Poe talk like Gollum as an Internet cat?"

The rest of the day passed slower than most, and I couldn't stay focused with all the things going on at home. I left the office that evening with some of the excitement of new home ownership still intact, but now the dread of something a little more sinister had woven its way through.

The weird thing was, I kind of resented the ghost for ruining what should be a great experience for me, and an indignation began to replace the fear.

Chapter 3

My truck's headlights swung around the side of the house as I pulled into the driveway; it was getting dark. As I shut the truck's door, I heard Ms. Keller's voice from behind our shared, overgrown hedge. I made a mental note to clean it up with some garden shears next weekend and tried to locate where she was.

"Hello, I'm over here," she said as she waved through the hedge and walked over to my yard.

"Hi," I said.

"I don't want to bother y'all while you're settling in, but I felt bad about delivering such dour news and ruining your big day. That was so careless. I shouldn't have been so tacky. Anyway, I baked you this blackberry cobbler. Hope you like it."

"Wow," I said, "thank you so much. You didn't have to go to all that trouble, and honestly, I'm glad you told me. Always better to know, I think."

"Oh, don't mention it. It's just what we do in this neighborhood. Y'all enjoy that cobbler now, and I'll talk to you later."

I waved to Ms. Keller and made my way toward the house

as I balanced the dish and fumbled for the keys. Unlocking the front door, I opened it to a living room shrouded in darkness. My smile waned as I used my free hand to search for a light switch. Maybe it was the situation, maybe it was years of scary movies and horror fiction, but I was a little creeped out.

No luck finding the switch, so I eased inside and made another mental note to unpack the voice-enabled lighting system. Although it was dark, I could still make out some large shapes I assumed to be furniture.

Furniture or monsters? Furniture.

I knew there was another switch by the kitchen. I just needed to find it. From the back of the house, I heard a creak.

Is it getting darker? Feels darker.

I paused, listening. Nothing.

I moved ahead slowly, protecting the cobbler, and deftly navigated my way around the couch and a few random boxes.

Another creak. I stopped and listened, quiet. I could make out a few outlines in the dark, but nothing out of the ordinary, and thankfully, nothing moving toward me.

Probably just the house settling.

My heart was bouncing around inside my chest.

How long am I going to be creeped out by my own house?

As I moved again, I heard the echo of footsteps from one of the bedrooms—no, not an echo …

"Max?" I called out.

I stood stone-still, looking into the inky black of the hall-way leading to the bedrooms.

"Max!"

I tried to control the seemingly irrational fear that some-one was in the house with me. If someone was, I might as well will it to be my best friend, right?

No response.

"Hello? Is someone here?"

Good night, did I really just say that? Do I want to find myself in a horror film?

Silence.

As swiftly and quietly as I could, I moved to where I thought the light switch would be, feeling for obstacles and balancing the precious baked cargo as I looked for something coming through the gloom. I made it to the wall, reached for the switch, and flipped it on to reveal an empty kitchen and living room still littered with unpacked boxes.

I set the cobbler down on the kitchen counter and worked through a breathing exercise. Thank god for the thirty-second meditation app. Freaking out wasn't going to help. Once I had my breath back under control, I turned and started to explore the house. Switching on a lamp as I moved through the den, I walked carefully until I stood in front of the door to my room.

It was slightly ajar.

My hand lightly touched the door and thrust it forward. The air in the room was tense, cold. It felt as though a set of eyes were peering out at me, breath held … waiting in the darkness. Hoping to exploit any wrong move.

I fumbled my hand over the wall until I found the light switch. A flick and the light burst forth to reveal a neatly made bed. The closet was wide open.

Nothing there.

Suddenly, I heard a noise from the front of the house and turned on my heel to face it.

Fear hardened to a kernel of courage, and I bolted to the living room to discover a shadow standing in the door.

Electric needles coursed through my veins and electricity

tingled and forked its way across my skin as a voice cracked the silence.

What are you doing here?

I steeled myself. My adrenaline spiked as my fight-or-flight response kicked in. I had nowhere to run, so I would have to stand my ground and confront the nameless enemy at my door.

"Since when do you beat me home from work?"

Thank god, it's just Max.

Funny how people adjust to situations. One moment, I was prepared to take on a faceless intruder, perhaps an evil phantasm, hell-bent on taking my life and stealing the essence of my immortal spirit. The next—dessert.

"Hey man, free cobbler." I pointed in the direction of the kitchen, relieved my soul was safe for another night, then thumbed the direction of the house next door. "Our neighbor, Ms. Keller, brought it over."

"Outstanding, I'm starving!" Max replied, walking to the kitchen at a pace just short of a jog. Sorting through drawers with one hand while undoing plastic wrap with the other, he settled on the most ridiculous implement available to cut into the pie-crusted blackberry treat. Pie crust, not bread. The best way to make cobbler.

"Maybe we should eat a sandwich first. Wait—are you seriously going to use an eight-inch butcher knife to cut a piece of cobbler?" I asked.

"I'm a grown man, Jonah. I'll do what I want. If I see cobbler, I eat cobbler. There is fruit," he said, opening the freezer door. "There is dairy." He snagged a half-pint of vanilla-bean ice cream. "And there is sugar. The three major food groups. Plus, I worked out today, so it all comes out even."

Max set the ice cream down on the counter with the knife on top of it and started rummaging through drawers for a spoon. I could tell he was looking for one due to his efficient and direct way of communicating: "Spoon! Spoon! Spoon!"

Opening the drawer nearest me, I grabbed a spoon and tossed it over while taking one for myself as well. Max handed me the knife as I grabbed a plate and slice of my own and put it in the microwave.

"You think of everything," Max said, apparently envious of my foresight to warm up the cobbler before putting ice cream on top of it.

"If the Scouts taught me one thing, it's to be prepared."

"You were in the Scouts?"

"Nope. How was your day?"

"It was great. Answered a bunch of emails, filed some files, and Photoshopped the ghost of this house atop Mount Wallet&Keys."

Max was a paralegal at a local law firm. He scored high on the LSAT but didn't make it into the Austin Law School, an enormous state-sponsored institution known for litigation (both in protection of its naming rights as well as its training of attorneys).

Plan B was to move to Austin, land a job at his current place of employment, make a connection with one of the partners who could put in a good word for him, and generally have fun with little to no responsibilities in the interim. He successfully accomplished three of the four, and was working to complete the set.

"Will you pass along my thanks to Nic for digging up that information for us?" I asked.

"You bet, if only to give her the opportunity to say something passive-aggressive about you. She destroys you when you're not around. How was yours? What did your bosses take credit for today?"

"She wrecks me when I'm there to hear it—I can only imagine what she says when I'm not. Eh, my day was fine, they were fine," I replied.

"Don't get me wrong—I think it's cool that you stand idly by while they grab hold of any innovation you create as their own. I just don't understand why you don't stand up for yourself like you used to."

"Well, they're my bosses, not some random guy mouthing off in a dorm. I count on them for, you know, money."

Max gave me a sarcastic "OK" signal as he scarfed down ice cream and cobbler.

"You think the house is haunted?" I asked.

It was a horrible transition.

"No, I think the house is great. The landlord is a little strange, but aside from that, it's fine. I don't believe in ghosts, and neither do you," he replied as he dumped his plate and spoon into the sink. "Now, let's go save the world."

Max rubbed his hands together, wiping off crumbs, and set off toward the living room to fire up the Xbox. I've known Max for a while and could tell he wanted to cheer me up, but he was wrong about one thing. I did believe in ghosts, and we lived with one. Well. We lived; the ghost was dead.

"Willard's a weird name," Max said, staring straight ahead at the TV.

"Your mom had a dog named Max growing up. You're named after a dog. You want to throw stones in a glass house?" I replied.

"Glass? I thought it was wood siding. Think it's still too

late for a refund?"

"Probably, but I'll—"

The click and thud of a door closing interrupted me. Max heard it too. Our heads turned to the source of the noise.

My room.

The sound of our characters dying from the first-person-shooter played on in the background. Both sides of the screen came up, asking if we wanted to respawn.

We sat silently as the game's soundtrack softly played in the background. *Why did it have to sound so eerie?*

A smirk grew on Max's face, as though he were about to break the tension, when we heard a clanging from the kitchen.

We looked at each other and rose off the couch as though we had years of military training. I even walked in a crouch.

Am I really doing this?

Moving noiselessly, I crossed the floor to the kitchen, taking a wide berth around the coffee table separating the space between it and the living room.

There, on the floor, was the eight-inch butcher's knife Max used to cut the cobbler. The pulpy filling of the blackberry cobbler made it look as though it was streaked with bloody gore, and it was standing handle-end up, the point of the blade stuck in the black-and-white checkerboard laminate tile.

"Probably just the foundation settling," Max offered. "Door shut, I had the knife on the counter … yeah, probably the foundation."

It didn't feel like the foundation. It felt like … well, it felt like the heebie-jeebies. It was quiet in the house now. Too quiet. Something was off, literally, because I should have at least heard the fan from the Xbox just five feet away. I walked back into the darker living room to find both the TV and the game system powered down.

"Did you turn that off?" I asked.

"No, maybe it's a power outage?" Max replied.

"The lights are on in the kitchen, and the lamp is on in my room."

"Maybe it's a breaker. Go check the circuit box."

"You go check the circuit box."

"Fine, we'll go together."

The quickest way to the breaker box was through the front door and the most direct route to the front door was across the living room. My skin prickled as I made my way between the couch and TV. Both the Xbox and TV came alive as I passed.

Max and I looked at each other, wide-eyed and slack-jawed.

"Oh goddammit, this house is haunted," Max said.

Chapter 4

Generally, I was a pragmatic guy. When faced with significant problems, I had a tendency to plan rather than freak out, and I definitely had a big problem: who would buy a haunted house when I was ready to sell?

Also, the immediate supernatural danger.

There was no way to deny it any longer, my normal life had taken a bit of a left turn. I walked into the kitchen, erased the word INVESTIGATE and scrawled PARANORMAL IN-VESTIGATION on the to-do list. I started toward the door and used my best nonverbal communication to indicate Max should follow me out. We hopped into my truck and slowly backed out of the driveway, then drove off down the darkened, tree-lined street.

"Shoulda packed a bag," Max said, his tone flat as he stared out the passenger-side window.

"Huh?" I responded, eloquent as always. "Oh no, we're going back. We just need to go to the store."

"Look, I get you want a balanced meal, but I don't think the cobbler threw us into hallucinations—or did it? What did that lady feed us?" he said, staring straight ahead.

I breathed out a small laugh. "Wasn't the cobbler, and we're going to pick up a Ouija board."

I'd known about Ouija boards for most of my life, from seeing them in movies to the stories we probably all heard about where someone we went to school with in junior high played with one at a sleepover, then suffered uncontrolled nosebleeds. Come to think of it, seemed like a lot of people had that friend. Maybe the story wasn't true after all.

The Ouija board, or some variation of it, has been used for hundreds of years in one form or another to talk to the spirits of the departed, but Hasbro has "Ouija" trademarked. *Take that mystics!* Luckily for us, they also sell them at huge, big-box retailers, which was where we were headed.

"A Ouija board, are you serious?" Max asked.

"Yes, I want to talk to this guy. Maybe we can help him move on … or move out. We don't need a roommate that won't contribute financially," I said.

"True, and with that guy's credit history—come on, how do we know it's even him? What if it's something else? I can't believe we're talking like this! Who has ghosts, and if so, who doesn't move immediately?!"

"I can answer that: us, and us. Dude, I just signed the next thirty years of my life away. Or at least the next two years if the market is still hot so I can use the homeowner's exemption to forego capital-gains taxes."

I said that. This is who I had become.

We merged onto the Ben White loop, or highway—whatever Ben White was in Austin—and drove in silence until we exited and pulled into the parking lot at the big-box store.

Some say the mark of true friendship is being able to abide comfortably in silence, so it's safe to say that based on those last fifteen minutes, Max and I were the best of friends.

We exited the truck on a mission, our faces set in action-movie mode. We walked into the store as though we were in slow motion, a camera in front of us documenting our every move as we geared up for battle.

"Maybe we should get some candles," Max whisper-growled as though Clint Eastwood was offering interior decorating advice for a séance.

"Unscented," I said in my best Vin Diesel.

We acknowledged each other with a slow-motion nod.

Tarantino-style music kicked off inside my head as we parted ways, Max to home décor, me to the toy section. Candyland, Battleship, Trivial Pursuit, Clue … I scanned the shelves for my portal to another world. Chutes and Ladders, Connect Four—pointing to help my eyes account for the games and check them off until—bingo.

Well, not bingo, that was over to the right next to Barrel of Monkeys. "Bingo" in that I found the Ouija board. Twenty bucks—reasonable.

The music in my head kicked back in as I pulled a box from the shelf and made my way back into the depths of the store, searching for my best friend. I found him, brow furrowed in consternation. He had gone back for a cart that was now filled with various sizes and shapes of candles, air fresheners, and Nag Champa incense.

"Oh my god, what have you done? Look at all this stuff," I said.

"Couldn't find any unscented candles and now I can't decide between lavender and vanilla. I just want to make sure we have options. What do you think of melon?"

He closed his eyes and sniffed the fragrance from a

five-dollar candle housed in a small bucket.

"I think edit down. The incense is a nice touch—grab that and the vanilla candles. Lavender makes me sleepy."

"You got it."

He put the incense in his back pocket and scooped up the vanilla-scented candles in his arms, leaving a cart full of various candles behind. It was kind of a dick move—someone was going to have to put those back—but now was not the time for store-etiquette lessons. Now was the time to check out ... and then communicate with an otherworldly spirit.

We exited through the automatic doors in near silence, the clattering of shopping cart wheels around the parking lot almost serving as a mantra for meditation as we headed out to the truck. We each stowed our bags, got in, shut the doors, and looked straight ahead.

We continued this way—focusing in, maybe zoning out—until Max finally broke the silence.

"What are we going to say?"

"Well ... we're going to ask who he is, why he's doing this, and what he thinks of our candle selection," I replied.

"We should have gone for the melon. I know it's a little out of season but it was sixty percent off, and the scent was just a delight."

"Do you want me to turn around?"

"No, I mean we're almost home. It's just such a shame," Max said. "Don't we already know who he is? Also, if you're not sure, why would you just assume the spirit is a he? Not very open-minded of you Jonah. I'm very disappointed."

"You make a good point—two good points. We need to keep an open mind about who or what we're going to encounter."

"Jonah, if I end up possessed by the spawn of Satan, I swear I am going to be so pissed at you. Since it would be your fault anyway, I would appreciate it if you would just let us take over the world. It's the least you could do."

"Of course, Max. I wouldn't dream of standing in the way of your co-world domination. Best of luck to you and your new overlord."

Once home, I pulled all the way into the drive and turned the truck off. Max and I entered the house through the kitchen and started unpacking the bags like it was our job.

I unlocked my phone and did a quick search for ways to set up a Ouija board for optimal results. I kluged together a hodgepodge of ideas that paired well with the materials we had on hand.

We needed a clear space, so we chose the empty breakfast area in the kitchen; plus, since both my wallet and keys turned up there after going missing, it seemed like a great fit. The search pulled up results that said incense both draws and repels spirits, but we'd bought some, so by god, we were going to use it. Hopefully, it was the type that attracted.

Max lit a couple and set them toward the back of the kitchen—just in case. I read that we should arrange our candles in a circle nine feet in diameter. We did our best, using a tape measure and some string, and set the board in the middle.

"Ready?" I asked.

"I guess. Jonah, I don't feel right about this. Whatever happens, I'm going to church on Sunday."

"If we make it until Sunday, muahaha."

Max rolled his eyes. "Let's light these candles and get this show on the road."

With the candles lit, we sat cross-legged on the floor with the board between us. I positioned the planchette (pointer thing, kind of like a plastic cursor icon) at the letter G, and put two fingers gently down on the middle.

The instructions I read suggested an opening greeting to invite the spirits in. I cleared my throat.

"Thanks to everyone for making it out tonight. Just want to let you know we have a great séance planned. Over here, we have my best friend, Max, on the planchette. Thanks, Max."

Max raised his hand and waved to the potential spirits in the room.

"We've gathered some of the best scented candles as well as the finest incense that can be found at America's largest retailer … just for you! I'm Jonah, your host for tonight. Now let's give it up for the supernatural!"

"You watch too much TV," Max mumbled under his breath.

The air chilled, and the planchette moved to "hello." We both jumped, knowing instinctively that neither of us moved it.

"How many spirits are here?" I asked.

The planchette moved to the number one.

"Did you used to live here?"

Planchette moved to "Yes."

"Are you Willard Hensch?"

Planchette moved away and then back to "Yes."

"Willard, I bought this house after you died. If I assure you that I will take care of it, will you move on?"

Planchette moved to "No."

I cringed. *Why was I so direct? Maybe I should have buttered him up first.* As if he was just going to say, "OK, now that you asked—sure."

"You have been trying to communicate with us. Is there something you would like to say?" I continued.

"L-E-A-V-E," the planchette spelled.

"Willard, I sunk all my money into this house—I can't leave. Is there a way we can all live together peacefully?"

The planchette moved quickly to "No."

"Why?"

T-O-O-L-O-U-D

"We could be qui—"

T-R-I-E-D-T-O-K-I-C-K-M-E-O-U-T-W-I-T-H-S-M-U-D-G-E

"Sorry about that, we didn't really think that one through. What can we do to make up fo—"

C-O-N-S-O-L-E-G-A-M-E-R-N-0-0-B-S

"Are you serious?" Max asked.

The planchette moved to "Yes."

"No one even talks like that anymore. Who cares about console versus PC?" Max replied.

I-R-R-E-G-A-R-D-L-E-S-S

"That's not even a word! What is wrong with you?" Max replied, slamming his hand on the floor.

W-H-A-T-S-W-R-O-N-G-W-I-T-H-M-E-W-H-A-T-S-W-R-O-N-G-W-I-T-H-Y-O-U

"OK, OK, stop it," I interjected. "I'm the one whose keys were stolen."

I-J-U-S-T-M-O-V-E-D-T-H-E-M

"Alright, let's focus here. Why don't you move on, Willard? Can you?"

I-L-I-K-E-I-T-H-E-R-E

"We do too. Let's just all agree to live together—you can have Max's room."

"Or the couch—living room, I mean. You can have the living room," Max chimed in.

His eyes went wide.

"Is 'living room' an offensive term to a ghost?" he asked in a whisper.

H-O-U-S-E-I-S-M-I-N-E-Y-O-U-L-E-A-V-E-P-L-
A-C-E-L-O-O-K-S-T-E-R-R-B-L-E-Y-A-R-D-L-O-O-
K-S-B-E-T-T-E-R-T-H-O-U-G-H

"Wow. Both screw you and thank you," I replied. "I worked hard on the yard."

I flashed back to Sunday when I spent the better part of the afternoon mowing, edging, weed-eating, and defining the flower beds with rocks I found around the neighborhood. I spent forever pulling weeds, and frankly, it was nice of someone to notice.

"Ha, you rhymed." Max pointed at me, then looked up into the air to address Willard. "And you misspelled 'terrible.'"

T-H-I-S-I-S-N-T-E-A-S-Y-A-N-D-T-H-E-R-E-I-S-
N-O-P-U-N-C-T-U-A-T-I-O-N

We laughed.

S-T-O-P-L-A-U-G-H-I-N-G-A-N-D-L-E-A-V-E-Y-
O-U-H-A-V-E-T-W-O-W-E-E-K-S-T-O-L-E-A-V-E

"Or what?" Max shot.

"Dude!"

"What?! He's being a dick!"

O-R

D-I-E

Chapter 5

I lost it. "Psshh, I knew you would say that. Typical hackneyed response, you're an awful ghost, and this séance is over."

Max got up, knocking over a candle as he left. He trudged off to his room and slammed the door behind him. I think Willard left too as some of the other candles puffed out, and the room warmed back up again. I blew out the rest of them and picked up around the kitchen before I went to bed.

I slept well that night, which surprised me. Something about a supernatural enemy using a tired horror-movie cliché to try to scare me actually made me feel better coming away from our makeshift séance than I did going in. My indignation from the day before reinforced my confidence. Sure, it would have been better if we'd convinced him to leave, or if nothing had happened and this was all in our imagination, but I now knew what I was dealing with—a hack. I could beat this guy—ghost—whatever. What was even more surprising was that I either forgot to set or slept through my alarm, and I was late for work.

A knock at the door woke me from my peaceful slumber.

"You still asleep?" Max said through the door. "Come look at this."

I looked at my clock. 7:15 a.m. *Dammit.* I shot up and followed Max to his bathroom. The room was still steamy from his shower. He pointed to the mirror.

GET OUT was scrawled in the condensation.

We stood there staring at the preternatural lettering.

"God, this-ghost-sucks!" I said.

"I know, this is so sad. OK, maybe I'm scared a little," Max replied.

"I'm more afraid of what my bosses will do to me if I'm late," I said over my shoulder as I hurried back to my room to throw on some clothes and head to work. Thankfully the unshaven look was in, so that saved me a few minutes. I hustled over to the kitchen as the last stop before I left.

"Dammit," I said under my breath when I found the coffee pot empty. I set its timer the night before so we'd wake up to the alluring aroma of coffee like in commercials.

Willard obviously turned both off. Forget the hackneyed messages; that was below the belt. No one messes with my coffee.

"Oh, you'll get yours, ghosty. You'll get yours," I said.

I grabbed my trusty traveler mug out of the cabinet and rushed out the door. I'd have to settle for the break room's generic bulk coffee at work.

I slowed down as I hit the break room just before eight, and yawned as I walked over to the little coffee station. The room wasn't much to look at: beige walls, cheap floor, and a few tables and chairs. The bulletin board in the corner displayed OSHA materials, announcements for this week's bake sale, and a crappy promo poster for someone's band. Debra sat alone reading, like she did every morning.

"How's the house?" she asked, still looking down at her book.

"Good, good. Bought some candles and incense last night," I said, pouring coffee into my traveler. "Smells nice. Real, real nice."

I took a sip and let the caffeine do its work. *I'm probably not addicted.*

"Sounds great, but you look tired. Forget to shave this morning? How are things with the undead?"

I looked down at the sad-smelling coffee and wondered if I wanted to have this conversation. So many questions and I'd only had one sip.

"Are ghosts undead? I thought that was the purview of vampires and zombies," I said.

"Just trying to make conversation here, Jonah. You obviously knew what I meant."

I pulled a chair out and joined her table. "I don't know how to say things are going, but we had a little séance last night. If I had to sum it up in one word though, probably—bad."

I described the series of events from last night.

"Then we're like, 'irregardless' isn't even a word!" I slammed home the punchline.

Instead of laughing, she just looked horrified. "Why would you do that? Why would you anger the spirit?"

I looked back down at my coffee. She was right. We probably should have thought it through. Maybe all we had to do was continue to ask nicely. Maybe I should take a look at myself, my life. I needed to grow up and be a better person.

"I don't know … he sucks. He was being a dick," I said instead.

It was too early to have a deep, introspective conversation. Besides, it was already done, and there wasn't anything I could do to change it now.

She shook her head. "This is bad, Jonah. This is really bad. You should never anger a spirit like that. It's dangerous. Has he acted out since then? Have you felt his presence? Is he moving things?"

I took another pull of my coffee.

"He has been moving things. And yeah, he wrote a message on the mirror this morning, turned off my alarm … probably … and turned off the auto-coffee maker," I said.

"What a dick," she said, putting down her book. "Listen, you need to find a way to de-escalate this situation. He could really hurt you beyond just depriving you of caffeine. I think I can help you though.

"I can come by tonight and lead another séance. This time, however, we're going to ask him *nicely* to leave or coexist peacefully. I have some friends that have dealt with this kind of thing before, and I think I can manage this. Now what did you use for your little ritual last night?"

I ignored the slight of "my little ritual" because it worked, right? She had a point though—I could have been nicer, and Max definitely could have been a better version of himself. I ran down the short list of materials and looked forward to having some help.

Our two bosses walked in about that time to let us know they weren't paying us to eat donuts and drink coffee.

"We weren't even eating donuts," I whispered to Debra as we walked out.

Chapter 6

I arrived home to find Max on the couch, playing our favorite international soccer game while trash-talking whoever it was he was playing. I'm sure they deserved it.

"My mom is an upstanding woman! How dare you." Max turned around to see me walking in. "Oh hey, how was your day?" He whipped his eyes back to the screen. "Come on, you heard me talking. You're really going to take that shot while I'm not looking?"

"Fine," I replied and walked to my room to dump my bag, then headed to the kitchen. "Bringing over some reinforcements for our roommate issue."

"Uh-huh," I heard from the kitchen. "Yeah, that's right. I'm an adult—yep—well—guess what? I can drive, can you? No, not for yeeeaarrrrrsssss. Uh-huh—yeah? Well, I have a job, unlike your dad, and I just beat you for the third straight time—alright, alright, that was over the line—yep, same time tomorrow—go do your homework, Timmy. Tell your mother I love her."

Max walked in as I threw a vegan burrito into the microwave. I wasn't vegan, but I figured those burritos were as healthy as I could get for microwaved food.

"What do you mean you're bringing reinforcements?" Max asked, opening the refrigerator.

"Friend from work seems to know about these things, said she could help."

Max grabbed a water and twisted the cap off. "Please tell me it's the Wiccan."

"Got it in one. We were probably a little disrespectful last night. Maybe we should apologize."

Max looked at me and took a swig from the plastic bottle. "So you think I should take down the pictures?"

I gave him a look, and he led me back to the living room and pointed. He'd printed out the meme he sent me along with a few others, put them in frames, and onto the walls.

I stared at him.

"What? I didn't have much to do today at work, and they're funny." He looked at me, mouth open. "Don't act like you don't think they're funny."

I did laugh. He'd improved upon his original work.

"Alright, they're funny. I'm just not sure our friend will see things our way. Nice frames though." I went back to the kitchen and started eating my burrito and thought out loud, "Do we have snacks? What's the social protocol for séances?"

"I think beer counts as snacks," Max replied from the living room where he was already back to another game, "or wine, probably wine. She sounds like a classy lady, and we have both."

On cue, there was a knock at the door. Debra had arrived.

"I brought snacks," she said as I opened the door, "some of my special candles, and wine." Debra had two bags in hand and was holding one out for me to take. *Mmm, snacks.*

"See?" Max said, getting up from the couch.

I made introductions as I brought the snacks to the kitchen and put them on a tray (yeah, I had a tray—my mom got me one). By the way—crackers, goat cheese, and an assortment of olives were apparently the snack choices for séances. Max was right. Classy.

I walked back in as Debra repeated my punchline from earlier in the day. "'Irregardless' isn't even a word!" She laughed, looking at me as I walked in.

"I said that," Max replied, looking at me in horror. "That was my thing. I said that."

"Whatever, Max, have some cheese." I set down the tray on our little coffee table, and said, "Debra, Max said the thing."

Debra nodded her head to Max in polite acknowledgment.

"That's right. I'm funny," Max said, dipping a cracker into some cheese.

We went about our snacks and wine while she prepped us on how things would go down. Debra walked us through the materials she brought (apparently ghosts like expensive red currant candles), showed us where to put them, and even picked a playlist of house music mixed with the sounds of nature to run in the background at a low volume.

She explained that we needed to apologize and be respectful. We were still going to use the Ouija board, but Debra would drive this time, so we expected a better outcome.

She went around the house, checking our candle placement while carrying around her own home-grown concoction of incense (she wouldn't divulge her recipe, but it smelled great, and she mentioned something about copal). Finally, around nine thirty or so, she felt like it was sufficiently dark enough for us to begin.

"Spirits are only active at night, so he should be ready by now," she said.

Debra lit the last of the candles and motioned for us to join her on the floor of the kitchen. She set up the board in the middle of a circle of five candles with plenty of room for us to sit inside. We all sat down and placed two fingers on the planchette and waited.

"Close your eyes," she said.

We did.

"We seek the spirit that abides in this house. Spirit, are you with us?"

We heard the sounds of breaking glass from what I guessed to be the picture frames down the hall, then seconds later the room chilled.

"Can we open our eyes now?" Max whispered.

"Um, sure," Debra said.

The planchette moved to "Yes."

"Yes, you're here, or yes we can open our eyes?" Max asked.

Debra shot him a look.

The planchette moved again to spell "B-O-T-H."

"Obviously, we already had our eyes open. How else—"

"Enough, Max. Thank you for joining us, spirit," Debra interrupted. "The living are here this evening to apologize for their behavior, and to ask you to allow them to live here in peace. We brought sweet-smelling offerings as an act of good-will. Do you accept our apology?"

The planchette moved.

I-F-T-H-E-Y-L-E-A-V-E

"Is there a way for everyone to live here together?"

The planchette moved quickly.

No.

"Why?" I asked. "I just signed the mortgage. This is my first house. Why can't we just work this out?"

T-O-O-L-O-U-D

"We can be quiet. I love quiet. I love naps. I get it."

A-L-S-O-D-O-N-T-L-I-K-E-Y-O-U

"Will, can I call you Will?"

The planchette moved even faster this time.

No.

"WILL you leave this house?!" Max interjected, looking supremely pleased with his pun.

I glared at him. "Dammit, Max …"

Debra froze, eyes wide. Her face changed, almost like she was going to sneeze. She seized, then settled.

Debra wasn't Debra now.

"You two. I've had enough." A different voice came out of Debra. A man's voice. An angry voice. Not a scary-angry voice, more like … I would describe it as—pissy. "You're loud. You're rude. You stay up at night spouting one-sided, insulting conversations."

"That's Max," I interjected. "I can get a new roommate, just give me a couple weeks."

Max looked at me and said, "Heyyy."

"No, no new roommates, no roommates at all, that's my whole point. This is my house. I built it, and I will remain here in perfect silence and solitude."

We sat quiet for a bit. The three (four?) of us. All looking at each other.

"You didn't build this house," I said.

"I most certainly did," Not-Debra curtly responded.

"You didn't. This house was built in the fifties. You just bought it."

"Semantics—"

"No, not semantics. I might understand the ghost of a man who put his life into designing and building a house by the sweat of his back for a loved one or family, but you just bought it, man. You need to move on—I am not leaving.

"I just signed a mortgage, so you can either leave, or hang out with me and Max for the next two years until I can make some money on this thing," I said defiantly, but then offered an olive branch. "Max is negotiable. I can find a quieter room-mate."

Max looked at me slack-jawed and whispered, "Diiiiiick."

Not-Debra seemed to mull my offer over for a few seconds before replying.

"No. I don't have much time left in this vessel, so now you hear me! Either leave alive, or stay and … *die!*"

"That's stupid," I replied.

Not-Debra cocked her head to the left. "What?"

"That's stupid. If I die here, I'm a ghost too. I'll just kick your ass for the next thousand years or so from the spirit world."

"No, you won't."

"I will. You don't understand the spirit that lives inside me. I overcome obstacles—however I can. Sometimes through sheer force of will. You quit life.

"I would make an awesome ghost. I've spent a lifetime reading and watching movies. *Poltergeist, Nightmare on Elm Street 3: Dream Warriors, Ghost, Ghostbusters, The Graveyard Book*—I am made for this," I said.

"I assure you, you would do no such thing. I have been a spirit far longer than you—" Not-Debra said.

"A year isn't that long—" I interrupted.

Not-Debra stood and shouted, "YOU HAVE THREE DAYS TO REMOVE YOURSELVES," then crumpled onto the floor as every candle blew out in the room.

Max and I rushed over to check on Debra. She was out of it, but OK.

Max quietly laughed, breathed in, and then loudly laughed as he pointed at me.

"You threatened a ghost!" More laughing, a deep breath, then, "What the hell?" More laughing. "I never really thought about that, but it's a real flaw to the whole death threat. What if you are a badass ghost? Even if you suck at it, you could still be loud and ruin his good time for eternity."

Debra started to come to. I looked at Max, smiling.

"We would be *hell* on him," I said. "I can't imagine being on your bad side for eternity. You show no mercy to random nine-year-old kids from the Internet. I would love to hear you let loose on someone who actually deserves it for—"

"Oh no, I am definitely out," Max said, shaking his head. "Yeah, no way, he just threatened to kill us. I think he's awake when I need sleep. Nope. I'm out. I can sleep on someone's couch for a while, no problem."

"That's good, Max," said Debra, groggily intervening, "and Jonah—Jonah, you should do the same. I've never dealt with anything like this. That was a good line about being a better ghost though. I've never thought of that either. That really could have worked. I may try that myself someday ... but no, you should definitely leave."

"I'm not leaving. This is stupid. He's a dick, but he's not a murderer ... Does it count as murder if he's a ghost and I'm not? Doesn't matter, I have too much tied into this house. Plus, I think I really would kick his ass if I was a ghost. I've seen the Patrick Swayze movie—recently, in fact. Max and I both just watched it. I could work in some ideas from the third movie in the eighties *Nightmare* serie ... you know, where they figure out they're in a dream and can just imagine whatever they want in order to fight off Freddy."

Max looked at me, condescendingly patted me on the shoulder, and helped Debra up.

"OK, Debra, we'll help you back to your car."

I gathered Debra's expensive candles and put them back in her bag as Max walked her out the door and to her car.

"Maybe there is a way to capture him, so he can't do anything," I mused.

"Like in the movie where the professors get kicked out of the university and start their own ghost-removing business?"

Max replied.

"Neither of you are scientists, and that's a movie," Debra chimed in. "You could try a dream catcher …"

Then we all laughed.

"Dream catchers … what are we, a bad tattoo?" Max said.

When we got to her car, I opened the passenger-side door and laid the bag of candles on the floorboard.

"Thanks for your help," Max said, opening her door and helping her into her late-model green Toyota.

"I wasn't very much help at all, unfortunately," she said, looking up at us as she sat in her seat with the door still open. "You really should leave, Jonah. I can't stress that enough. However, if you are bound and determined to stay, these spirits rest when the sun is up. Make your plans then. Bye now, see you at work tomorrow."

"Actually, I may take the next three days off now that my life depends on it. I'll call in sick tomorrow," I replied.

"That makes sense, Jonah. I'll make sure to tell the bosses I saw how ill you were," she said.

"Thanks, Debra—"

"That you had diarrhea and were in terrible condition."

"Diarrhea … Debra, what? Don't—" I tried cutting her off.

"She's right. No one questions diarrhea, Jonah," Max interjected.

She looked at me with a wizened grin. "OK then, I'll tell everyone you have diarrhea."

She shut the door and started the car. Max and I watched her drive away and stood in silence.

"Am I supposed to believe she knows so much about this stuff just because she's Wiccan—"

"Shut up, Max."

"That's just the diarrhea talking, Jonah. Make sure to stay hydrated."

Chapter 7

We walked back inside and discovered that Willard had indeed smashed out the glass from every picture frame holding one of his memes, so we cleaned up the mess and started crafting a plan of attack. Debra warned us about Willard being able to overhear us at night, so we implemented the cunning deception of whispering. We figured we would know if he was close because it got cold when he was near.

Max decided he would stay up as late as he could playing video games and talking as loudly as possible while I went to bed to catch some sleep. I would need some rest over the next few days. Once I shut the door, my room was pretty quiet, so I wasn't sure why Willard said we were too loud. Then I began to wonder if he was in the room with me.

Was it colder than normal?

I turned on my TV and tuned it to a home-improvement channel. Even though I liked most of them, for some reason, I was always able to sleep through their shows. Plus, everyone on those shows was either off-the-charts upbeat or annoying—sometimes both. Either way, I was pretty sure Willard would hate it and leave me alone. We had a deal: three days.

I woke up the next morning inspired and determined—nothing like a death threat to keep you on your toes and focused. Hopping out of bed, I made my way to the kitchen to find the coffee maker off again. He wasn't breaking the deal by doing that, but it was definitely a dick move.

I manually started the coffee maker and poured a bowl of cereal that I took with me to the living room. Then I unlocked my phone and brought up a search page.

OK. Hmm ... now, what to search for?

Psychics seemed like a good place to start, so I took screen shots of the names and contact info for the top results with micro breaks for cereal. Madame Lisette, Jake the Spiritual Life Coach, Mistress Zoe and her team of Psy-kicks (looks like a martial arts mash-up there—I'm into it).

I finished my cereal and dialed the first number. No luck, left a message. They weren't open at a quarter till seven in the morning. Second number: strike two, left a message. Third time was the charm though; on the fifth ring, someone answered out of breath.

"Mistress Zoe," loud breathing, "and her," breathing and a swallow of air, "team of Psy-kicks. How can I help you?"

"Zoe?" I asked.

"No, this is Tammy. Are you looking for Zoe? Are you calling for a reading or a class schedule? If so—"

"I'm calling about a ghost problem."

"What? Say again, please?"

"Ghost, I have a ghost problem. My house is haunted, and I'm looking to do something about it."

Muted laughter on the other end of the line.

"Please, this is serious."

"Fine," Tammy presumably pulled the phone six inches

away from her face, "Zooooee! Zooooee!" I think she covered the receiver with her hand, although not well. "Got a call for the crazy side of your business … says his house is haunted."

I could hear a whispered argument on the other side of the line.

"Hello," a new voice said, "this is Zoe. Sorry about Tammy, she's new. She's my cousin's friend and a great kung fu instructor, but she needs to work on learning the other side of the business—you don't want to hear this—I'm sorry, how can I help?"

"I have a haunting. We've had a few séances, and now the ghost has given me three days to move out, or he'll kill me."

"What's your address?" Zoe asked, down to business. "Exorcisms cost $400 for the first attempt, $300 for each subsequent attempt. Cash only. We can be there at 8:30 p.m."

The word *attempt* didn't exactly instill confidence, but I needed to try something. I gave her my address and more details about the previous séances. The rest of the call remained strictly professional with Zoe asking about the size of the house, my history, and more details about my encounters with Willard so far.

I hoped this worked because I only had $1,900 left in savings and I still wanted to eat if I made it past the next three days.

Exorcism? I thought those were just for demons.

I snapped my fingers and entered a new search. I wasn't Catholic, but if even half the movies I watched were true, I was sure a priest would be willing to help, and probably for free. I hit the shower and changed into my Sunday clothes. I was going to church.

"Hey, keep it down out there. I was up all night." A muted,

whiny yell surfaced from behind Max's closed door just as I was leaving my room.

"You're not going to work today?" I responded, walking over and leaning into the door.

"No, I just called in and said I had diarrhea. Didn't even question it. Kim just said, 'Gross. Stay home,' and hung up."

Huh. Not sure who Kim is, but maybe diarrhea really does work every time.

"Are you going out?" Max asked, still in that annoying, whiny tone.

"Yeah—need anything?" I replied.

"Can you get some waffles?"

"You got it, anything else?"

"Juice."

"OK, bud, anything else?"

"No."

"OK," I said.

"Jonah?"

"Yeah, Max?"

"Can you get the waffles with blueberries?"

"Yeah, Max."

"Thanks, Jonah, you're the best." His voice trailed off, and I assumed he rolled over and went back to sleep.

"OK, buddy," I said.

I pulled into the parking lot of Austin's largest Catholic church, St. Raphael's. I'd met a priest from there before and thought he was cool but rude. That said, I'd take rude over St.

Michelangelo's—they just like to party.

I walked into the nave—which I had to look up as I was a recovering Southern Baptist. We had sanctuaries, classrooms, and basketball courts.

The actual experience of being inside the church was new to me, but I'd seen a lot of movies where people go to these churches, so I walked over to what I recognized as confessionals. I stepped in, closed the door, and waited. Soon, I was joined by a priest.

"Forgive me, Father, for I have sinned," I began.

"How many days since your last confession?" a voice replied from behind a screen. I could pretty much see him. This wasn't like the movies at all.

"All of them, I guess. This is my first time," I replied.

"You're Baptist, aren't you? What did you do?" the voice from behind the screen accused. *Sounds like he had some sort of history. Wonder what that's all about.*

"Nooo. I'm not Baptist," I answered, which was technically true because I hadn't been to church in a while. There were some great morning shows on Sunday, and I liked to party. OK, mainly the morning shows, and I liked to go to an early spin class.

I continued, "I haven't done anything, per se, except buy my first house, which turned out to be haunted, and the ghost threatened to kill me in a couple days."

"OK, get out."

"I thought this was your thing though. Don't Catholics do exorcisms?"

"We do, but demon possessions, not ghosts. Try Jake the Spiritual Life Coach."

"I did."

"You did. Really?"

"Yes, I called Jake but wasn't able to get hold of him. I did reach Mistress Zoe and the Psy-kicks, though, and they're coming over tonight."

"Sounds like you're on your way then. I used to work out with them before they hired a new kung fu instructor."

"Yes! Tammy, she's the worst."

"Awful. Completely unprofessional. Hey, Father Chandler, could you be any slower?"

I laughed, "Could this be any weirder?"

"Get out."

"Sorry, I didn't mean it. It's just kind of fun to say."

"No, I mean, get out. Let's go get some coffee, and you can tell me your story."

I shook Father Chandler's hand as we exited the confessional and followed him for what seemed like half a mile through the church to their own nicely appointed little break room with stained wooden walls and a huge Gothic arch in the ceiling. He poured coffee into a plastic foam cup and offered it to me, then motioned to a station of sugars and creams. I took it black.

He sat down in a comfy, overstuffed leather chair and invited me to sit in an identical chair across from him.

"So, you have a ghost problem," he started, taking a sip of his coffee. "Tell me about it."

I gave him the details about us moving in and the window cracking, making a mental note to fix that if I made it through this whole thing.

"Red currant candles, you say?" he asked rhetorically, musing over his personal mug of coffee. "That's a nice touch. I like those."

"So, can you help?" I asked.

"Yes. First, don't use Ouija boards. You are inviting trouble. You could call a demon, and then you really could use my help. Second: move."

"I can't. I just sunk everything I have into that house."

"No, it's not that you can't; it's that you won't. There's a difference."

"So I should just leave it for someone else? Put them in danger, have them sink their savings, hopes, and dreams?"

Father Chandler looked down at his cup, appearing to contemplate my question.

"You could rent … No, you're right. I understand, Jonah. I just can't help you. Demons get scared when we show up. We're bringing the light of God with our faith, and they hate that. They were cast out of Heaven and can't stand to be reminded of what they're missing out on—it's too much. What you're dealing with is an ex-accountant who sounds like a total asshole."

"You can say that?"

He laughed. "I wish I could be more help, but I tell you what I will do—I'll pray for you."

"Thanks, Father," I said, standing up. "I appreciate you taking the time with me this morning." I shook his hand as I made my way out.

"Anytime, Jonah, you'll be in my prayers."

I noticed a bank of candles outside the chapel on my way out, so I stopped and lit one before I left. The faint smell of melon filled the air. Max was right. It was nice.

Tess Keller came through her door, waving, as I pulled into the driveway around noon. I rolled down the window. "Hi, Ms. Keller."

"Hi, Jonah, so glad to see you're feeling better. I understand you weren't feeling well earlier."

I gave her one of those weird, confused smiles, where there's about a millimeter of space between your top and bottom teeth.

"Uh, what?"

She shook her head and waved a hand as she stepped closer to the truck.

"Max told me," she began, dropping her voice to a whisper. "Max told me about the di-uh-ree-uh."

Freaking Max. What the heck? Wow, one trip to church and my language sure did clear up. I noticed Ms. Keller was holding a casserole dish. Please be cobbler, please be cobbler.

"So I made you this peach cobbler," she said.

Yes! My favorite.

"Thank you, Ms. Keller, that is so sweet. We enjoyed the last one so much."

"Max wrote me the most delightful note when he returned the dish. I'm just so glad to have you boys as neighbors."

Max strikes again. Way to show me up, buddy, but that was really nice. He always was one of the most secretly kind people I'd ever met.

"Thanks again, Ms. Keller, I need to get in and take my meds."

I looked down at my stomach and made an awkward face, which happened to be a great move because she handed the cobbler right over. *Seriously, does diarrhea get you out of anything?* I waved goodbye to Ms. Keller and pulled all the way up the drive.

Max was on the floor eating a cheeseburger when I walked through the door in the kitchen. I set his waffles and juice down on the counter and gave him a stern look. He looked back up at me blankly. I looked at him, then at the waffles, then back at him again.

"Sorry, man, I forgot," he said.

"Blueberry waffles—I had to go to three stores."

He sucked in air through his teeth and offered me half his burger. I didn't really go to three stores.

"Oh, and Ms. Keller next door made us another cobbler. It's in the truck."

Max was out the door almost before I could finish my sentence. Hustling back in, he took some plates out of the cabinet, slid over to the freezer and grabbed some ice cream, then moved to open a drawer. And closed it. Opened another drawer, and closed it. So on and so forth around the kitchen. Then again, backward. He looked at me.

"Huh. Where's my big butcher knife?" he asked.

"Max, that's not the knife to use."

"Oh really? Show me a book where it says what knife to use for a cobbler."

I pointed to the top of the fridge where Martha Stewart's visage smiled down at us from the cover of a cookbook my sister gave me as a gift a few Christmases ago.

"It says that in there?" He looked at me skeptically, eyebrows raised.

As I took a bite of burger, Max looked at me sideways, then from another angle, eyes squinting.

"OK, OK. You win this round. So what utensil do I use, Mr. Disciple of Martha?"

"Please," I said, "call me Jonah. Mr. Disciple of Martha is my father."

"Cute."

"Use a spatula. Also, I was bluffing. I have no idea what's in that book. My sister gave it to me and I never read it."

"Still, I need to find that knife. It's Japanese and expensive," Max said.

"I know … it's a great knife," I said, watching Max expertly cut squares of peach cobbler out of the casserole dish. "Oh, look how much better that spatula is working for you—and it's such a fun word to say—*spatula*."

"Spatula," he said.

"Spatula."

"Hey, Jonah, maybe you should think about leaving. I'm staying at Dean's for a couple weeks until I find someplace to land. I'm sure he wouldn't mind you sleeping on his floor."

Dean Calhoun was a friend of ours from college. He dropped out and left for culinary school in Austin, from which he graduated, and he now worked as a cheese monger for a high-end restaurant downtown. Nice guy, someone you could always count on if you needed something.

I never really had anything bad to say about Dean, except, "Dean smells like cheese."

"Well, yeah, that's his job."

"What if you start smelling like cheese, huh? You want to smell like cheese? There goes Max. He just walked behind you. How did you know it was Max? Because he's the only one that smells like cheese at a law firm," I said.

"You're going to get killed by a ghost," Max said. "Those are real words coming out of my mouth. I know I was encouraging you to stand up for yourself earlier, but do you understand how strange this is? Do you remember *Poltergeist*? They left. Not soon enough, but they left, and then their house got sucked into a vortex. Do you want to get sucked into a vortex?"

"Depends."

"Depends on what?"

"Do you know what a vortex is?"

"Jonah, of course I know what a vortex is."

"OK, Max, just explain what a vortex is. Maybe I don't know."

"Screw you, Jonah. I'm just trying to help."

"I know, I know."

I calmed down and took a bite of burger. I chewed it. It was good. This place really got the portion right, and the pickles were amazing.

"Hey, I called some people to help tonight. They're coming over for an exorcism. Is this P. Terry's?" I asked.

P. Terry's was an Austin institution with cool midcentury-modern-designed spots all over town. Great burgers, shakes, and fries.

"Yes. Isn't that for demons?" Max asked and handed me a plateful of cobbler.

I warmed it up in the microwave. "P. Terry's? No, it's for everyone. I don't know. They seem to think it will work, and don't worry about the house, Max. It's not built on a burial site—we're just haunted by the ghost of an asshole."

After finishing off my half of the burger and a truly excellent piece of cobbler, I sat on the couch and scoured the Internet for plausible ways to evict a ghost from your house. Max spent the afternoon putting his things back into boxes and garbage bags for his move over to Dean's.

"Mind if I use your truck to move this stuff?" Max asked,

holding two garbage bags of laundry.

He was just inside the front door with his hand already turning the knob, which meant he was using my truck whether I said "yes" or not. I realized he was wearing a new T-shirt with one of his Willard memes screen-printed across the front.

"Sure," I said. "When did you make that?"

"Oh, a couple days ago. We have a printing office downstairs, so I made a few. People thought they were pretty funny, so I ended up selling them and taking orders for more."

"What? You took orders for more? How many?"

Max looked up at the ceiling. "I don't know … about forty-three."

"About forty-three? Not exactly forty-three?"

"Exactly forty-three."

"You're a legend."

"It doesn't suck to have a printing office downstairs that faces South Congress—people just kept walking in. Guess they recognized my memes."

South Congress is one of the major streets in Austin that starts at the Capital and makes a straight shot south through downtown. It also happens to be one of the few major thoroughfares with heavy pedestrian traffic in Texas. That's not commentary on urban planning; it's just one of those things. It's hot here, and cars have air-conditioning.

Hold on—people recognized the memes? I pulled up my favorite news aggregator app on my phone, and sure enough, Willard memes were trending. I found Max's username in some of the top posts, but the Willard memes had taken on a life of their own.

"So, I'm just going to go," Max said, slowly sliding out

the door.

"You'll need keys. Max, why didn't you tell me about this? It's amazing. Your upvotes are insane."

"I have your spare set. I hung pictures around the house, Jonah. You're looking at them. Besides, you have a lot on your plate. I felt weird saying anything because of everything going on. Willard memes are huge—who would've thought? What's even better is that I set up an online store with shirts and mugs and I have hundreds of orders."

I'll admit, that made me jealous, but Max was my friend. I should have been happy for him. It's not his fault that I was threatened from beyond the grave—hell, he was too. He just had the freedom to leave without suffering the lifelong financial repercussions of walking away from a thirty-year loan.

"That's great, Max. That's really great. I'm happy for you. Since when do you have a spare set of keys?"

"Since I knew I was moving and knew exactly where you kept them. I know all your secrets, Jonah," Max replied, ominously raising his head in a way that allowed him to look down on me. "You're a sick man, Jonah, a sick, sick man."

"Fine, but I'm not helping you move anything, and have it back in one piece tonight—no scratches."

Max slipped out and let the door close behind him, leaving me alone for the first time in a long time. The house felt darker somehow. I noticed every creak or crack, every shift, every scrape of a tree limb. Suddenly my situation felt very real. Sometime soon it was going to come down to just me and Willard. I thought I should take a nap before Mistress Zoe and her team showed up. I was sure Jason Bourne would do the same thing.

Brian Corley

Chapter 8

I've heard it said that we only remember the dreams we're having right before we wake up. Even the long ones occur only seconds before we open our eyes, synapses firing off like crazy as we come to. My synapses must have given it all they had that night.

I found myself encompassed in a brilliant light and what looked like an angel reaching out to me with a message. It was stretching out from my ceiling as I emerged from a deep nap on the couch, awakened by a knock at the door.

Slowly, the light faded from my eyes as darkness took its place. What time was it? I reached for my phone. Eight thirty exactly. Damn, Mistress Zoe was timely. Impressive.

I rolled off the couch and slowly ambled toward the front of the house. I'd gone to an ATM earlier in the day to grab some cash for tonight and had it ready as I opened the door. I turned on the porch light, revealing a small group of people— about a half-dozen or so.

They were in their early to late twenties and led by a short, athletic woman dressed in a white, collared, short-sleeved shirt striped in various oranges, reds, and pinks, wearing either long

shorts or short gray pants with black, lace-up, rubber-soled
boots. I presumed her to be Mistress Zoe . . . or Tank Girl.

"Hi, I'm Zoe. Are you Jonah?" she asked.

Nailed it.

"Yeah, I'm Jonah. Thanks for coming on such short notice,"
I replied.

I offered her a roll of twenties totaling $400 and opened
the door wider to invite the group in. Zoe entered with an
air of authority that gave her a presence larger than a person
standing five foot six should have. She didn't swagger; she just
had an easy self-confidence backed by an unspoken power.

The rest of the team filed in behind her. The Psy-kicks
seemed like a group of kids you'd find in an independent
bookstore after yoga class while recovering from a night out
at one of Austin's dwindling few live-music venues. There was
cool haircut guy, cool haircut girl, tall guy, nondescript girl …
I couldn't remember all their names, so I just decided to tag
them all as Psy-kicks for the time being.

Zoe walked around the house while the rest of us huddled
together in uncomfortable silence, exchanging some awkward
smiles and nods as we waited for her to get back to us. After a
walk-through inspection of the house, she rejoined the group
and turned to face me.

"Your house is a little creepy. Do you always sit in the dark
by yourself?" she asked.

Only then did it dawn on me that the only light we had
came the front porch.

"Sorry, I was taking a nap. Let me get some light going.
Computer: *lights*," I said, glad that I remembered to unpack
and install my voice-enabled lighting system. I'd heard people
complain that those things listened to every word you said. If

so, it was about to hear some crazy shit.

Zoe directed cool haircut guy to retrieve her bag from the van and started giving instructions to her team. Once cool haircut guy was back, she unzipped the oversized military rucksack and started handing out bundles of incense to the group—smaller, slightly acrid-smelling bundles for every room of the house other than the kitchen. There she placed a larger, sandalwood-smelling bunch in the spot where we held our previous séances.

"This is where most of the communication occurred, right?" Zoe asked, making sure she understood my previous rundown. I nodded, and she knelt to light the incense in an ornate ceramic bowl.

She explained, "Some of the bundles we're setting up around the house will act to repel your spirit while the larger one here in the kitchen will attract it. We'll let this burn for a while, then use its ashes to communicate with the spirit, much like you did with the Ouija board."

"Why not just use the Ouija board?" I asked.

Zoe bristled. "I studied under Master Kevin Yang for ten years. Since then, I've borrowed from his techniques and rituals, combining them with some of my own. Our method has all the upside and none of the down of the Ouija board."

I didn't know if ten years was a lot or not or if I should know who Kevin Yang was, but Zoe and her Psy-kicks were here and I'd already paid them.

Walking over to her bag, she continued, "We will attempt to communicate with the spirit and, once again, ask it to leave. However, there will be consequences if he doesn't leave this time."

She pulled an ornate wooden sword out of the bag and

handed it to me. Its "blade" was about four feet long and decorated with detailed carvings. The "blade" wasn't sharp and looked more like an ornate cricket bat than a sword.

Zoe watched as I felt the carvings and turned it over.

"The carvings describe the story of Izanagi no Mikoto. You paying attention?"

I nodded.

"Good. Legend has it that Izanagi no Mikoto's wife, Izanami no Mikoto, was killed in a terrible accident. Many years after her death, he still missed his wife so much that he traveled to Yin Jian—the underworld—to see her. When he came upon her at a distance, she appeared just as she did the day she died. See?"

She pointed a finger at a carving on the sword and moved it along to correspond with the story.

"Upon seeing him, she begged Izanagi no Mikoto not to look at her and made herself invisible. It was dark then, so he lit a single light and looked upon her face. Izanami no Mikoto's face was swollen and festering with eight kinds of thunder-gods resting upon it.

"Izanagi no Mikoto was terrified and fled, but the thunder-gods pursued him. Down the road they went, until Izanagi no Mikoto's strength and stamina began to fade. A large peach tree grew by the side of the road, and in one final desperate act, Izanagi no Mikoto plucked a peach from that tree and hurled it at the thunder-gods, and they fled in terror."

"He threw a peach at them?" I asked.

"Yes, he threw a peach at them. He was desperate. Imagine being in a situation so dire, so hopeless, you threw fruit at someone—much less a god."

"Damn."

"Can I continue?"

"Yes, sorry."

"It's OK. Bewildered by his good fortune, and fearing they might return one day to find him, Izanagi no Mikoto tore a branch from the tree and returned home where he carved a sword from it that told his story and to protect himself and his family from the spirits should they find him where he lived."

The room fell into silent reverence for the story, but I was more than a little skeptical.

"So that's the sword of Izanagi no Mikoto?" I asked.

"Oh no, this is from Fredericksburg," Zoe replied with a little bit of her Texas accent breaking through on burg. "My family always went to the same orchard there to pick peaches every summer, and after hearing the story from Kevin and see-ing him use his own sword in ceremonies, I decided to make one from the largest tree I could find there."

Fredericksburg, Texas, was a small, old German town about an hour and a half outside of Austin known for their peaches.

I turned the blade over in my hands. The carvings were im-pressive, intricate—it was good work.

"You made this?" I asked.

"Oh no, Quinton made this. He's an art student over at Austin U."

Cool haircut guy grinned and shrunk modestly. Guess that's Quinton. Turns out that peaches are good for more than cobbler, and I had to respect Zoe's dedication to locally sourced items.

Zoe gathered her team into a circle around the bowl she placed on the floor in the kitchen and sat cross-legged on the floor. Everyone followed her lead. She pointed for me to sit directly across from her, the fog of incense rising between us. It smelled nice, and I felt at ease as we sat in the circle. She set her sword on her lap, the blade resting on one knee and the pommel on the other. Placing her middle fingers and thumbs together with her hands facing up and resting on each side of the sword, she closed her eyes and bowed her head, so we did as well. After a few minutes, I found myself more relaxed than I'd been in days—maybe ever. So this was meditation? I was into it.

"Willard Hensch, show yourself," Zoe said in a stern but respectful tone.

A few seconds passed, and the temperature of the room lowered significantly. I peeked through my eyelids to see the smoke of the incense stir as though someone had walked through it. My eyes widened as I saw a form through the fog.

"Willard Hensch, you no longer have a claim on this place. It was over once you passed on to the next plane."

She leaned toward the bowl, plucked the incense with one hand, and emptied the ashes from the bowl to the floor. She placed the bowl and incense to the side of the mound of ashes and, with some ceremony, began to spread the mound flat with her hand until a circle of ashes about a foot in diameter was now centered and concentric within our circle.

"Speak to us, Willard. Will you leave peacefully tonight?" she said.

The ashes began to stir as Willard began to write in them.
No.

"Willard Hensch, we are here to ask you to leave this man in peace. Will you leave peacefully tonight?"

The ashes below his first answer stirred again.
No.

"Pinyin!" she cursed. "Three times we will ask, then we will ask no more. Willard Hensch, will you leave here peacefully tonight?"

The ashes stirred, covering up the previous answers. New letters emerged in neat print:

I listened to the story of your sword. I heard everything.

The ashes stirred, covering the script, and new letters formed:

I am not scared of your sword, and I am not afraid of you.

Again, the ashes stirred, covering the previous reply, and new letters emerged:

This is much better than the board. It's nice to be able to use punctuation.

That at least got a smile from most of the group, and I had hope for a moment that we could find common ground.

"Willard, let's just find a way to coexist," I offered. "Max moved out. You can take a room, and I can take a room. I'll be asleep most of the time you're awake anyway."

The ashes stirred, covering his previous replies, and new writing emerged:

Nothing has changed. You will leave, or there will be consequences. I will not warn you again.

The ashes scattered as though someone blew them toward me. Again, I saw his ghostly form in the fog of incense. Zoe jumped into action and took a swing into the smoke with the peach sword. We all heard the thud of meat and the crack of bone as she connected with something.

I looked around wildly. *Did she just hit one of us by mistake?* No one seemed to be reeling in pain. Cool haircut girl was closest to the opening that led from the kitchen to the living room. Her hair blew back as though someone just rushed by her, and the temperature in the room rose back to normal.

Zoe lit off in the direction of the exiting spirit, with the rest of us following behind. She paused in the living room, crouching in a warrior's stance, the sword held firmly in front of her while her eyes scanned the room. We were spectators now, watching as she moved from the living room to my room. From my room to the hallway. From the hallway to Max's old bathroom.

Again, we heard a crack and felt a rush of air a few seconds later with Zoe quickly in pursuit. Back to the kitchen, where she seemed to lose the thread. She scanned the house a few more times, relaxed her guard, and rejoined the group.

"I don't think he's gone, but he certainly wasn't expecting this," she said, grinning and twirling the sword in her right hand. "The incense burned out. I can't get a good look, and it won't do me any good to go around swinging wildly. Lin?"

She looked at cool haircut girl, who I knew to be Lin.

"Lin, do we have any more sticks left at the office?"

Lin shook her head, no.

"We could always go up to the gas station and buy some Nag Champa," I offered.

The group collectively shook their heads no this time.

Zoe replied, "It's not the same. We have a special mix that allows us to establish a connection with the spirit. I'll make some calls, but we may have to wait until morning."

Zoe spent the next hour or so on my couch making calls, while I made some tea and doled out what was left of Ms. Keller's peach cobbler to the group. Zoe shuffled back to the group, who were spread out in various cool leans around the kitchen, with sunken shoulders and hair frazzled from a hundred frustrated finger combs.

"Looks like I'm not going to be able to get anything until around ten tomorrow morning," she said.

I offered her the last of the cobbler and tried out my own version of a fashionable lean against the kitchen sink.

"Jonah, we have a cot back at the office we can set up for you. Take advantage of that, stay with a friend, or get a hotel room. I would not recommend staying here tonight."

Cool haircut Quinton offered, "You can stay on my couch if you'd like."

I thought about it. I thought about calling Max and staying at Dean's cheese-infused apartment—hell, I even thought about reaching out to Nic. My pride got the better of me though. *This is my place. It may not be a dream home, but it's mine.* I decided to take a stand.

"No thanks, Quinton, I'm staying here. This is where I belong."

Zoe stared, twirled the sword in her hand, then offered it to me.

"Fine, suit yourself. Hang on to that tonight. I want it back, but it may come in handy. For the record, I think this is the absolute height of stupidity, but it's your life. I'll give you a shout in the morning, and we'll make plans and try again tomorrow night."

"Sounds good," I replied.

The team gathered their stuff and headed out the door.

"Remember, $300 for tomorrow's attempt. Cash. I have a few ideas and think we can get him out. I'll talk to Kevin tomorrow when I pick up more supplies. Good night."

She shot me a casual two-finger salute as she closed the door behind her, and I found myself alone again.

I was toweling off after a shower when I noticed the room was colder than normal.

Willard is here.

"Pretty gross that you're watching me towel off, perv," I said out loud, hoping to embarrass him into leaving.

The room didn't get any warmer, so I grabbed some clothes out of my dresser and went back into the bathroom to get dressed. *Who knew I was so modest?* I hung my towel up over the shower curtain and started brushing my teeth, scanning the mirror for any new messages from beyond the grave.

None materialized.

Back to my room, I grabbed the peach sword and walked down the hall to check the thermostat. It had already adjusted to seventy degrees for the night, but it seemed much colder. I grabbed an extra blanket out of the linen closet in the hall and padded back to my room.

"Joke's on you, I like sleeping cold," I said.

I laid the blanket down on the bed, pulled back the covers, and tucked myself in with the peach sword at my side. I did feel safer having it around. I turned on the TV and tuned it back to the home-improvement channel. A guy with spiky hair was gesticulating wildly around a room, pleading with a couple to see his vision for the house. Perfect. I hoped Willard hated it.

When I woke up earlier than normal the next morning with a sharp pain in my neck, my right hand shot up to find the source of my discomfort. I pawed, pulled, and removed the source of irritation.

I realized, too late, I was holding on to the handle of Max's missing butcher knife.

A warm pool of blood formed around my head and neck, and I sat up quickly.

Chapter 9

Immediately I felt light-headed and lay back down. I was getting cold, sleepy. The peach sword to my left offered me no help as I gasped for air, getting colder by the second.

Dammit, why did I stay here? Why didn't I book a hotel room? I should have taken Zoe up on her offer, or Quinton, or Max. Why do I always stand up to confrontation? Why couldn't I have just let this place go?

It just cost me my life.

I pulled the knife from my neck but didn't feel pain—probably because of the endorphins kicking in. I knew I was in a dire situation. My mind raced. What can I do? I couldn't think of anything. I was bleeding everywhere and couldn't find my voice. I needed to try something.

I fought to get up, to move.

I had no strength left but continued to struggle.

Acquiescence.

Peace.

Finally, I closed my eyes to rest.

A bright light roused me, and I opened my eyes to a brilliant white light emanating from a door that didn't belong in my room. I instinctively knew that I was supposed to walk through it.

I sat up in bed and faced it.

I thought back on my life, my friends, and my family. I was a good son, a good brother, and a good friend. I made a lot of mistakes, but I felt as though the scale weighing my deeds leaned toward good overall. Time to rest.

The door began to pull on me like it had a magnified gravity of its own. I didn't like being pulled like that and struggled against it.

The pull intensified. The power of the light was overwhelming, and my ears filled with a sound like someone opening the door to a plane at 30,000 feet.

Even through all this, the promise of the door remained: peace, rest, reunion with family and old friends gone too soon.

No.

I'm not ready.

The door pulled, and the light began to overcome me. It was all I could see.

I pushed forward and reached out for something to hold onto, but there was nothing to grab.

I can't go yet, I have unfinished business here.

The pull immediately released.

I shot across the room and slammed into the wall. The light died down, and I began to get my bearings. The new door in my room pulsed with a soothing light as the deafening din calmed to a steady thrum.

I stood up—no, I hovered and looked down on my bed. A horror show. My body was splayed out, a knife in one hand, a ceremonial sword just out of reach of the other.

I looked to my right.

There he was—Willard Hensch, with a smug, satisfied smirk across his narrow face. I instinctively reached for the peach sword on my bed. As I clutched it, Willard's expression changed. Confusion? Terror? *Why is he looking at me like that? If I'm a ghost, how can I hold this sword?* More light—too much light—the room began to fade—no, I began to fade as the sun came up.

As night fell, I rematerialized. The doorway with the bright light was still there; however, everything else looked very different. My body was gone, blankets and linens were gone, the knife was gone, the sword was gone.

I wasn't floating anymore.

Someone had found my body. My heart sank as I wondered who discovered it. Was it Max? Zoe? I hoped it was Zoe. I didn't want to think about my best friend discovering my body the way it was.

Willard.

I'm going to make him pay for this.

I bolted toward the door to my room, but my hand couldn't grip the knob. It took me a moment, but finally the thought occurred to me that I no longer needed to concern myself with doors.

Testing my hypothesis, I reached my arm out to the other side. Satisfied with my experiment, I stepped through with my whole body into the tiny hallway, looked toward the living room, and immediately made eye contact with my murderer. Willard Hensch. He looked just like the picture from Max's memes: young, skinny, with hair plastered down around his head. The same smug look on his face as he sat in a tufted

Brian Corley

leather wingback chair that did not belong in my living room. The rest of my furniture was there, however. Interesting.

"I see you no longer have your sword," he said.

"Not that I need it," I replied.

My anger took over, and without thinking, I flew forward and, with the fiercest right uppercut I could muster, sent him and his chair over backward.

Willard floated slowly upward, a sneer on his face, and flew toward me, fists raised. His punch connected and knocked me back—hard—through a wall and into Max's old room. I bounced off the back wall that faced the outside of the house and onto the floor next to Max's softball bat. Like the sword, I instinctively reached for it.

However, unlike the sword, I grabbed a ghostly facsimile of it while the original stayed in place. *Hmm, interesting, but now it's payback time.*

I floated back through Max's wall into the living room where I found Willard floating comfortably. He was waiting for me, arms crossed and smirking. His expression contorted when he saw the bat in my hand.

"How are you doing that?!" he exclaimed.

He bolted toward me, arms outstretched, and tried to grab it from me.

I swung wildly and connected with a crack reminiscent of a juiced major leaguer taking one out of the park. Willard flew backward and bounced off the outside wall of the living room and onto the floor. My mind started clicking a few things into place.

One: we both bounced off outside walls to the house, but could move freely inside it. There must be some sort of boundary there. Two: Willard seemed to have the advantage in hand-to-hand combat, but I could do something he couldn't— grab things around the house, at least facsimiles of them.

80

Advantage—me.

Never in my life would I have imagined hitting some-one with a baseball bat—I could really hurt them. I certainly wouldn't have swung at their head—I could kill them.

That said, I was dead now and so was Willard, and neither one of us was getting any deader. I promised him a miserable afterlife, and it was time to deliver.

I made my way toward Willard as though I had all the confidence in the world. I knew he couldn't figure out how I had this bat in my hand, and that scared him. I wondered if he had any of his own tricks hidden up his sleeve.

"You should have taken the door, Jonah," he seethed through gritted teeth and lunged at me again.

I took another swing, and he went down.

"Why? We're just getting started. I warned you, Willard, remember?"

I took another swing as he lunged for me again. It felt good—I was good at this.

Should I be doing this? It feels so easy that I almost feel bad. He did murder me this morning though ...

This went on for a couple hours until he got tired of fight-ing back. He lay down against the outside wall, exhausted, and frankly, I was ready to stop.

Now what?

I know I said I threatened to do this for an eternity, but I was already bored. Then an idea struck me, and I floated over to the utility room where I ghosted a facsimile of a roll of duct tape. I set the leather tufted wingback chair back up right and dragged Willard over to it, set him down, and taped him up without a fight.

Time for some answers.

I couldn't even touch the doorknob in my room, so how was he able to break the window that first day? How was he able to break the glass in the frames, and how the hell was he able to use Max's butcher knife?

So, I asked him.

He smiled as he looked up at me, punch-drunk and exhausted. Then he dropped his head again as though he was going to take a nap. Dammit.

I thought back to the Patrick Swayze movie Ghost that Max and I just watched, where he played a ghost that hadn't moved on. I also thought back to how my dad found it while flipping channels one afternoon, and we watched it as a lark. It was a lot different watching it again with my mom and sister after he died.

What would Swayze do? Let's see, he learned to move stuff and communicated through a medium. Check and check, Willard had done both of those, although we brought the medium to him.

I wondered if he'd watched the same movie. I remembered the ghost that taught Swayze on the subway just got pissed in order to move stuff, so I decided to try it.

I looked around and decided to focus on the TV remote sitting on the coffee table. I thought of my mom, my friends, missed opportunities—Laura from marketing—my entire life cut short. I balled all those feelings together and reached out hard.

I spun the remote.

I couldn't believe it worked.

I walked around the house looking for small objects to practice on. I made my way to the kitchen, and something on the counter caught my attention. Salt shaker—boom, knocked over. Shot glass! Nudge. Nudge. Nudge, aaand onto the floor. Smash.

I was like an Internet cat, knocking things over left and right. I was making a mess and should probably stop. *One more shot glass though.* It bounced. *Dangit, what a way to end my streak.*

Not even a full night into being a ghost and I was already

bored. Is this my life now? I floated back into the living room. Willard wouldn't look at me but seemed to be resting somewhat comfortably in his chair.

I crashed onto the couch just like I would in life. I wished I could watch TV, then thought maybe I could. I got good and pissed and punched my finger toward the power button on the remote. Success. I did the same thing three more times to punch in the cartoon channel. It was probably one of the few channels at this hour that still was still broadcasting original programming instead of paid advertisements. One of my favorites was on: a slapsticky, fast-cut show about teenage superheroes.

Willard bolted up as straight as he could while the ghost duct tape held true to his chair. His eyes widened.

"No," he whined. "Please, no. Why?" He slumped back down in the chair. "Why couldn't you have just passed through the door?" he said.

I muted the TV.

"Better?" I asked.

He nodded.

"Tell you what, I'll keep this on mute if you give me some answers."

"Fine," he said, "what do you want to know?"

"When I … woke up, as I am now, all I saw was the door. It offered me peace, quiet, and tranquility, which seems to be all you want. Why wouldn't you take it?"

He looked away and said, "It doesn't appear for me anymore. It stopped after a few days, weeks—months maybe—I'm not sure. Time doesn't mean what it used to anymore. I don't have anywhere to be, nothing to see. I just appear here, night after night."

"Yeah, but I had to tear myself away from the door, Willard. I had unfinished business—with you." I pushed the issue. "Why didn't you go through?"

"I don't know. I was scared, I think. I wasn't religious growing up, and I didn't expect there to be an 'after.' I don't know what lays on the other side of that door for me. I had a hard life," he said.

"Life isn't easy for most people, Willard. What makes you think you had a tougher road than anyone else?" I replied.

He went on to explain that he'd never really fit in at home or at school. He was an accident—they actually called him that—and they resented him. He was picked on in school and ran home most days to avoid getting beat up. He'd go straight to his room to study, making sure he was quiet when he got home, so as not to disturb his mother.

He excelled in school, won a scholarship to Austin U, and stayed in town after graduation as a programmer at the local branch of a large accounting firm. He bought this house shortly after. Unfortunately, things at the firm were much like they were for him in high school, only this time the bullies were his bosses. They took credit for most of his work and mercilessly taunted him. One day, he stood up for himself, but they fired him. He went home to the only place he ever found peace and decided to end it all there ... here.

"Then you arrived with your friend," he said, "all bluster and bravado, walking around my house like you owned the place."

"I did," I softly interjected. "I did own the place, but you took that from me too."

He nodded.

"One thing though," I added, "I thought you were an accountant."

"No, just worked for that dreadful firm." he replied. "Why?"

"Nothing. It's just what it said in your obituary."

His face dropped, and his shoulders hung limp.

"I guess there was no one there to correct them."

We sat in silence for a while, then began to fade as morning arrived.

Chapter 10

I felt refreshed and had a newfound empathy toward Willard as I faded in the next night. However, the look in Willard's eyes returned no such understanding. Apparently, he awoke renewed and refreshed with a seething bitterness toward me. Luckily, he was still bound to his chair.

"Untie me," he raged.

I decided that may not be a good idea and thought it best to ignore him—which just upset him more. I wandered around the house and looked in on my old room. The bright-white-light door was there again, but for how much longer? I thought about going through and leaving Willard tied to that chair for eternity ... or however long ghost duct tape lasts.

I wondered if Willard could see my door and if he could go through it even though it was meant for me, so I floated back into the living room and asked him. I guess the question ended up sounding more like a threat because he went on a tirade, telling me I was just like all the others, but I would get mine—typical mustache-twirling villain stuff.

Hell, I'd already gotten mine—I was dead. Still though, I had a choice to make: I could wallow in my own rage or deal with my new situation. I'd worked out a lot of aggression last night, and it just seemed pointless to continue on that path. Staying mad at Willard wasn't going to change my situation; in fact, I kind of felt sorry for him. It didn't change what he did, but being on the other side gave me a new perspective.

Also, I had to admit that being able to float around was kind of cool. I started testing what I could do, seeing if I could ghost-grab a ghostly facsimile of the remote and watch ghost TV.

Turns out I could ghost the remote alright, but there wasn't ghost TV. *Disappointing.* I set it back down and started testing the outside walls, but couldn't get through.

"Can we leave?" I asked.

"Why would you want to?" Willard replied.

I understood why he didn't want to leave, but I felt differently. I floated to the front door, put my hand against it, and discovered that I could push through.

Once outside, I found that although it was dark, I could see fine—as well as I could in the day in my first life, like somewhere between an overcast day and a well-lit outdoor space at night. Other than the chirping of crickets, all was quiet in the neighborhood. There usually wasn't much going on this time of night, and most people would have fallen asleep a while ago—which made it all the more noticeable when I saw a guy standing out in front of the house on the corner, staring at me. I looked behind me just in case there was something going on there—nope. I looked between him and me to see if maybe his dog was out taking a leak. No to that too.

He waved me over then walked behind the house, so I floated ahead to follow him. When I made it to the house and around the corner, I didn't see him anywhere. I checked to see if he'd ducked into the backyard, but I saw only a chain-link fence and one of those old clothesline carousels.

I heard something, though, something faint, a consistent noise—crying. It was coming from inside the house.

Now is the time in the movie where you should leave. Just go. Why investigate a noise? Especially crying.

I knew it might not end well, but I was already a ghost and wasn't getting any deader. I floated up the back steps and through the door to investigate.

There, in the ghostly outline of a chair that I could tell wasn't there physically, sat an old woman, her head in her hands, softly weeping. Her hair was up in an unintentionally messy way, and she wore a conservative flower-print dress with a lace collar from another era. She looked up with hope in her eyes as tears rolled down her kind face.

"Can you see me?" she asked, her voice shaking.

"Yes," I said as compassionately as I could muster, which wasn't hard, given how frail and feeble she looked sitting there.

"Oh my word," she said and smiled, "I haven't been able to talk to someone in years—maybe thirty or forty. What year is it? No, don't tell me."

She motioned for me to join her.

"Come have a seat, young man, and visit with me for a while."

The room was not well furnished and had clearly seen better days. I would hazard to guess that the current occupants rented this place, and on the cheap. That's not to say that renters don't take care of a place or that homeowners can't be slobs, but this place had a very disposable feel to it: torn-up carpet, walls that hadn't seen a fresh coat of paint in years, etc.

I sank down in a ratty chair across from the old woman.

"I'm Jonah," I said gently. "I used to live a couple houses down from you. I'm still there, just not living obviously."

She smiled at my small attempt at a joke.

"Nice to meet you, Jonah. My name is Angela."

I nodded. "Nice to meet you, Angela. How long have you been here?"

"Oh, a long time I suppose," she began and noticed me taking in the state of her house. "It didn't always look like this though." She laughed and began to rock a little in her over-stuffed, La-Z-Boy recliner. "I moved here with my Francisco in 1962—he was an engineer at the base."

She was referring to Camp Mabry, an old military base on the west side of town that had been in Austin since the late 1800s.

Angela continued, "We bought this house and raised a family—two wonderful children, a boy and a girl. Frank, after his father, and Gretchen, after my great-grandmother."

"That sounds amazing," I said. "How long did you live here?"

"Oh … quite some time, quite some time. Long enough for Frank and Gretchen to grow up and go off to school, get married and have kids. Francisco and I did everything together. We loved to go on walks, at least two every day. He always said it was important to keep that blood pumping, but I think he just liked to spend time with me." She winked and continued, "See that tree in the front yard?" She pointed out the window at an old red oak. "Francisco planted that tree when we first moved in here. He said our children and grandchildren would play under it one day, and don't you know, that's exactly what they did!"

She laughed as she looked up toward the ceiling. I could

tell she was remembering better days.

"I remember a storm in the '70s that knocked out our power for days—the whole neighborhood. Francisco used it as an opportunity to get to know the neighbors. He went out and bought hot dogs and hot dog buns and came back and just started grilling. People came from blocks around because some of them started running out of food, you see? That's just the type of man my Francisco was." Her voice quivered as she trailed off.

"I just couldn't bear to leave him the morning that I passed. I saw the door with all that beautiful light. Glorious. But I just said to myself—not without Francisco." She softly tapped her right hand against the arm of her chair to emphasize the last three words.

"You know, I think he knew I was still here. He would get up early—four in the morning—and sit at the breakfast table and talk to me just like I was there." She looked off to her tiny kitchen. "I miss our little coffees together." She gathered herself up to continue her story. "The children began to notice that he was forgetting things. Started out as misplacing his keys or wallet.

"I tried to help. He always kept everything on his nightstand, but sometimes he would forget and leave his wallet here or his keys there. I would always move them to where he could find them, of course, but after he started forgetting the grandchildren's names, Frank or Gretchen—maybe both—decided to move him to a home where someone could look after him.

"I woke up one night, and he was gone, and I knew the children must have taken him away earlier. I didn't know how to find him or what to do. I worried that maybe he couldn't find me. Then I thought that maybe he would come back here, to this place one day. Before too long, Frank and Gretchen's husband came with some of their boys and moved everything out of the house.

"Frank stood at that door right there and said goodbye to me one last time, and I to him. They sold the house to a lovely couple who just moved to town. After a while, they had a baby and decided to sell the house.

"So on and so forth … I saw people come and go. Families, couples, students from time to time." She laughed. "Those students could get so rowdy. You know, they had such a good time, but they sure were hard on the house."

She darkened.

"There was one family that lived here—a young couple—that had a little baby. That man drank too much. Every night he drank. He would drink himself into a sorry state—he was a mean little cuss. He would get to drinking, then start hollerin' at his wife. One night it got real bad, and I thought he was going to hurt her, or that little baby.

"I just knew I had to do something. Just as I thought he was going to go too far, I cut the lights out on the house. I'm not sure how I knew to do it—I just did it. One minute he was hollerin' up a storm; the next, he got real quiet. He went outside to check that old breaker box and brought the lights back up. He got to drinkin' some more and started hollerin' at her again. This time he threatened her, and I cut the lights off again.

"I scared him then. He stopped yelling and ran outside again. Thankfully that gave her enough time to grab the baby and get out. She went over to our neighbors, the Crenshaws, and they took that girl and her baby in for the night. Those two split over it, and he was out of here before he could do any more damage. I'm proud of that."

I took note of what she did with the lights and filed that away for later.

"After a while, someone bought the house and just started renting the place out. At first, a few nice families came through. I remember one young couple stayed here for a while—the Diaz family. I liked them a lot. Well, one night, the Diazes were out for one of their date nights, and a couple of hoodlums broke in through that back door there in the kitchen. Well, I just thought to myself that I had to do something, so I did. I turned on the TV, and wouldn't you know it … the police were on a show, and those boys lit up out of this house just as fast as they could go—more scared than a cat at a dog pound, I tell you what." She looked at me, laughing, her face fading to a grin.

"There've been others that obviously haven't taken care of the place, and now the four men that live here couldn't care less. I'm so tired, Jonah. I'm so tired of being here. I miss my Francisco."

I took her hand.

"What if you could use my door?"

She looked at me, her hands over her mouth.

"Oh now, Jonah, that's your door. I couldn't do that."

"Sure you could, or we can go together."

She sat back, thought for a second, and said, "Well yes, Jonah. I think I will take you up on that. I believe I am ready to go."

Immediately a bright light filled the room as a door appeared in front of us. Her door. There was no question; there was just something about it that let us both know it was for her.

She smiled, and her eyes brightened as she took on the appearance of a much younger woman in her prime: dark hair in a wave of curls, and a light-blue wool dress with oversized buttons that was the height of fashion somewhere around the mid-60s. She stood up, straightened her jacket over her skirt, and turned to me.

"I best be going on to see my Francisco," she said, looking toward the door like a bride about to enter a sanctuary. "I think it's time we had one of our walks."

Off she went, through the door and gone. The light in the room dimmed.

My chest felt like it was in a vice. I wasn't ever one to cry—hadn't in years—but in that moment, I wished that I could.

Chapter 11

I got to my feet again and slowly made my way through the front door of the house, noticing that I was walking now instead of floating along. I got the feeling I could float if I wanted to, but I just wanted to feel the steps for now. Outside, the man from before was leaning against an old red oak in the front yard.

"Father Chandler told me about you—asked me to help you," he said.

"What?" I replied.

The man stepped out from underneath the tree to reveal himself. I would say he was anywhere from his mid-forties to early fifties, a guy that looked older, but not old if that makes sense. He was tall, in shape, and was dressed in an understated fashion in a plaid flannel shirt, untucked and over worn jeans—not like someone trying to dress young, just cool.

I could tell there was something different about him. He wasn't a person, but I got the feeling he wasn't a ghost either. Whatever he was, I felt like I could trust him, like I should listen to what he had to say. He had an air of effortless authority around him.

"I said Father Chandler told me about you," he answered. "Well, kind of—he was talking to my boss's boss's boss, but I was in the room, and here we are."

I put it together.

"Father Chandler said he'd pray for me."

He nodded.

"So now you're here."

He nodded.

"But I still died."

He raised his eyebrows in acknowledgment and nodded again. "Yeah, sorry about that. I wish I could have been here earlier." He plucked some leaves off a low-hanging limb and walked toward me. "What you did in there is important, you know. You made a difference."

"Was that a test?"

"No, actually, I wanted to show you something else. What you did, though … I didn't expect that."

"What did I do exactly?"

"You gave her hope, Jonah. You gave her hope, and she wanted to move on from where she was and on to the next place."

"What would have happened if I hadn't gone in? If no one went in?"

He shook his head. "Nothing good. Maybe she'd have turned bitter, mean. Maybe she'd have given up, withered away, spent the next few hundred years or so floating around that old lot. We don't have to guess now because you helped her. That counts, Jonah. That means something."

"Where does the door go?" I said, finally asking the real questions.

"Why would I know?"

"I get the feeling you know."

"Yeah, yeah, I do know. It goes to where it's supposed to go. Some say Sheol or Hades—a place of rest. Some, like your friend Zoe, might say they go on to Yin Jian. Some say Heaven; some say Hell. You get where I'm going with this." He nodded like I actually got where he was going with this.

"No, I don't. That's why I was asking where it went."

"Only one way to find out. That look on your face tells me that you're not quite ready to discover that, though."

I looked down at the ground and back up to him. "Nope, not yet, I guess. So what is it that you wanted to show me anyway?"

"Christmas, Mr. Scrooge, I've come to show you Christmas."

Oh cool, he was going to take me through what life would be—

"Eh, I'm just kidding. I wanted to show you this kid that was showing off for his girlfriend and was about to do something stupid. He's gone now, but it was funny. Come on, let's get you home before the sun comes up. If you're caught outside when it does, it's over."

I panicked. "Really?"

"No." He leaned over, laughing, and straightened back up, waving me off. "No, man, come on. I'm sorry. I'm just messing with you. Seriously though, you may want to wake up in familiar surroundings tomorrow."

We got to the house, headed up the walkway, and slipped through the front door.

Willard's chair sat empty. *Uh oh.*

Suddenly he rushed through a wall in the living room but stopped in his tracks when he saw us. He obviously didn't expect me to bring company.

"Who is this?" he asked.

"This is … uh … my friend." I looked at the guy next to me. "I don't know your name."

"Call me Seph," he replied, hands in his pockets while looking Willard straight in the eye.

"What are you?" Willard asked.

So he got that impression too, interesting.

"I'm an angel," Seph replied, as normal as you or I would say, "I'm a plumber" or "a student." *Hmm. Makes sense.* I guess I kind of put that together for myself already.

"No," Willard said. "No, there are no angels—"

"*Behold,*" Seph thundered as a blinding light illuminated the room.

I fell to the floor and covered my eyes. I couldn't move. I'd never felt anything like it. It was as though I was pinned by some unseen force. I was terrified.

The light faded and a transformed Seph stood in our living room, rigged out in all sorts of armor. Sword drawn and shield at his side, he beamed down at Willard, who was on the floor too, shielding his eyes.

As the light began to fade, the downward force on both of us relented, and Willard squirmed his way to the kitchen and out the side door into the night. I sat up to one knee, blinking. "Blinking," I guess. I didn't need to blink anymore, but I was shaking off the effects of what I just witnessed.

Seph laughed to himself. When I looked back to him, he was wearing the same clothes as before. He walked over to Willard's chair and flopped down into it.

"Sorry. I didn't have a lot of time to argue and didn't feel like trying to convince him with words. He wouldn't have believed me otherwise."

"You scared him. You didn't have to do that. He had a tough life, he's been through a lot."

"You're right," Seph reflected, looking up at the ceiling. "He's kind of a dick though. Anyway, do you want to check out your funeral?"

Did I? Yeah, kinda.

"Where's it going to be? Is it here in town? Will I need to travel? If so, how am I supposed to travel? Most funerals I've been to are during the day. How can I go if it is?" I asked.

Seph held out both hands to calm me down.

"OK, OK, good questions. First, it's during the day, but I'm giving you a little hall pass. I kind of run things for the area and have some leeway. Second, it's here in town over at St. Raphael's. Father Chandler stepped in when he heard what happened to you. He feels bad, even though he gave you good advice." His hand was resting on one of the arms of the chair, but he lifted a finger to point at me. "You should have listened to him. Third, yes, we'll need to travel downtown."

"That's a long walk."

"It is a long walk, but lucky for you, we're not walking. Did you notice earlier how you floated toward me at one point, and then we walked back to this house at another?"

"Yeah."

"It's because you thought you could do it."

"OK. So if I think I can fly there really fast, I can?"

He smiled. "Yep."

"OK then, could I just think myself there?"

He laughed and clapped. "Yes!"

"So why didn't Angela just blink herself over to the nursing home with Francisco?"

Seph shook his head. "Because she didn't think to do it. It may not seem like much, but I'm giving you a lot of information here. You instinctively knew to grab that sword and that bat last night and the night before last. That was good. You figured it out on your own. Others do that, or something like it, but most have help. They learn from other ghosts. Very few figure it out on their own."

Ah, I see. So I'm special. I knew I would be good at this.

"No." He shook his head, stretched his arm out, and shook his finger. "No. You're not special."

Could he read my thoughts? I didn't say that out loud.

"You're not the chosen one. There aren't going to be letters from some wizard school flying through the mail slot. You just figured some things out faster than most. I'm giving you pointers because you really shouldn't have died the way you did. I've only seen a handful go like that, and all of them moved on. You stayed behind and fought the guy who took you out. That's ballsy."

"I don't know, Seph. Sounds like you're saying I'm special."

He rolled his eyes and muttered, "This is what happens when everyone gets a trophy." Seph stood up and straightened his clothes. "I'll be by tomorrow to wake you up for the funeral—big day for you." Seph walked toward the door and disappeared, and I went to my couch to watch cartoons until the sun came up. *I didn't even have a mail slot.*

"Willard?" I asked in a loud voice.

No response. I was pretty sure he was gone. Poor guy.

Chapter 12

I faded into my room, which was flooded with light. Daylight seemed so much brighter now that I was nocturnal; it was almost overwhelming. Seph was leaning on my doorframe in a perfectly tailored dark suit.

"Up and at 'em, I see. Good," he said. "Are you going to wear that?"

I realized I was wearing what my mind instinctively defaulted to: a navy-blue T-shirt and jeans. No one was going to see me, so why should I care? Still, it was my funeral, and you only get one of those—probably. I thought about a look that I associated with high fashion and success: a slim-fit navy-blue suit with a bright-white button-down underneath. No tie, but a crisp collar. I checked the mirror, but couldn't see myself.

"Looks great," Seph said. "I think you're getting the hang of this."

I'm special, I thought. *He's impressed. I'm good at this.*

"You're not special," he grumbled and looked off in a half eye roll. "Let's go. They've started."

Blink. Just like that, he was gone. And just like that, I was back with him at St. Raphael's.

"Nice turnout," Seph said while he pulled a face and gave me the OK sign.

I floated up to get a better view, and he was right; it was a nice turnout. People I hadn't seen in years. Teachers from high school, elementary school, and a couple of professors from college. The group of guys I hung around with from high school. We'd lost touch, but they'd rallied to come pay their respects. I appreciated that.

Oh … Aunt Mindy, ugh, pass.

Nic was there, by herself, looking at her phone in the back. More friends, acquaintances. *Ah, there's Valerie. We dated in high school, kind of.* Blah blah blah, old church friends, people from work—Debra.

Debra was crying and telling the person next to her she told me to get out of that house. *Sorry, Debra.*

Hank was there with my two bosses, blah blah blah—was that? Yes. Yes! Laura from marketing. Laura from marketing was there!

"Seph, Laura from marketing is here!" I yelled from across the sanctuary.

Seph gave me an embarrassed wave of acknowledgment. *What are you embarrassed about, Seph? No one can see us.*

Back to Laura—she was crying. Did I have a chance with Laura from marketing? *This—this is my biggest regret.*

Max.

Max's head was bowed, and he had his arm around my mom and was comforting her. My heart broke as I watched her and my sister Taylor hold each other's hand and cry. We lost our dad when we were younger, and now they had to go through this with me. *Damn, it wasn't fair.*

Max looked over, almost as though he was looking at me.

But he wasn't looking at me.

He was looking at Laura from marketing. *Hands off, Max, you sonuvabitch*! He gave up trying to make eye contact with her after a few seconds and went back to comforting my mom. *There you go, Max, back into best-friend territory.*

A massive pipe organ dominated the front of the sanctuary at St. Raphael's, only making room in the middle for a stained-glass installation depicting an angel with a sword above his head. I would say he looked like Seph, but that's probably a little too on the nose. I was probably just a little starstruck, having met my first angel, so I thought every angel was him or something.

The organ played "Shall We Gather at the River." *I hate that song. I've always hated that song. Who chose this playlist?* I scanned the room again. An old friend here, Allison over there—*nice of her to show up.* She was handing her card over to my cousin.

I noticed Zoe and the Psy-kicks right around the time Father Chandler cleared his throat and the room fell silent.

"Thank you all for being here, even in this tragic time, it's good to be around those we love …"

Then he said a bunch of other things, people cried, it was moving. I was ready to go, so I floated back to Seph.

"You worried about your friends?" Seph asked.

I nodded.

"Don't. Death comes for us all."

I shrugged. "Not you."

"Eh. You know what I mean. Come on, it's not so bad. You can fly, wear whatever you want—"

"Alright, you make a good point."

"Besides, they'll be here soon enough."

"What?!"

"Sorry. Sorry. Bad concept of time over here, I'm billions of years old. A couple months doesn't seem like a long time for me."

My eyes widened.

"Just kidding," he said with a chuckle. "You ready?" he asked.

I nodded an affirmative and faded out.

I faded in again that night and looked for Willard, but he wasn't at home. I decided to tour the neighborhood to see if I could help someone else like I did last night with Angela. It didn't take too long before I was drawn to a house a couple streets away. This time it was a guy about my age. I listened to his story for half an hour or so, and pretty soon his door reappeared for him too. He thanked me and moved on. Good deed done.

With that behind me, I wanted to try to have some fun, so I decided to check out the scene on Sixth Street, a strip full of bars, like Bourbon Street in New Orleans where people go to get hammered and make bad decisions. It was a real shit show, and everyone loved it.

I decided to take the scenic route rather than just blink over, so I took to the air at about fifty miles per hour.

I'd always liked Austin. Growing up, we'd drive over to get new clothes for school. In college, we would travel over to go out and have a good time. I had good memories of the city, and it was a sight to behold from the air. I swooped down and hit the sidewalk at a perfect pace, right at the corner of Congress and Sixth. I'd taken maybe four steps before I heard a voice beside me.

"You're a little overdressed, aren't you?"

It was Seph.

"Hey man," I said, patting him on the shoulder as I changed from my blue suit into some jeans and a pearl-snap button-down. This ghost clothing thing is cool.

"Heard about what you did earlier, Jonah. That's good. That's really good. I'm proud of you."

It was early still for Sixth Street to get going, but I noticed there were just as many ghosts out as there were people—and they were having a good time. Up and down the sidewalk they went, laughing and drinking.

I was confused. I hadn't had to eat or drink anything as a ghost the past few nights, not to mention go to the bathroom. It was kind of great, to be honest.

"They're not actually drinking," Seph said.

He can read my mind. I bet he's reading my mind.

"It's just an affectation," he continued. "What else are you supposed to do out here?"

I shrugged in agreement, and we kept walking until I heard music that sounded a little louder than what was coming from the bars. It seemed to be coming from a weird place though, behind a wall and not a door. Seph smiled and nodded toward the source of the music. We went through the wall— and the front door—of a phantasmagorical club.

The place was packed, and a band played on a stage at the opposite end of the club from us. Seph pointed to a ghost guy surrounded by a group of smiling ghost women.

"That guy," Seph said, pointing again at each word, "that

guy is great. He made this. In the physical world, this is just another junk bar with a light-up floor playing the same music you would find anywhere, but this guy … he can make an entire scene."

"Cool," I yelled over the music. "So does Stevie Ray Vaughn ever get up? Will I get to hear him?"

Seph shook his head and ushered me outside again so we could talk instead of yell. "Look man, Stevie moved on. He lived a complete and fulfilled life. The guys you see in there are great—don't get me wrong—they're amazing. But those guys are the ones that didn't make it for some reason. Some OD'd. Some killed themselves. Some quit music, took regular jobs, and regretted it for the rest of their lives."

He walked me down the street.

"Most, like ninety-nine percent, of the people you've read about from Austin moved on. Ann Richards was gone as soon as she saw that door. She led a great life and was fulfilled. She probably wouldn't even care that they named a bridge after her. Lady Bird Johnson? Same deal. Gone. She led a complete life and left the world better off having been here.

"This town is beautiful because of what she did. Town Lake—Lady Bird Lake—it was a cooling area for the power plant, just a dammed-off part of the river. She planted trees all around it, and now it looks like it's been that way forever. Trust me—it didn't always look like that. You get what I'm saying to you?"

I didn't. I mean, I understood what he was saying, but I wasn't sure why he pulled me out to say it.

Seph punched my shoulder. "You want to go see a movie?"

I did, actually.

"Yeah, let's go see a movie."

We floated over to a movie theater on Sixth that was owned by a local chain of cinemas. They sold food and alcohol there and had a good reputation for their choices in films. We found a couple empty seats in the back of one of the theaters and acted as though we were just ordinary people watching a movie.

It was pretty good. It took place in space and had decent dialogue and great special effects. About thirty minutes in, the guy next to me got bored and started spouting off jokes whenever things got quiet. It didn't look like the girl he brought was too impressed with his observations, but that didn't stop him from making them.

After about the tenth comment, I balled up my rage and tapped his beer glass over into his lap. The girl he was with, probably relieved to finally have something to laugh at, did so, but with a bit more gusto than necessary. He stood up, arms out, and set the glass back upright. Searching for napkins without success, he left to go to the bathroom—I guess. He didn't come back.

I hate it when people talk in the theater. Seph casually looked over, gave me a thumbs-up, and focused back on the screen.

We caught another movie afterward as it was still early for us, and frankly, I was really into seeing movies for free. It was a swashbuckler, and I floated to the middle of the theater to watch it in optimum comfort.

A voice emerged from the back. "You make a better door than you do a window, pal."

I sunk down to an open seat close by Seph, who leaned forward so I could see him, his mouth open and eyes wide as he gave me a condescending thumbs-up while waggling his eyebrows and nodding his head in the affirmative.

♥

"So, you thought we were the only ones to think about seeing a movie?" Seph said, mocking me on our way out of the theater. "Opening weekend too," he said and laughed.

"I thought it would be comfortable."

"It looked comfortable—for about thirty seconds—until the entire theater turned against you."

"Asshole," a girl jeered from a small group floating by us.

I nodded my head with my hands out to indicate I was sorry. The group floated on, and we continued to walk our way back down Sixth headed toward South Congress.

"Ever been to the Paramount?" Seph asked.

"Yeah, of course," I said.

"Not sure if you're into this, but they have an amazing orchestra playing tonight with a couple hundred years' worth of accumulated talent."

"Sure, let's go."

"OK, so the guys in the club we saw earlier are really good. Really good. Would totally make it as a world-class band today, but they're drawing on less than about a hundred years' worth of song-writing style and accumulated knowledge of those instruments. Not to mention there were only a couple guitars, a bass, and a drum set up there. Now—"

Seph stopped and hovered over the sidewalk.

"Think about an orchestra. Hundreds of years of material and knowledge to draw from, right?"

He started moving again.

"This guy Karnowsky was traveling through town in the 1860s and died here of pneumonia. He could have been one of the greats. Amazing composer and conductor, his life was cut way too short. He put together a symphony sometime around 1870, and they played in the Capitol building until the Paramount was built in 1915. He's been recruiting talent ever since, and you will not believe the sound they make. Seriously, if you've never heard a live orchestra, it will change you."

"Sounds good," I said.

Seph was too excited to stop going on about how great this Karnowsky guy was. He wrote his own music, performed the classics, made *improvements* to the classics. *Oh my. Can't wait.*

My attention found its way to my surroundings. It was late enough that the police blocked off the streets so that people could stumble around basically wherever they wanted to with a significantly reduced chance of being hit by a car. The undead mixed with the living and everyone was having a good time.

It almost felt like a theme-park ride. Ghosts of the Central Texas Party Strip: Dead Men Tell Plenty of Tales. Really, they won't stop talking.

Seph was still rambling on about Karnowsky when we reached Sixth and Congress. I seemed to catch the attention of a beautiful girl across the street. Her dark hair was tied up in a high ponytail, and she wore black from head to toe: black motorcycle jacket over a black top, cool faded black jeans, and black boots with a heel. She had amazing style, and there was something about her that I felt like I'd never seen before.

We made eye contact, and I smiled with some sort of newfound undead confidence. She nodded back, and a dimple appeared on her left cheek. I tapped Seph as casually as I could, and for some reason, as though I thought she could hear me from across the street, I said under my breath, "Seph, do you see that girl?"

Seph noticed the direction I was looking and casually glanced that way, then stared for a couple seconds.

"No," he said and slipped back into whatever he was saying about Karnowsky.

A bus passed between us, and she was gone. Just like a movie. I hated movies like that; they don't make any sense. That never happens in real life.

Seph gently pulled me in the direction of our destination, at least I was fairly confident it was the right direction due to the brightly lit sign that read PARAMOUNT in front of us.

It was well past midnight now, and the theater had been closed for hours. We entered a packed house of ghostly apparitions and searched for some empty seats. I observed that it was perfectly fine etiquette to float up to find a space to sit, but you had to be in a seat to enjoy the show (no spiritual loitering like my episode in the theater). We found two open seats in the upper balcony and floated our way toward them.

I sat next to a guy dressed in a top hat and tails straight out of the '20s who was with a woman sporting a short, bobbed haircut and wearing a flapper-style dress and a long string of pearls. Seph leaned in and said, quietly enough to be understood as a whisper but loudly enough to be overheard, "Hey Jonah, do you think the couple next to you lived during the '20s?"

The man in the top hat swallowed and gave us an appropriately smarmy side-eye.

"Maybe I should be in my Greek-style robe and sandals," Seph continued.

The guy turned his head to look at us. Seph stared back,

smiling, and whispered, "I'm billions of years old." Then he cracked up laughing.

The man and his date floated to another location, giving us as many passive-aggressive glances as they could.

"So what *did* you wear billions of years ago?" I asked, genuinely curious, and now free to talk a little louder than a whisper.

"Shut up, it's starting," Seph replied as the room hushed to the tapping of a baton on a music stand.

After three and a half hours of music with no intermission (why would we need one—we don't eat, drink, or pee), I can honestly say I've never heard music like that before. Great … hooks? I don't know what word you would use to refer to a melody that stays with you from that type of arrangement, but I hummed what seemed like classics to me on the way out of the theater.

Also, it struck me—as a newly minted ghost—that getting out of a theater is so much faster when anyone can go in whatever direction they want. Up, down, sideways, slantways— there were as many exits as directions in a great glass Wonka- vator. No more waiting in the aisles like cattle. Instant egress.

Seph clapped me on my shoulder as we hovered out over Congress. "Alright man, that was great. Did you have fun?"

"Hell yes, that was a good time. Karnowsky is amazing! Thanks for that."

"Good, good. Alright man, I need to get to work a little earlier than usual, so I'm going to head on out."

"Work?"

"Yeah man, work. Remember I said I was in charge of this area? I'm kind of in the military here. Most of our work takes place during the day when people are all up and going, so I can usually let some of my lieutenants handle things if I need them to at night."

"When do you sleep?" I wondered out loud.

"I don't need to. Not bad, right?" he said, then bolted.

It was nice out. I would guess it was on the cooler side for a summer night—I guessed because I didn't feel temperature anymore, another welcome perk to the ghost life. I decided to head home, taking the slow, scenic route again, floating south out of downtown, over the Colorado River/Town Lake/Lady Bird Lake (all of these names apply), down Congress and over Ben White, and finally down to my little neighborhood. I wasn't tired—I wasn't sure if I would ever feel tired again—but I decided to lie down on my bed and watch some television. It was early morning now, so I could probably catch up on some news. I faded out as I caught up on the world's events.

Chapter 13

I faded into a terrible smell, which—living or dead—is never a good thing. It was also the first time I'd smelled something as a ghost, so I was immediately on guard.

My doorway to the great beyond stood like a monolith in my room, beaming its promising white light, but I felt compelled to get out of there as quickly as possible. Nausea hit even though I had no stomach and nothing to expel. I carefully made my way out of my room and into the hall where I quickly realized I wasn't alone. Candles and incense burned around the house—acrid smoke in every room but one: the kitchen. So, naturally, that's where I went.

There, sitting cross-legged on the floor, were seven familiar faces: Zoe, Lin, Quinton, um … the rest of the Psy-kicks, and Max. Six of the group of seven looked nervous—tight shoulders, shifting stances, eyes closed but opening every so often to check around the circle. One of them pulled their sweater tighter around them, and I recalled how the room cooled whenever we communicated with Willard.

Zoe, as usual, was centered, determined, and at peace—humming a quiet mantra. The peach sword was back with her and sat across her knees, her middle fingers and thumbs touching, hands resting on opposite ends of the sword. She began to call for someone. I sat still, listening, waiting, and watching.

Oh … she was calling for me. I remembered how it was done.

"Spirit or spirits, come. Speak to us," Zoe invited.

I saw the ashes and began to draw with my finger but quickly had a better idea. I blinked to my room and ghosted a pen out of my work bag, then blinked back. I began to write in the ashes.

Hi.

It wasn't exactly as neat as I was going for, but it was better than the chicken scratches we endured from Willard, so I was happy to add a little value to everyone's lives.

"Willard, is that you?" Zoe asked.

I thought it best to move it along. They were my friends, after all. Well, Max was my friend. I paid Zoe and the Psykicks. I mean, they did show up at my funeral, so maybe we were friends?

No, it's me, Jonah. Willard left a couple nights ago and hasn't been back.

I could see the tension leave the shoulders of most of the group. Max relaxed, then tensed again. "How do we know it's really you?" he asked.

Because?

"Tell me my favorite video game," he demanded.

I don't know, either college football or the world soccer one? Willard could have probably said as much though.

"Dammit, he's right," he said, looking up to the sky for inspiration. "What's my favorite food? What is the name of that girl you work with from marketing, and what number am I thinking of?"

Tacos, but that could be just a good guess. Not telling you—back off, leave her alone—and I have no idea. I can't read your mind.

Max sighed in relief. "Math checks out, guys. It's him."

The mood in the room shifted, and everyone relaxed. Some of the Psy-kicks even smiled—in a cool, casual way, of course.

Zoe cleared her throat and asked, "Why haven't you moved on? Is there anything we can do to help?"

Leave it to Zoe to ask the good questions.

I don't think I have enough room in the ashes to answer fully, I began, smoothing back the ashes and writing again. **I've found a purpose here, and actually like it. I can help people.**

"Waitaminute," Max said. "That doesn't sound like Jonah at all. I'm going to need you to tell me the name and number of that girl you worked with from marketing."

I drew a closed fist with the middle finger extended into the ashes.

Max grinned. "I'm not dropping this. I will find out. Look, Jonah, I wanted to see if Willard was still here, or if you were here, or moved on—" He stopped to gather himself; I wasn't sure, but I thought I saw tears well in his eyes. He let out a deep breath. "Your mom has to sell the house, and we wanted to make sure that whoever bought this place didn't find themselves in the same position you did. Anyway, maybe not just whoever, I was thinking about buying it from her."

Yes, yes! Do that!

"I mean, two people died here in the past few years. I can probably get a good deal—"

MAX! Do not do that to my mom! I burst forward to basically just blow some air in his face. The incense wavered, and the candles' flames moved in one direction toward him.

He smiled and held his hands up. "Easy, easy. I'm just kidding. I wouldn't do that to babe Ruth."

Stop calling her that. How are you going to afford this place?

"Alright, alright, I'll stop. My business has really taken off, but you act like this is some sort of mansion. It's a nine-hundred-square-foot bungalow. I got it. I don't even need a roommate, but I was thinking about asking Dean to move in."

He smells like cheese.

"Yeah, I know, but he stepped in when I needed a couch and his place is a dump."

Zoe cleared her throat again. "What is it like for you? What are you doing to help people—people or ghosts?"

Honestly, I feel like a borderline superhero. I wiped away the ashes. **So far, I've only helped ghosts move on, but I saw the new pirate movie last night.**

Zoe inhaled, ready to respond to me, but Quinton interrupted. "Is it good? I want to see it. Lin, do you want to go?" he asked.

It's OK, I guess. Spoiler alert: they get away.

Zoe cut in, "Hey! What? Quinton, stop. We don't know how much time we have with him."

Zoe breathed in to continue while Quinton mumbled, "It's not a spoiler alert if you don't give me time to look away."

Zoe clenched her teeth and gave him a side-eye, then relaxed, closed her eyes, and took a deep breath. "What do you mean you're like a borderline superhero, and how are you helping spirits move on?"

I can basically just imagine where I want to be, and I'm

there. I wiped away the ashes. I can walk or fly, and make ghostly facsimiles of real-world items. More wiping of ashes. I can imagine whatever I want to wear. More wiping of ashes. With all that said, I've basically just listened to people and given them hope to move on. More wiping. Then a door appears, and they go through it. Wipe, wipe. **Not exactly 100% on the mechanics.**

"Interesting," Zoe said aloud. "What does the door look like?"

Big rectangle made of light. A lot of light.

I could see Max stifling a Carol Ann comment. Not out of discipline, but probably because he couldn't think of how to make it funny enough to voice. I couldn't read minds, but I knew Max well enough to know that.

The group looked around, eyebrows raised and nodding. Zoe continued, "Anything else?"

I befriended an angel.

Zoe looked either confused or concerned. It was a new expression that broke through the façade of an implacable front. "What do you mean? How did you meet it? Is it trying to help you move on?"

I don't know. He was just around. He's shown me a few things. Wipe, wipe. Kind of a guide, I guess.

"What has he shown you?" she asked.

How to dress. We went downtown and listened to some music, saw some bands.

One of the Psy-kicks piped up, "My band was on Red River last night. Did you see us?"

No, sorry, didn't make it out. : (

I wondered if I was the first ghost to use an emoticon.

Zoe pressed further. "What is the name of the angel, and

are you sure he's an angel?"

I began to write down the name of my angel friend, but my hand wouldn't move. In fact, I couldn't remember his name. I remembered everything else. Everything.

Yes, I'm sure he's an angel. No mistaking it—take my word for it.

I flashed back to that moment in the living room. I'll never forget that physically—or spiritually—crushing light.

"His name," Zoe pressed, "what is his name?"

I couldn't write it. *Hmm. That's interesting.* I had an idea.

Father Chandler kind of introduced us.

Zoe nodded and looked satisfied with that answer, and I went on to tell her and the group as much as I could about what I'd been through so far.

In an effort to expand my horizons, I asked Zoe some questions about some different neighborhoods I could check out and their histories. I wanted to start meeting other ghosts and see if I could help out around town. Since she was a native Austinite, she was able to give me a decent rundown on a few. It was frustrating using the ashes—it took forever.

The group dispersed to go their separate ways around midnight or so, and I decided to head out and see what I could do to help those in need. On Zoe's recommendation, I thought I would start with the Tarrytown neighborhood in central Austin.

Chapter 14

I did my best Superman impression and flew to the locale, landing around 9th Street. I explored the carefully cultivated but modest homes and noticed something out of place: a three-story, Frank Lloyd Wright–inspired architectural masterpiece. A waterfall flowed out of the bottom floor and everything.

I'd actually seen a Frank Lloyd Wright house before when I was younger and visited some family in Jackson, Mississippi. What was different about this house was that it wasn't really there. It was built like the club on Sixth Street, a preternaturally fabricated showpiece.

I could hear bass and the noise of electronic music coming from what sounded like the backyard and decided to have a look. I floated up high and over the house, looking down into the yard. A series of three tastefully lit, rectangular pools, stacked so that one cascaded to the other, descended from the back of the house. The landscaping itself was all based on structured straight-line formations working in perfect cohesion with the pool.

The back of the house was predominately made of glass with what looked like steel supports. I had no idea what the

material was, but I assumed it was the same stuff as the ghosted items I made.

Through the glass, I could see a hip couple in their late
thirties or early forties dancing together. The lady noticed
me and alerted the guy to my presence. He wore a snug-fit-
ted black wool sweater, gray wool pants with a sharp crease
and cuffs, and what looked like very expensive black shoes. I
remembered that I didn't have to dress for the weather anymore since I couldn't feel temperature any longer, so I blinked
together a look as cool as I could think of, complete with a
stylish leather jacket to illustrate just how little I cared about
the weather.

He walked up to the glass and raised his voice. "No, thank
you," he said while looking me up and down to nonverbally
communicate he didn't think my look was as great as I thought
it was.

"What?" I replied. "'No, thank you' to what?"

"No, thank you, we're not interested in whatever you're
here for. Bye," he said.

His partner wore a form-fitting light-gray wrap dress and
black strappy heels. She looked a little annoyed, but also a little
embarrassed. She gave off the vibe of someone who was used
to entertaining and didn't want to be rude, so she motioned for
me to come in.

I phased through the glass as politely as I could. I don't
know ... I guess I bowed my head or something.

"Well?" asked my exasperated male host, arms raised.

"Yeah, sorry. I was just walking the neighborhood and
noticed this house. I've never seen anything like it—did you
make it?"

My other host smiled, and if ghosts could, she probably
would have blushed.

"First things first, my name is Deirdre Kunkel. But please,

call me DeeDee." She walked forward with her arm out-stretched to shake my hand, adding, "and this is my husband, Jeremy Randolph."

"Hi, I'm Jonah," I said and shook her hand.

"Hi Jonah," she continued. "Thank you, and this is my master work." She gestured with her arms out, indicating the house was her creation. "I am an architect … we're both architects," she said, motioning to her husband, who gracefully acknowledged her gesture. "Like I said, this is my master work and I—" she looked at Jeremy, "—we wanted to live in this neighborhood ever since we moved to town."

"I'm a landscape architect," he added.

"This looks incredible," I said as I scanned the room.

"Let's take you on a tour then," DeeDee offered, to Jeremy's visible chagrin.

I could tell he wasn't into it by the way he slumped onto the couch, his body hunching into a disinterested slouch. His face fell flat, and he looked off toward the beautiful, long, thin bricked fireplace that was open to each side of the wall in which it was housed.

DeeDee ignored Jeremy and started the tour by walking me up a floating staircase (in the architectural sense, not supernatural … OK, fine, both senses) with a wire and metal railing. She showed me room after gorgeous room—a bedroom overlooking the cascading pools and an amazing view of downtown, two sets of offices with various drafting boards and models, a general-purpose room with a view similar to the bedroom's, and back downstairs.

I noticed bathrooms and a kitchen were conspicuously absent, but we didn't have a need for either really, so I guess she didn't feel the need to include them in her design.

After a half hour or so, we ended up back in the living room with Jeremy. DeeDee took a seat next to him on the beautiful sharp-lined couch, and I sat in a wood-paneled, black leather lounger. I was fully up to speed on the inspiration for every lamp, railing, and light switch in the house. It may sound boring, but it was impressive as hell—DeeDee knew her stuff.

She was originally from Virginia and went to school in Atlanta for architecture and engineering. In Los Angeles, she met Jeremy, a native Angelino, and they decided to move to Austin to start a business and a family. The business apparently started out great but was cut off before it could thrive after an ill-fated drive home from a holiday party. Messy scene, apparently.

When the conversation turned to me, I decided to present my new occupation of saving after-lives rather than my prowess with a spreadsheet.

"We're good," Jeremy said.

"This place," DeeDee explained, "is our 'unfinished business,' as you described. Now that we're here, we have everything we want. Why would we move on?"

They had a point I couldn't argue—the place was amazing. They had each other and their dream. What would they move on to?

Jeremy stood up from the couch, indicating it was time for me to go, so I stood as well. As they walked me out the front, DeeDee had a flash of inspiration.

"I have something for you." She whirled around. "Four houses down is a group of—gentlemen. You may want to drop in on them."

Jeremy's face flashed surprise. "Oh! Yes. Jonah, if you can move them on along … wow. We would owe you—so big."

OK. It's a case, I guess. A case? An assignment? Something to do? I felt more comfortable calling it something to do. I confirmed the address and description of the house and floated that way.

I didn't have to go too far to find it: a light-gray, smooth-plaster, flat-roofed house with floor-to-ceiling windows ten feet across on either side of its black front door. The yard was perfectly manicured with lush green grass and a rectangular gravel bed around the perimeter of the house. I could hear loud voices and laughter from the street—no wonder DeeDee and Jeremy wanted these guys gone. I approached the house feeling a little like the cop that's about to break up the party— or maybe the Jehovah's Witness, ready for a challenge.

What I mistook for the sounds of a party morphed into something ominous as I drew closer: grown men's voices taunting like schoolyard bullies pulled straight from an old movie of the week.

Although the house was well lit, it felt dark, sticky. A man and a woman reclined on their couch, drinking wine and watching TV, oblivious to the noises coming down the hall … save one.

"Mommy?" a small voice whined from behind a half-opened door.

"Back to bed, Eric," the woman replied from the couch. "I'm not going to tell you again."

I heard crying, and then the footsteps of a young child running as the door slammed shut behind him. I moved swiftly down the hall as I heard disturbing refrains coming from Eric's bedroom.

"*Mommy!*" a voice mocked.

"Mommy!" another voice repeated.

Menacing laughter erupted as I discreetly phased through the door to scan the room. I watched as a rotund, bearded ghost of a man in his late fifties knocked a stuffed animal from a shelf. Eric looked up from his covers and pulled his head back under, making himself as small as possible.

I lurched back out of the room as quickly as I could before someone noticed me, and I frantically searched the house for something I could use. I floated through a closet in the hall but discovered only games and linens—nothing helpful. In the garage, though, I found some golf clubs, so I ghosted a nine iron and then made my way back through the house. Again, I felt the darkness creep over me, as if the air's viscosity changed. I floated toward Eric's room, alert and on guard.

Phasing through his door again, this time I entered the room with as much bravado as I could muster. The room fell silent as the gang of ghosts took notice.

"Welll," drawled a voice. I looked to its source to see a big bald guy—six foot two and muscular—wearing a plain white T-shirt (somehow soiled) and jeans. He was fully tatted out, though the ink had no cohesion; it was a series of what looked like homemade illustrations.

"What do you think you're going to do with that?" he asked, rising from the child's dresser he was leaning against and sauntering toward me.

"I bet, right about now, you're wondering how big a mistake you made coming to this house," he said as he circled me.

I should probably have said something.

The two other guys in the room were pretty big as well. There was the fat one I described earlier in cutoff sleeves, a biker vest, jeans, and boots, and a wiry guy in jeans and a button-down shirt missing its sleeves who sat on a toy box in the corner. Sneering.

I was just about to say something perfect—I can't remember exactly what it was, but I just knew it was going to be good—when two hands suddenly grabbed my left shoulder. Just before I flew fifty feet or so only to stop (hard and im-

mediately) against the far wall of the house, I remembered
(a little too late) that there were supposed to be four guys in
this house. Good thing I couldn't get a concussion … at least I
didn't think I could get a concussion.

"Bitch!" I heard from what was now the far side of the
house for me. Then laughter. Laughter that got louder as it got
closer. I'd lost the nine iron somewhere between here and the
boy's room and found myself defenseless as the four ghosts
phased their way into the room—a beautiful room, by the way.
It was a cool house.

"Hey, hey," squawked a new apparition—another wiry
one—as he entered the room. He seemed kind of dirty, greasy
even, with a cock-sure swagger that an education cut short
after the eighth grade probably helped reinforce.

"Hey," he said again.

I heard him the first time.

"I heard you the first time," I said as I got up and dusted
myself off. After a few seconds, I realized I didn't need to do
that (no dust for us ghosts), so I stopped mid-motion kind of
awkwardly.

"You lose this, boy?" he asked, twirling my nine iron.

"Yes, thank you," I said in as friendly a tone as possible,
smiling and holding my hand out as if to retrieve it. Maybe I
shouldn't have been so sarcastic.

He took a full swing that connected right under my chin
and knocked me back through a wall and into a huge walk-in
closet. I definitely shouldn't have been so sarcastic. I looked
around to get my bearings and found myself in a closet filled
with suits and dresses, all perfectly placed on hangers. Shoes
rested on risers, and there were drawers for shirts and sweaters.
I believed it was cedar-planked, and I wished I could smell
it—then something in the corner caught my eye. The un-
mistakable stock and handle of a twelve-gauge pump-action

shotgun.

God bless Texas.

I ghosted a version of the shotgun as well as the closet door. I needed something to kick out for the perfect action sequence.

I reentered the bedroom in amazing form as I kicked out the ghosted door and pumped the shotgun.

"Come get some," I sneered.

The room fell silent. I didn't see anyone laughing now.

I should have waited to pump the shotgun. Now would have been a better time while everyone was quiet.

My four adversaries regained their composure as they each pulled their own pistols.

Right. I wish I had a bigger gun.

I noticed the dirty, wiry guy's eyes widen a little as he looked at my gun.

I followed his gaze. It was bigger. My gun was bigger, like I was in a damn cartoon.

Of course, this is just like the clothes.

I quickly blinked a gun belt with grenades attached and two bandoliers of bullets across each shoulder. I thought of Stallone with two huge machine guns, and without looking, I knew that I already had them in my hands. I started shelling, and the room erupted with noise, bullets, and flying casings.

One of the goons managed to get off a shot or two on their way out of the room and hit me. *Damn, that stung.* I wondered what it felt like to get hit with the big ones I was shooting. *Probably bad. I'm guessing they hurt.*

I smiled as I pursued my quarry down the hallway and out the front door, guns-a-blazing. Two of them fell in the yard and held up their hands, hoping I would accept their surrender. I'm not exactly sure how we process damage as ghosts, but we can definitely get hurt.

The fat one walked back, hands up, to join his friends.

"Loyal, I guess I can respect that," I said.

He nodded and collapsed onto the front lawn.

"You want to tell me what you were up to back there?"

The fat one, now flat on his back, spoke between breaths. "Kids can sense us way better than adults. More fun to scare 'em."

"That is so messed up. I don't know where to begin. That ends tonight. You're never doing it again … right?"

They mumbled amongst themselves.

"Right?" I repeated. "You're never doing it again. Say it," I repeated, this time aiming an even larger gun at the group.

"We're never doing it again," they replied in unison.

"Good. That's better. Now, you're going to leave, and you're not going to come back. Understood?"

They all nodded, but I wasn't sure I believed them.

"If I catch you here again, I'm going to take you back with me and put you down in a very dark place for a very long time. The kind of place where the only music is weeping and gnashing of teeth. Do we understand each other?"

They all nodded again, but this time I believed them. Good thing they bought into my dark prison bit, although I guess it wasn't that big of a jump, given what I'd just conjured in front of them.

"Oh, and make sure to pass the message along if you see your bald friend," I said.

"Don't worry, we will," the greasy one said, "but we'll make him wish for what you just described if we ever see him again."

"Alright … well, y'all go ahead and get moving," I said.

"Have a nice night, sir," the fat one said.

"Real sorry," said the greasy one, "you'll never see us again."

The last one just gave me an awkward wave and avoided eye contact, and I watched them fly off to the north. Once they were sufficiently small enough on the horizon, I walked back inside. No need to phase my way in through Eric's door this time as it was open, his mother spooning with him on his little bed and stroking his hair. Yep, I was done here.

I floated up and followed Baylor Street until I ran across the public art installation called Hope Outdoor Gallery. It's a few hundred feet of walls that graffiti artists use as their canvas, but it's something to behold.

I decided to stop and check it out for the first time up close, examining individual pieces and looking for their tag. I wasn't there long before I caught movement out of the corner of my eye. My head whipped around, and I thought I saw the girl from the other night on Congress, slightly obscured by a tree.

I squinted (not that it helped—no real eyes) to try to discern if it was her or not, but she walked behind another tree and disappeared. She wasn't concealed by its trunk; it was too young a tree for that. She was just gone—Cheshire Cat style.

I shook my head and floated above South Lamar, a north-and-south street, and made my way south. It was a scenic route that took me by the edge of downtown and across the river to the south side of town.

Once I arrived back home, I decided to challenge myself to phase down from the roof and directly onto my bed, like I did when I was in junior high at my desk with wads of paper and a trash can. If I could land directly and perfectly flat on my bed, then I was the grand champion of champions.

I missed, but just barely.

Chapter 15

I faded into a familiar smell. Bleh. I hated waking up to smoke. Zoe and her team must be at the house. I ghosted my trusty pen out of my work bag once again and headed straight for the kitchen where I found the welcome space I expected—sandalwood-smelling incense, candles, and eight familiar faces circled around a bowl with a crackling old transistor radio from some sort of ancient time—like the '80s—set beside it. I didn't wait on Zoe to summon me and headed straight for the ashes. Sweaters and knitted blankets were tightened (they were prepared for me this time).

What's up?

Zoe smiled. "Plenty, but try saying it."

What? What did she mean, "say it"? Oh yeah! Why didn't I think about this before? The ol' spirit talking via white noise trick, of course!

Going back to the early days of radio, there have been accounts that detail mysterious voices coming through speakers, accounts that continued on with the advent of television. I used to love to watch "ghost hunting" shows where they walked around old houses yelling into the air and then listening to recordings for phantom replies.

"Testing, testing, is this thing on?" My voice crackled through the old radio. "Want to thank everyone for coming out tonight. Show of hands, who here is from out of town?"

Zoe leaned back and shot a sideways look at Max with a victorious smile as he took a twenty out of his pocket and passed it around the circle until it made its way to her. She mouthed "thank you" and graciously bowed her head.

"We were kind of getting frustrated with the ashes thing, buddy," Max explained into the air, as though he were looking at me. He wasn't, and it entertained me more than it should have.

He was right. I was already tired of writing everything down. It was getting to be a bit of a mental beating, and I was beginning to wonder how long we could keep that up—kind of like how we could easily call our old friends to catch up, but we didn't because talking on the phone seemed like such a hassle. Or like texting someone that wouldn't let the conversation end. Anyway, we had a new solution, and I liked it.

"Jonah," Zoe said, "we have a business opportunity for you."

"Cool, I'm listening," I said. "But I don't need money, so I'm not really sure what's in it for me. That came out sounding more selfish than I meant. I just mean that my motivations—"

"OK, I get it. Just let me finish the thought," Zoe said.

She was looking at me. Maybe she could see me, and maybe it was just the smoke from the incense, but it seemed like more than a good guess. She continued, "OK, I'll put it this way—I have a proposition to keep you busy."

Max chimed in, "I went to talk to Zoe today about researching some other ways we could communicate with you. She had to take a call during our meeting, and I figured out

they were talking about another haunting. So I had this idea—
why don't we help? We've got a ghost … he's doing this stuff
for free right now … why not help people and make a little
money?"

Zoe continued, "So I agreed to let y'all in on my business,
if you were up for it."

I floated around the room as I thought it over, the tips of
the candles' flames following me. It was a pretty cool effect.
Hmm.

"Sounds a little self-serving though. I mean, right now I'm
just doing it because I like to help people."

"You said it yourself," Max began. "You can't use money,
so it's not self-serving at all. You could—say—give your cut to
me."

I guess Max had more of a head for business than I gave
him credit for.

"Why would I let you keep the money when I could give it
to Mom or Taylor?" I replied.

"Good question. Why would you give your cut to me
instead of your family?" Max said, repeating the question aloud
but to himself. "Because it's how you'll cover your part of the
rent here—and I think the loan officer for the mortgage company would like to see another stream of income other than
the slightly-above-minimum hourly wage I make at the law
firm and the lucrative—but still new and unproven—revenue
from Meme in my Coffee."

"You named your company Meme in my Coffee," I
laughed—not hard, it wasn't that funny. "OK, if I'm helping
you and the fine, upstanding ghosts of Austin move on, I suppose that keeps me firmly in the do-gooder category. Kind of
like a police officer or firefighter."

Zoe added, "Don't forget our clients. You're helping them too."

"Alright, I'm interested. How do you see this going down?"

Zoe and Max filled me in on ideas from their brainstorming session earlier in the day. The general premise was that they would spend time sitting and talking with the client in the home while I talked to the haunter in residence. They thought it was a good idea to continue with Zoe's prepared ceremony, including the incense, because it would help the Psy-kicks see spirits through the fog. Also, that whole bit really set a mood, and it would probably make our customers feel like they were getting their money's worth. I insisted they just use the sandalwood-smelling kind for every room though. I got sick just thinking about the other smell. At some point in the night, the spirit would need to move on, consider moving on, or we would make them leave the house.

"Oh, and we have an all-inclusive package now!" Zoe said. "$3,000—all in—for the exorcism. No need for the per-attempt charge now that we have a guy on the inside."

"That was my idea," Max chimed in, scanning the room and making sure everyone knew. "That was my idea."

Zoe rolled her eyes. "That was Max's idea, and a good one." Zoe placated Max with a gentle high five.

"Yeah," cool haircut Quinton added, "maybe now some of us can afford to eat three meals a day."

"When do we start?" I asked.

"How about now?" Zoe offered.

I agreed, and the group broke to stand, stretch, and extinguish the bundles of incense around the house. Zoe collected the little transistor radio and left it on as we all filed out of the house toward an old but clean, white, fifteen-passenger van.

"Shotgun," I crackled through the whining old radio, looking at Max as he threw up his hands in frustration. I was always better at getting the drop on calling the passenger seat, and it was good to know I still had the knack—even from the great beyond. Zoe started the van and tuned the radio to static so we could communicate on the way to our first client's house. I wondered if that made me a Psy-kick now …

I began to sing through the radio.

"Don't make me turn this off," Zoe threatened as her hand shot to the volume knob, but it was too late. Max picked up where I left off, and cool-haircut Lin joined him. Before too long, the whole van minus Zoe crooned along to Survivor's "Eye of the Tiger" from *Rocky III* while I sang the guitar part. Dun! Dun-dun-dun!

Zoe stopped the van about a block short of the client's house and asked me to go scout it out. She showed me the address and a picture of the house on her phone, and I floated down the street to find it.

Our client's house was a split-level built in the '70s in the Zilker neighborhood—a small community in South Austin. I phased through the front door and started scanning room to room, looking for the source of our client's problem. I found our client, a young woman in her twenties. She hadn't fully changed from work, but was wrapped in a well-worn knit sweater. A small, scruffy, black-and-tan, mixed-breed dog sat at her feet, looking up as she made a late dinner over her stove.

I dropped down to the bottom floor of the house and into a wood-paneled and rock-walled multipurpose room. There, on the far side, sat a teenage boy in bell bottoms and a green-and-yellow ringed T-shirt, moping around, trying to tune a busted-up old guitar. He didn't notice me, so I floated back up and made sure I'd checked every other room to confirm there weren't any other spirits hanging around. Once satisfied that the kid was my case, I floated back to the van.

"It's a teenager," my voice crackled through the speakers. "Looks sad, what have we heard from the client?"

"Our client works in tech," Zoe said, "and bought the house after she sold an app she'd been working on since college. Strange things have been happening with her electronics—her TV cuts off constantly as well as her music. She's had people over to look at them both, but no one can figure out why. Her room downstairs gets colder than the rest of the house at night, and she's been through multiple A/C and insulation guys who can't solve those problems either. She mentioned that she always gets a little sad when she goes down there, so she stopped using it altogether. Most recently, she thought she heard a voice in the house. Her dog sitter said the same, and recently quit."

"OK, I'll go talk to the kid," I said.

Zoe turned around in the driver's seat. "Alright, everybody, let's do this."

She turned the key and drove the van the rest of the way to the house. The Psy-kicks, which now included Max, piled out of the van and headed toward the front door. So did I, but I didn't wait with them and just went on through. I heard the doorbell ring as I floated over to the stairs.

To reduce the risk of scaring him, I decided to walk down like a normal person, and my efforts succeeded. He acknowledged my presence with a nod, and I returned the gesture with another. He told me his name was Ozzy, and he died in an electrical accident in the house while trying to wire up a few guitar amps he'd collected to make sure the entire neighborhood could hear him play instead of just the fifty houses within closest proximity.

He felt protective of his little brother Kyle, who was four at the time of the accident, and didn't feel like he could move on and leave him behind. Kyle grew up and went off to school, and his parents sold the house shortly after that and moved to Florida. Ozzy never figured out how to leave the house and found himself blocked in. He instinctively constructed the guitar he was still tuning but didn't understand what I meant when I asked him how he did it. Maybe it was such a critical part of his identity, he couldn't imagine being without it.

He hadn't figured out how to change clothes either—maybe he wasn't able to. He just stayed in the same house night after night. Bored. He copped to turning our client's shows off because he thought they were annoying.

"Just all these plastic-looking phonies talking about how they're the right one for some stupid guy—so dumb. And why are people orange now?" he asked. I didn't have a good answer.

He said he turned off her music because it "sucked."

I shared with him what I'd been doing for other spirits around town, and it didn't take long before his door appeared. He gave me a wave and a nod of the head as he strolled through, and I noticed his teenage façade break for a moment as he saw the other side. Whatever he saw moved him.

Feeling good about myself, I floated back upstairs to find the group circled in deep meditation. Zoe felt like she needed to stay in practice, and it was yet another thing that made the customer feel like they got their money's worth. The group reacted to the change in temperature as I entered the circle and opened their eyes to see the words:

I'm sorry I scared you. Wipe, wipe. **I'll move on.**

The client teared up and buried her face in the little scruffy dog. I floated out of the house and back to the van, settling just above the passenger seat to wait for the group. Zoe returned with an envelope overstuffed with cash and opened the driver's side door as the rest of the Psy-kicks piled in from the side.

"We even got a tip," she said as she got in and turned the key to start the van. Max opened the door to the passenger side.

"Still shotgun," I said through the speakers.

Max shook his head, slammed the door shut, and piled in the back with the rest of the group. The van slowly pulled away from the curb and out into the night.

We were waiting at a stoplight, about to head south out of the neighborhood, when I noticed what looked like a fun ghostly gathering at a little strip mall on the west side of Lamar.

"I'll catch up with y'all later," I announced through the speakers.

I heard a few "be goods," "okays," and one loud "shotgun" from the van as I floated off in the direction of what looked like a fun time.

Chapter 16

I heard voices and laughter and saw groups of ghosts hanging out in the parking lot. Music spilled from an open door. Calling it a strip mall may have been a little generous as it was really just three buildings close together, owned by different people, with a converted gas station beside them that had been turned into a fast-food burrito joint.

The outside of the shops had been recently renovated with a stucco application to bring the disparate looks together. I floated toward the open door and found it propped into place by a box fan that kept the area cool. I guessed it must have been a nice night, temperature-wise.

I walked into a pottery workshop with work displayed along the walls and items on tables in various stages of progress. On the far side of the room, in front a kiln, played a band with two singers, a guitar player, a drummer behind a small kit, and a little string quartet. In the middle of the room sat four stations of pottery wheels, all attended by local artisans with faces fixed in looks of focus and determination.

Behind them at each station—very closely behind—sat ghosts with their arms wrapped around each person as though they were helping guide their hands along the clay. Each ghost mugged for their friends and various onlookers as they cheered them on. It was about that time that I recognized the band was playing "Unchained

Melody" from the Righteous Brothers.

I rolled my eyes, laughed, and turned to leave when I noticed the girl I'd seen the last few nights directly behind me. Dressed in all black again, this time with a perfectly tailored leather motorcycle jacket, jeans, and dingo-style boots, she looked stylishly tough and intimidating as hell.

She smiled when she saw me.

"Can you believe they've been doing this for like thirty years?" she said. "Same song, for hours, until they finally close up shop."

She spoke in a rich voice with a bit of a scratch and a hint of an accent that I couldn't quite place. Maybe Middle Eastern—Israeli, I thought.

"Thirty years," I replied. "No wonder they have it down so well. These guys are good."

"It's kind of a thing. Newbies come for fun while the old-timers come to make fun of it and pretend they're not having a good time."

"I'm Jonah," I said, offering a hand.

"I know," she replied, shaking it.

"I've seen you around, haven't I?"

"Yes," she said, and I realized how much cooler this conversation would be if we had drinks in our hands so we could take sips in between our exchanges while posing in nonchalant stances. She continued, "I've seen you around."

Damn, she was mysterious. *What should I talk about ... the weather? No. Books? No.* I wondered how I could read books now, and if I could ghost one. Then, I focused back on the conversation.

"So, what did you do?" I started with a terrible question and continued with, "You know, before—all this."

She looked somewhat amused.

"Ah, before this," she said, looking around and acting as though I meant the pottery shop. "Before this, I was a soldier."

That would explain her ability to carry herself in such a way as to simultaneously attract and terrify me.

"What brought you to Austin?" I said, cringing inside as soon as the words came out of my mouth. *God, I am boring—this sucks.*

"I was reassigned," she replied and volleyed back, "what about you—what did you do?"

"What do you know about spreadsheets?"

"Very little."

"Then you may be impressed to learn that I was a business analyst."

"No. Not really, that sounds boring."

"I'll have you know, it not only sounds boring—it is."

She looked down and laughed, and I started to feel as though I might actually be able to hold a conversation with this girl when I noticed a familiar face outside—Willard Hensch.

"Something wrong?" she asked, looking behind her.

Willard noticed us looking and tried to obscure himself behind a group of ghosts hanging out in the front.

"Would you mind excusing me?" I said.

She nodded. "Of course," she said and mingled her way toward another group.

I floated up through the roof for a better vantage point of the parking lot and saw Willard standing behind a group of spirits with his knees slightly bent so as not to be seen from inside the building. Some of the ghosts in the group observed his presence but ignored him. I made eye contact as I floated down.

"What's up?" I said before touching down on the asphalt, pleased with my pun.

Willard didn't seem to get it. He straightened up, looked me in the eye, and said, "Hello."

"Little surprised to see you here," I said. "Doesn't exactly seem like your scene. You know, being around other people—outside."

"Yes. Well. I have been forced to try new things as of late. I was just passing through, and I noticed this—gathering—so I thought I would look in."

I didn't know Willard well, but I felt like we'd spent enough quality time together to get a sense that he wasn't telling the truth. Something was off.

"So, are you living over here now? I mean, have you found another space?"

"Yes. Yes, I found a nice quiet house owned by a man that is rarely home. Travels a lot for work."

I could tell he thought he really nailed that delivery as a look of self-satisfaction spread across his face. He had changed though—literally. He was wearing something new, probably for the first time in years. A gray button-down, dark-gray slacks, and some sort of sensible dress shoe with a rubbery sole—on the athletic side of the orthotic shoe continuum.

Wasn't a good look, wasn't a bad look. In fact, I would describe it as a look for someone that didn't want to draw attention, which fit Willard quite well, actually, and was a step up from before. So good for him.

"Well, good, I'm glad you found a place," I said. "You know where to find me if you ever need anything."

"I certainly do."

Then he was gone, just like that. A couple ghosts in the group beside me noticed as well, and I took note that Willard's blinking out surprised them.

"Huh," I said out loud to myself.

Seph taught me how to do it, and I wondered how Willard learned. Politely nodding to the group, I made my way back inside to find—I forgot to ask her name.

I floated through the door to the familiar tune of "Unchained Melody" and scanned the room for the Cheshire Cat girl. There were new ghosts at two of the stations and the other two sat empty. It looked as though people were heading home for the night, which made sense because it was late.

I looked around a few minutes more before giving up. She must have left, so I decided to head home.

I was ready to be back and didn't feel like taking the long way, so I just blinked myself there. Finding the house quiet and dark when I returned, I floated to my room, turned on the TV to break the silence, and watched three little superheroes save a town from a turban-wearing monkey until I faded out into morning.

Chapter 17

The next few nights were fairly uneventful. Max and I hung out a lot and watched TV, cracked a few jokes, and played a few games. Max would set up my cards facing away from him, and I'd guide him to which one I wanted to play, crackling my moves through a portable radio. We always liked getting groups together to play board games, and he was good at finding new ones before they really caught on.

Zoe, Quinton, and Lin would sometimes stop by after class and play with us too. I'd set out after everyone left or Max went to sleep to scan the neighborhood, but there didn't seem to be any more listless spirits in the area for me to help. I ended up back at the house, flipping channels between twenty-four-hour news stations and cartoons.

I discovered that I couldn't ghost a book to read because I was just making a copy of what I saw. If I didn't know the words—all the words—I couldn't ghost a book.

Max was kind enough to set up my old computer so that the screen wouldn't time out. I could tap the space bar to start and stop an audiobook whenever I wanted to. We downloaded a few like *The Hobbit*, which had always been one of my favorites and read like a new book to me every few years I went back to it. We added some Neil Gaiman and a couple Douglas Adams books. Of course, as part of the process, I had to give him my login. He went on to make a big show of what he could do now that he had access to all my old apps and spent a significant amount of time checking my browser history.

Thankful for private browsing, I wandered around the house looking for something to do while he entertained himself. I noticed he had a glass of water on the nightstand next to his bed, so I went ahead and knocked that over and onto his pillow for him.

Finally, the weekend came around, and we got a call with a new case. We were headed back to Tarrytown to help a family that recently noticed some very strange things. Zoe brought the van by to pick us up, and we met her outside. Max thought ahead and didn't bring a radio outside with him, which allowed him to proclaim "shotgun" in a loud, clear voice as the van rolled to a stop and which prevented me from beating him to it.

Max strode victoriously over to the passenger side of the vehicle while I phased through the van. Once inside, I hovered between Zoe and Max as she gave us the rundown on our clients for the night: a young couple, Barb and Tim, thirty and thirty-two respectively, with a four-year-old little girl named Haley. Within the past week, they'd noticed strange sounds and cold spots around the house—particularly in Haley's room—and she'd started talking as though someone was in the room with her. After checking in a few times to find her alone, Barb took her to a psychologist as well as her priest. Apparently, this case was a referral. *Thank you, Father Chandler.*

We came to a stop down the street from their modest bungalow, with another perfectly manicured lawn.

When I phased through the front door, I found Mom and Dad on the couch and heard a gruff voice down the hall. Sensing a familiar energy, I floated down the hallway and stopped short of what I guessed was Haley's room to overhear what was being said.

"Then, right after you fall asleep, that's when I'll get ya." The gruff voice of a six-foot-two bald man boomed over the shoulder of little Haley.

I looked into a stereotypical little girl's room: pink walls with a mural of a castle on one side of the room, and two sliding-door closets that took up the width of the other side of the room. Stuffed animals and toys lined shelves up and down a wall, and there was a custom toy box/bench built in underneath a picture window with stylish shades and gauzy white curtains for the fourth. An antique wrought-iron bed sat against the castle-painted wall and took up most of the middle of the room. Haley sat on a cute purple rocking horse while she brushed the hair of a blonde plastic doll. Unlike Eric, she wasn't scared at all. She rocked back and forth, smiling.

"No, you won't," she said. "You can't do anything. You're just a ghost, silly."

The burly ghost mumbled a string of inaudible curses and kicked his leg out in frustration, barely making a small stuffed dog wiggle on the floor. Little Haley had transformed the muscle-bound apparition to the afterlife equivalent of Sweetums from the Muppets.

Impressed with our youngest client, I phased out of the room and hurried back toward the van.

"Alright," my voice crackled over the speakers. "I got this. He probably won't move on, but I don't think we'll have any trouble getting him to leave."

"Copy that," Zoe said, turning the key to the van and putting it in gear.

The van pulled in front of the client's house, but I decided to go topside and through the roof to check on Haley and bald biker Sweetums.

It wasn't long before Tim and Barb gathered Haley to meet the Psy-kicks in the living room, and I watched my case slump onto the bed with his feet still on the floor and his head in his hands. I peeked through the ceiling.

"What's up?" I said.

He looked up slowly, initially failing to register my pun, but slowly shook his head as recognition dawned.

"Damn, son, I'm beginning to think you like me."

I floated down to the floor.

"Yeah," I said. "On opposite day."

"Wow, really nailed that one," he said sarcastically.

"Look, they can't all be gems," I replied. "One-liners are more of a numbers game for me."

He nodded. "What did you do with my friends?" he asked, standing up to loom over me.

"We came to an understanding," I shot back, as cool as I could muster. "I'm pretty sure they're looking for you though."

"Good. And when we—"

"I'm pretty sure you don't want them to find you," I interrupted.

Judging by the way I found myself flying through the house and bouncing against the wall to the garage, I could tell he didn't like the way I talked to him. I got up as quickly as I could, but it wasn't long before he was in the room with me.

The garage was neat and organized, with everything in its

place. Lots of cleaning supplies lined the shelves on the walls, but I didn't notice any tools. One black hybrid car and a silver minivan took up most of the space in the two-car garage and were the only things between me and big bald Sweetums over there.

He looked at me with wild eyes, shoulders squared, "muscles" flexing.

Quinton opened the door, walked through him, and set down a bundle of incense. My shiny-domed adversary looked surprised as Quinton walked back through him into the house. The burly ghost took a whiff of the incense, and I watched his expression change as he registered that he could actually smell something for the first time in what I guessed was a long time. He nodded his head as the corners of his mouth descended.

"That's really nice," he said.

"Sandalwood," I replied, "and some other stuff. I think this guy Kevin makes it?"

"Huh," he said.

His face hardened, and he stalked toward me, all brawn and determination. I wondered if I could take him one on one and decided to close the distance between us. I took my best swing and could tell I hurt him, but I could also tell he'd been in a lot of fights because he punched me back three times before I registered what was going on. After the third, he just pushed me back against the garage door and laughed at me.

Fighting isn't like the movies. It helps to actually train—or get in enough of them that you know what you're doing. Most of the fights I'd been in during my life were broken up before too much could happen. In fact, by this point, Vice Principal Walker would have already been between us and leading us back to his office, but I didn't expect him to show.

I got to my feet with a plan. I'd been wanting to try some-thing for a few nights now, and this was the perfect time to experiment. I held my arms up and said, "Wait, wait, don't hit me yet."

"Alright," he said and started circling the room, surveying its contents. The minivan was backed into the garage, and he seemed to find something interesting toward the back hatch.

"So, we can do this the easy way or the hard way," I threatened, though I think it came out hollow because he just chuckled as he reached into the van and pulled out a ghosted tire iron. His eyebrows shot up as he turned the tire iron over in his hands, smiled, and looked back to me. It looked like he didn't know he could do that. I think I inadvertently taught him a valuable lesson I was about to regret.

He went on to pull the classic bad-guy move of holding the iron in one hand while menacingly tapping it in the other. I guessed it was a classic for a reason: it looked pretty scary.

"Let's try the hard way," he said, moving slowly toward me.

I smiled as energy began to flow around my hands, and I summoned my inner Goku and prepared to perform the Kamehameha.

Little by little, I saw my adversary's shoulders drop, as though memories of our last encounter dribbled down his mind like yolk from an egg cracked atop his nefarious bald noggin. His face was lit from the reflected light of the energy I was gathering in my hands, and out of the corner of my eye, I noticed frost forming on the windshield of the hybrid.

WHOOSH!

I released the pent-up energy all at once, throwing him up, back, and maybe out of the house. I flew straight up and past the roof as fast as I could to see—yes—he was definitely out of the house and arcing across several others.

Cool, it worked. Years of watching *Dragon Ball Z* finally paid off. My homework might not have been as detailed at the time, but knowing how to shoot a beam of energy from my hands sure trumped a fourth-grade book report at the moment.

I pursued him as fast as I could and dropped down next to him where he lay in the middle of a street.

"What are you, like some low-rent Pennywise?" I asked.

"I don't know who that is. It's just that kids can almost see us," he replied.

"They're kids—and you've never read or seen *IT*?"

"Oh yeah, are you talking about the clown guy?"

"Yep."

"What the hell? No. No, man, I'm not some pervy clown. I just want to be acknowledged. I want someone to know I'm there."

"Whatever. You don't mess with kids," I said.

"We've done it for years."

"That's not a valid argument."

"Fine."

"So, you're done now, right?"

"Sure," he said.

"I don't believe you."

"I'm done. I promise."

"If I catch you back here, or hear about you messing with kids again, things will go a lot worse for you than they did tonight."

"Oh yeah? How so?" he asked.

"I've got a deep, dark pit full of big bad dudes way worse than you. I catch wind of you pulling this kind of stuff, or that

you're back in this neighborhood, then you're joining them …
for a long time. You won't like it. It won't be fun."

"I've been to prison before," he said.

"Not like this, nothing like this. Pennywise has nightmares
about my pit."

His forehead relaxed as though he were no longer thinking of a comeback, but of terrifying consequences. I was lucky
enough to have my supernatural jail bit work again.

"We're done here, then," I said. "You're off to another
neighborhood, no more messing with people, no more haunt-
ings. Say it."

"Fine, I'm out of here, and I'll keep to myself."

"You don't have to keep to yourself. You could consider
doing something beneficial."

He laughed. "Like what?"

"I don't know … help someone find their wallet or keys
sometime."

"Alright, fine, maybe I'll do that. What's your name, kid?"

"Jonah."

"Jonah, are you going to keep kicking me out of places I
want to live?"

"Not if you keep to what we agreed to."

He nodded and flew off to the west. Once he was far
enough away, I floated back to the house to write in the ashes
and let Haley know that the ghost was just being silly and
was going to go away now. She didn't seem to care that much
and skipped off to her room. Her parents, on the other hand,
demonstrated a mixture of relief and consternation at their
child's ability to handle the situation.

The Psy-kicks went about the house and collected the incense bundles, cleaning what they left behind, while Zoe was

handed another overstuffed envelope. Cool-haircut Lin called shotgun, much to the visible chagrin of Max, as the group piled into the van. We were headed to a 24/7 diner on Congress known for their banana pancakes, migas, and omelets. Apparently, they went there when we parted ways after our last case and decided it would be a tradition.

The diner was an old Austin institution with a pithy neon sign that welcomed you by apologizing for being open. Inside was an assortment of tables and booths with wood-grained Formica tabletops. The room was decorated with layers of hand-painted murals. I distinctly remembered that it smelled like hot coffee and a well-seasoned griddle from when I was alive.

We ordered a round of drinks—a mix of coffees and iced hibiscus mint teas. The excited chatter of the group hushed as Zoe pulled out the overstuffed envelope for distribution. She counted out that night's takings in front of everyone twice, then pulled some rubber bands out of her bag to wind individual bundles to dispense.

Zoe cleared her throat and began what sounded like a well-rehearsed speech.

"Another solid night of work, everyone."

A couple of Psy-kicks smiled and pantomimed excited applause. Zoe acknowledged them with a nod of her head and continued. "This is for the house," she said, holding up the largest bundle of twenties that would go toward the business expenses, rent, and so on. "This is for our intrepid spiritual guide and his sidekick."

Max bristled for show.

"Just messing with you, Max," Zoe said, turning her attention to Quinton, who was sitting next to Max. "This is for you," she said, tossing Quinton his cut and then going around the table doing the same for everyone else.

After everyone had their cash from the night's job, she raised her glass of iced hibiscus mint tea and made a toast. "To the best damn people I know—living or dead."

Smiles and the clinking of plastic glasses and thick ceramic mugs echoed around the table.

At that moment, I missed being able to eat or drink, and deliberately diverted my attention elsewhere in the room. It was surprisingly full at this hour, with people coming in as a final stop before going home from a big night out. A couple tables were full of students deep in their books, studying while nursing their coffees with endless refills.

Next to a podium by the entrance, a man waited to be seated: medium-length hair, slightly sweaty, wearing jeans and a T-shirt. I got the impression he was there to see someone, and he scanned the room in such a way that he wouldn't actually make eye contact with anyone—so unnoticeable that he was noticeable. There were plenty of apps to put people together, and who was I to judge? A waitress came to take him to a table, but he apparently had his heart set on another as he politely gestured and walked to one on the far side of the room.

I turned my attention back to Quinton, who was deep into a joke and about to deliver the punch line. "So anyway, the bartender said to the ghost, 'You want the same thing as your friend, the skeleton?' And he said, 'No, I'm just here for the boos.'"

The table cracked up.

"Hey," I crackled through a portable radio, "I'm right here. Sure, it's funny when the skeleton orders a beer and a mop because there are no such things as skeletons. Well, I mean, there are, just inside bodies."

The table fell silent.

"Hey man, I'm really sorry. I didn't think …" Quinton started.

"I'm just kidding. I love that joke," I said.

Some awkward smiles were exchanged as eyes looked anywhere around the room other than the radio and Quinton. Max ordered chips and queso for the table, and the festive mood returned. More jokes were told, stories were exchanged, and anecdotes shared about that night. Apparently, Tammy almost set the curtains on fire in the master bedroom. Effing Tammy.

I couldn't help but notice the guy sitting alone at the table on the far side of the room. It had been over an hour, and he was still just sitting there, nursing a coffee while watching us have a great time.

Around the diner, groups started breaking up, and tables began to empty while he sat waiting on someone that probably wouldn't show—poor guy. It eventually got late enough for us to leave. Zoe paid for the meal and dropped most of the group back at the office/dojo where they filtered out to their various vehicles and rideshares. She drove Max and me back home while we traded stories of the weirdest endings to nights out we'd ever had. Max finished his story as we sat parked in front of the house.

"So I pulled up to her apartment, and she just sat there with this confused look on her face. It took me a few seconds, which felt like forever in retrospect, to realize that I'd taken her back to my ex-girlfriend's apartment. You'll be shocked—no second date."

Zoe breathed a laugh out. "You're an idiot. G'night."

Max grabbed a radio and left.

"You never told me that one," I said on the way back to the house from the van.

"Yeah, Lisa Underwood," he said, shaking his head.

"Whooaa, Lisa?! No wonder you never said anything. Dude, that is hilarious. I guess that was after Kara?"

He nodded. "Please don't tell anyone."

"Max, you should know your secrets are safe with me. Partly because you're my best friend, but mainly because I can't tell anyone—because believe me, I would tell everyone we know about this."

Laughing, he shook his head as we entered the house and headed to his bathroom.

"Night, Jonah," he said, closing the door behind him.

I floated back to my room and picked up where I left off on *The Hobbit* audiobook and laid back on my bed until the sun started to come up.

Chapter 18

I faded in the next night with the bright light from my door-to-the-other-side illuminating the room and realized for the first time that it was always there when I woke up and disappeared at some point during the night. I wondered when it went away, and if it was some sort of countdown, disappearing earlier and earlier until it stopped showing up altogether. Not letting myself dwell on it for too long, I drifted around the house to see if Max was home. I found a note on the fridge that let me know he was out and wouldn't be back until late. No work for us tonight then.

I floated into the living room to find a familiar form sitting on the couch with his feet kicked up on the coffee table.

"Hey Seph," I said, hovering by the TV.

"Hey man, hope you don't mind. Thought I'd stop by and check in. Heard you've been busy."

He heard? Alright, not bad, so word is getting around about me. That's cool. Feeling upbeat and emboldened, I floated down with much ceremony into a mock Eames lounger I decided to create, modeled after one of the pieces I'd seen at DeeDee and Jeremy's house. Sure, it was a little ambitious and out of place for my little house, but I liked it. To complete the look, I blinked into a velvet smoking jacket and silk pajama pants, while holding a straight-handled pipe in my hand. A plume of ghostly smoke wafted from its bowl.

"To quote a great spaceman—don't get cocky, kid," Seph deadpanned. "You're acting as though it's a good thing I've been hearing about you."

I cocked a ghostly eyebrow. "Is it a bad thing?"

"TBD," he replied. "See, we have a set of rules ... maybe not rules ... but a code we like to live by between ... ahh ... how should I say ... planes."

Planes? What did he mean—

"What do I mean by 'planes'?" he said.

Damn—he was good.

"So let's say Max walks in right now. He looks around, and from his point of view, it's an empty room. He can't see you, he can't see me. For the sake of the illustration, a plane is just another word for a flat surface, and you can layer surfaces— like animation cells. Now stay with me." He stacked his hands one on top of the other. "On this layer—this plane—we can see him, but he can't see us. We're on a different plane. Make sense?"

I nodded. "Sure, makes sense. The layers are on top of each other, and Max can feel when the layers get close because it gets cold."

"Kinda," he said, pausing, his brow strained. "What you're talking about with the cold has more to do with energy. You're interacting with the other plane and that takes energy. Heat is a neat and efficient form of energy, so you cool down a room. Kind of like how you burned calories from food for energy when you were alive."

He stopped to think again before continuing. "I'm over-simplifying. Let's skip the science right now so I can continue on to the point I'm trying to make."

I nodded, took a ghostly drag on my pipe, and made some Baggins-esque smoke rings.

"That's cute," Seph acknowledged and continued. "So take me, an angel. I have access to entirely different planes, and I'm able to interact with both yours and the living's should I want or need to."

"So how come I don't feel cold when you're around?" I asked.

"You don't feel temperature at all, Jonah. Remember? That said, I'm a bit of a different animal altogether. You wouldn't feel a temperature change, but you would—and probably have—noticed a difference being around me. Like the night we met, you probably thought there was something unusual about me.

"Again, let's not get bogged down in scientific detail for now. Living humans, on the other hand, would only notice what I would want them to notice. We may be casual observers or a test of their hospitality. On occasion, my kind have been heralds of events to come."

"Like Gabriel," I interjected.

"Like Gabriel," he affirmed.

I flashed back to the other night when I tried to talk about Seph with the Psy-kicks but couldn't. "Why can't I remember your name or talk or write about you when I'm around my friends?"

He looked down and fidgeted with his jeans. "There are names that are to be known, and names that cannot be spoken. All for different reasons. There are reasons why Gabriel, Michael, Lucifer, or Uriel should be known on the mortal coil."

"Or Legion," I interjected again, trying to further prove that I knew things.

"Pssh," he scoffed. "Legion—could that be more over-played in modern pop culture? That was a name they used to illustrate the point that there were a bunch of them controlling that one guy. People act like it's super creepy and scary to say 'Legion.' It's an army formation made up of a few thousand soldiers—that's it. Then those jerkoffs went on to kill a bunch of pigs. *Oooh, big show of power!*" He made mock spooky hand motions on either side of his face. "Idiots. Alright, let me get back on track. Think of Jacob—do you know that story?"

"Kind of."

"Genesis tells the story of Jacob wrestling an angel but doesn't give his name. Two things—maybe three—to take away from that. One: Jacob started wrestling a guy—a regular human guy—that he later realized was an angel after he put his hip out of socket and gave him a new name. Two: the writing never mentions the angel's name. Three: it's a weird story that doesn't give much detail. It just makes it seem like some random guy goes up to him and they start wrestling—all night. There had to be more to the story than that."

He made an interesting point. Did Jacob just wait around for people to come by and wrestle?

"Alright, but how?" I said. "I couldn't even remember your name in the moment."

Seph's eyes sparkled a little, and he clapped. "Aha! Yes. Be-cause you don't have the authority. You're on a different plane of existence now, Jonah. There are different rules, but they're not written down. This is a no-man's land.

"There is a set of rules for the living—whole books of

them. You live your life, and then you move on. However, you decided you didn't want to move on. Do you realize the will you had to exercise to do that?"

Apparently it was a rhetorical question because he picked up quickly where he left off.

"You're beholden only to basic universal laws now. The one you want to know about just happens to be what humans— flesh or spirit—can and cannot be aware of. Not should not— cannot."

I nodded my head, acting as though I understood, but I didn't really.

"Which brings me to my next point—you're bumping into one of those laws now. Humans are supposed to live their lives and make their choices based on the world they're living in. With few exceptions, they're not supposed to be influenced by otherworldly interactions."

"What are you talking about? Me talking to my friends and clearing out spirits from people's homes?"

"Yes to both, and add the fact that you're in an actual business with them."

"I don't understand though. The people we're helping are already interacting with spirits. If anything, we're helping enforce the law by stopping the interaction.

"Also, you said they're not supposed to be influenced by otherworldly interactions, but you just talked about two of them with Jacob and Legion. In fact, there are examples all through the Bible of God intervening in humans' lives—testing this guy, delivering this nation, condemning this one. Playing favorites left and right."

Seph fidgeted with his jeans again.

"Trying to figure out how to dumb it down for me?" I asked.

He laughed, looked down at the Xbox controller on the coffee table, and held it up.

"No, no, sorry. You made a good point. This is an imperfect analogy, but maybe you'll follow. You know that college football game you love?"

I nodded, trying to help the story along.

"You play in a mode where you start with the existing teams, then recruit guys to build it up over time. The school you pick isn't the best, so you have to start that first season with two-and three-star guys, then you get better prospects season over season as you win more games, right?"

"Yep," I replied.

"You find yourself getting attached to that three-star talent who overachieves, remembering all those rounds of recruiting visits and the day you got him to commit. You start him immediately because of his upside, and he becomes your go-to receiver as a freshman even though you have higher-rated players on the roster, right?"

I nodded, "Uh-huh."

"So, you still love your team, but you're playing this guy because you recruited him last season and he was the first person to say 'yes' to your school in the game."

He took a breath to see if I was following. I nodded my head yes, and he continued.

"OK. Now you decide to create a player and name him something crazy to make your friends laugh when they watch you play, a player that you use all the time so they can't miss it—like a quarterback or defensive end. Dozens of guys on the roster, but you pick your favorites."

"Yep," I replied, wondering where he was going with this.

"Or your soccer game. Your players message you and tell

you they're unsettled and they want more game time, so you give it to them because they asked. Or you loan or sell them because they keep asking, replacing them with players you scouted and put in your academy, again putting players on the roster because they're young with upside and you're the one that found them. Sometimes you sim games, or even seasons, and sometimes you want to be involved."

"OK, so God plays favorites."

"Well, yeah, occasionally. He created everything. He can do what He wants. You play favorites when you create players within a game you had no hand in designing. They're simulations—they're not even real. Imagine if you came up with the idea, created a world—beings with free will—and then set them loose to see what happened. It took six billion years to get this planet ready for a few thousand years of civilization.

"He's busy, you know? This isn't the only place He created. You look at the stars in the sky, and you have to know some of those support life. Earth is just His favorite. He created humans in His image, as flawed as you all are, and He picks favorites sometimes. Moses, Abraham, David, Paul: He intervened in their lives and plenty more that aren't written down."

"Don't forget John, George, and Ringo."

"Nah, Paul is obviously the favorite."

"OK, we'll talk about that another time. So I still don't get how I'm breaking any laws by intervening. The people I'm interacting with have already been influenced by otherworldly forces."

Seph nodded and gave me a sympathetic look.

"It's a gray area. Look, you have to know by now that if angels exist, then so do demons—right?"

"I hadn't thought too much about it actually," I said.

He gave me a strange look.

"What?" I said. "Don't look at me like that. I've been having a good time. Besides, some of these ghosts are bad enough. Why would I want to think about worse things out there?"

"There are worse things out there, Jonah, and some of them are starting to petition to take action against you."

"Petition? Are you serious? Are they canvassing South Congress to get signatures? How many do they have so far?"

"Funny," Seph said, standing up and stretching. "You're funny." He began to pace around the room. "Do you know the story of Job?"

"Yeah." A little, I thought.

"OK, so Job was this guy—good guy, another one of God's favorites. But Lucifer—always quick to point out that God's favorite creation could be flawed—asked God to give him a shot at testing him."

"Yep." I nodded. "I've heard this."

"Ever think about how he asked God to do that?"

"What do you mean?"

"Most people think that Lucifer—Satan, the Devil—is some dark, gross, spiny-horned, bat-like demon sitting on a throne in Hell. That he's bitter and figuring out how to ruin people's good time on Earth. They're partly right—he's definitely looking to ruin someone's good time. But he's not some grotesque-looking creature. As a matter of fact, he's quite handsome, and a lot of fun to be around."

I cocked a ghostly eyebrow. "What?"

"Seriously, he was and is supremely impressive. I mean, you should see his hair—it looks fantastic. That was always part of his problem. Anyway, his confidence turned to pride, and his pride let him think he had a better plan to run things, and that's what got him booted from the Host.

"He still comes around from time to time to try to illustrate his original point—or maybe just to be a contrarian dick. Part of me wonders if God allows him back to eventually work out for himself that he's wrong. Anyway—so Lucifer saw that Job was God's favorite and thought the guy had it too easy and that maybe with a little bit of adversity, Job would start to turn on Him. Well, we all know he didn't, and Lucifer went on his way to do whatever he does with his time.

"Point is, that type of petitioning occurs all over. Most things stay local, but sometimes issues bubble up to those two. Imagine it as kind of like the Supreme Court here in the US."

"So you're saying that demons are starting to petition to come after me?" I asked.

He took a beat and nodded. "I just want you to be aware of what's happening around you."

I nodded back and looked down at my ghostly silk pajama pants while I zoned out to think. Just when I thought I had it figured out—I thought this was just going to be fun.

"Speaking of being unaware of what's happening around you, did you know Electric Fern is playing tonight?" Seph asked.

"Who's Electric Fern?" I replied.

"Wow—it's worse than I thought. First off, technically it's who are Electric Fern? They're a band. A great band. Your afterlife isn't all about secret clubs and symphonies. You get fantastic views of actual great living bands too. Want to go?"

"Sure," I responded.

Why not? What else did I have to do besides sit here and worry about demons coming after me now?

Brian Corley

Chapter 19

We made our way downtown to a club on Red River Street known for its barbeque and live music. There were two stages: one inside that held a couple hundred people, and one out back that overlooked a gravel-covered open space fenced in by scrap wood and sheets of corrugated metal.

Red River Street ran perpendicular to Sixth Street and was one of the last bastions of live music downtown. The show was on the stage out back and was packed with a couple thousand people in attendance.

The band walked out to thunderous applause and played a solid opening set. I couldn't believe I hadn't heard of these guys before now, and they had been touring steadily forever. I also couldn't believe we could go wherever we wanted—no backstage passes needed. Chalk up another perk of the after-life.

I looked at the smiling faces singing along in the crowd. The ghostly contingent made a pretty good showing as well. We had the luxury of a 180-degree point-of-view spectrum to choose from. Some chose a ground-level view in the crowd in front of the stage, while others floated around above and behind the stage.

Taking it all in, I noticed a familiar face toward the back of the lot. Somehow managing to isolate himself even in a c rowd was Willard Hensch. Maybe moving was the best thing to ever happen to him. He was actually out in the world—around people.

He noticed me looking and was gone almost as quickly as I saw him—as fast as the moment between blinks.

I turned my attention back to the band and enjoyed the show, trying to sing along to a catchy chorus that was new to me, but obviously not to the crowd. The crowd shouted in unison, some with their arms raised toward the band. It was then that I noticed another familiar form across the stage.

Leaning forward against a railing, holding a beer and looking down at the band from a deck built to hold VIPs, was the man I'd seen at the diner the other night. The one sitting alone at the table. Again, he struck me as someone who was there by himself, quiet and stoic as those around him danced and sang along with the band. He vacantly looked on, took a pull on a long-neck beer bottle, and walked away into the crowd, presumably back inside. *Did he just see me and walk away? Am I paranoid?*

Probably, but news that a demon attorney has their sights set on you can really do a number on a guy.

I wrestled my attention back to the present and to the amazing show in front of me. Damn, these guys were great. After a couple encores, the band called it a night, and the crowd started to disperse.

"What did you think?" Seph asked. "These guys are alright, huh?"

"Yeah, they're amazing. I can't believe I hadn't heard of them before," I replied.

"That's good," he said, poking me in the chest to make a point. "It's nice to discover things out there we never considered before, huh?"

"Subtle as a hammer, Seph."

He laughed. "Hey look, man, I gotta get going. Think

about what we talked about tonight, and watch yourself."

"I did that once," I replied. "It was weird."

"You're funny," Seph said, floating off. "Hope you stay that way."

What a night, I thought as I floated out and onto Sixth Street. It was one of those times I really missed being able to drink. Eventually, I got to Austin's premier ghostly nightclub and phased through the wall to a packed house—looked like some serious overflow from the concert along with the regulars. There was a big band on stage—four-piece horn section, two guitars, bass, keys, and a singer all dressed in black suits—and they were killing it.

Out of habit, I walked over and leaned against the bar. There were others there, some on stools, some standing, and some with drinks in their hands. It looked right for a bar, but I just couldn't get into it. Why have something in my hand I couldn't really use?

"Hey you," a voice purred from beside me.

It was the Cheshire Cat girl I kept running into—my night was looking up.

I looked over and tried to play it cool, acting surprised, as if I didn't recognize her voice immediately from the one con-versation we had.

"Hey," I said like a real Cyrano de Bergerac. "Great band." I nodded toward the stage.

"Yeah," she said, nodding back and smiling, "they're one of my favorites here."

"You come here a lot?" I asked.

"Yes, quite often actually," she replied.

What a great accent. I steeled myself. It was time to draw on a trusty pickup line that had been passed down to me from an old friend in high school. Well, maybe not old, but he was a senior when I was a junior—that isn't important.

We'd been through many a battle before, me and the pickup line, and it was time to call upon it once again. The cavalry trumpet in my mind blared, and we charged into the fray.

"So you've probably heard a thousand pickup lines before, maybe even a couple hundred right at this spot."

When her eyebrow rose, I knew she was wondering where I was going with this.

"So I shouldn't even try one of those," I said.

"I'd advise against it," she replied.

"So I should really just try to get to know you."

"Good idea."

"If you could be any animal in the world, what would you be?" I asked.

"Hmm. Good question. Land or sea?"

"Land."

"OK. I'd say an elephant because I would be smart, formidable, but still social," she said.

"Interesting answer. An elephant, huh? OK, same question, but now the ocean," I replied.

"Oh, that's easy—orca. Same reasons as before. Did you know that they can kill a great white shark?"

"Yes! I've seen a video of that, fascinating," I said.

"Mm-hmm."

"OK, last one. If you were a fruit, what would you be?" I asked.

"Tough one, tough one. I think I'll go with tomato," she said.

"Did you say that because most people don't think it's a fruit?"

"Maybe … what?" She punched my shoulder. "What?"

"Nothing, I just think you're more of a fineapple," I replied.

Yes! Near-perfect delivery. Every pause in delivery, every nuance, played right into my hand.

"What is a fineapple?" she asked.

My ego turned to ice while my sense of irony touched it lightly with a small hammer, disintegrating me internally into a million different pieces. Dammit, the accent was a dead giveaway. *We're from two different worlds. Why did I think that would work?*

I started to explain, "See, it's a dumb play on words—"

"I know," she laughed. "I'm fucking with you, idiot."

"Nice one," I said, thankful I couldn't blush anymore. " Nice one."

We had a Cameron Crowe-ian moment as we turned our attention back to the band while we enjoyed the music and the proximity of each to the other.

The band finished their set, and we decided to take a walk down Sixth. It was a nice night, the sky was clear, and the moon was almost full. We were a few blocks down the sidewalk before either of us spoke.

"So," she started. "There is a lot of talk about you, Jonah."

Cool, she remembered my name—maybe not the takeaway here, but cool.

"Really? What kind of talk?" I replied.

She turned to look at me as we walked, and then turned back. "Some say you're going around kicking people out of their homes—like some sort of vigilante."

"Like Batman," I offered. "Do you think I should wear a cowl?"

"So it's true," she said with a soft smile. "Yes, it would improve your look."

"Hey," I shot back, a little hurt. "I guess I could see how it could come off that way. Mostly I'm just trying to help people."

"By kicking them out of their homes?"

"I don't think I've actually kicked anyone out of their homes, but I've definitely ushered out some unwelcome other-worldly houseguests."

"I've heard that too. They say you can do crazy things, make things appear from nowhere."

"You mean like a nightclub with bands playing phantom instruments?" I said sarcastically and pointed behind us. How were my abilities any more remarkable than the guy who created what we just left?

"It took him years to create that club. It takes a musician time to create their instrument, and they have almost imprint-ed on them anyway from years of practice. From what I hear, you can just make things." She splayed her hands out in front of her face like an expanding flower. "Poof."

Huh. I didn't think of that.

"Who are 'they,' by the way? They sure know a lot," I said.

She smiled. "I have my sources. Maybe a little bird told me. Perhaps you could show me, Jonah."

"What," I said, "here?"

"Sure, why not?"

"Nah, not here—too many people."

I had the idea that the outdoor art gallery would be a perfect spot at this time of night, plus it had the added symmetry of our having met there once already—kind of. She agreed, and we floated up and over in that direction.

We landed on the sidewalk along Lamar and walked the rest of the way over. A bottle on the ground caught my attention.

"See, one way to do it is to grab at an object that's actually there." I stopped, reached down for the bottle, and came back with its ghostly facsimile. "See?"

"Impressive," she remarked. "What else can you do?"

"Hmm. I can do this," I said as I turned the bottle into a paintbrush, waggling my eyebrows, inviting an impressed response.

She breathed out a polite laugh. "OK, I can see how that would be useful here."

In a moment of inspiration, I grew the paintbrush four feet in length and tossed it toward the bottom wall of the outdoor gallery. The brush sailed through the air and started applying a ghostly message across the surface with the flourish of a form at the far end: the image of Maximus Decimus Meridius from *Gladiator*, his arms outstretched with a sword in one hand. The inscription read: "ARE YOU NOT ENTERTAINED?" in bold block letters. It was good work, and I didn't even know I could pull it off until that moment. I turned to her and then back to the painting, my arm moving in a showy presentation, then I collapsed into a dramatic bow.

She gave me a polite round of applause and a small bow in return.

"Very good," she said, "very impressive."

She floated over and stalked the length of the wall, inspecting my work, stopping to take in the detail of Maximus and nodding in appreciation. She took a breath and turned to face me.

"I'll be going now, but I'm sure we'll be seeing each other again soon."

I thought she was joking and tried to express as much by leaving my mouth open in a dumb grin, but she walked behind a tree and disappeared like the damn Cheshire Cat again.

I waited around for a few minutes just in case, but she didn't come back. Dejected, I blinked back to the house.

The lights were off when I arrived, and Max was probably asleep. I floated through the door to my room—the physical one, not the one to the other side.

Floating over to and above my bed, I wondered when I'd see what's-her-name again, and decided to flip through some channels to take my mind off her until the sun came up.

Chapter 20

The next night I faded into the sounds of people talking, laughing, and other general hallmarks of a good time. Something about waking up to those sounds really sets a guy off in a good mood. I floated out of my room to see Zoe and Max on the couch in an intense, but obviously entertaining conversation. Max was telling a story, his upper body leaning forward, his hands making wild flurries of gestures. Zoe was leaning in toward Max, hanging on every word and looking highly entertained. I floated on into the kitchen to find—a kitchen table!

It was a smallish '50s-modern-style circular table, wrapped in chrome, with a pearloid plastic top that had slightly yellowed with age. It had four chairs, all chromed out, and what looked like red vinyl upholstery for the seat and back. Each chair held a Psy-kick in various stages of reclining or posing, and they were playing a card-based board game. They cracked up after almost every hand that was played. Cool haircut Quinton leaned back on the counter in repose, sipping coffee and taking in the scene with rapt attention.

"Hey everybody," my voice crackled through a small radio set on top of the fridge in the kitchen.

The smiles around the table dimmed. Apparently, my voice

meant that the game was over and it was time to work. Quinton straightened up and looked around, as if he was going to be able to see me, and returned my greeting.

"Hey Jonah, good morning." He raised his coffee mug in a mild salute.

Zoe and Max joined us from the living room. Zoe had an unslung messenger bag in her hand and indicated with a nod for the Psy-kicks to make some room on the table. She set the bag down, released some sturdy plastic fasteners, and opened the bag to the satisfying sound of strong Velcro. Unzipping a pocket, she pulled out a manila folder and started passing around sheets of paper to the group. She'd typed up a rundown of our job for the night and started walking us through what we should expect.

Max took his sheet and leaned against the kitchen counter next to Quinton as Zoe told us about our clients: Judy and Glenn, a couple in their mid-forties. They lived in Hyde Park, the last refuge of Austin's aging and fading hippy community, just north of campus. The neighborhood used to be a mix of craftsman- and bungalow-style homes, but as prices in the neighborhood increased over time, the type of buyer changed as well as the architecture.

Larger, contemporary craftsman homes replaced some of the smaller houses with an increase in sleek modern architecture as well. Old Austinites pointed to this neighborhood, as well as Barton Hills and Zilker, to complain about how Austin was losing its charm. That said, there was nothing more Austin than complaining about how it was much cooler in another, bygone era.

Judy was the CFO for a regional bank in town, and Glenn was a VP of HR for a large tech company based out of California. They bought the property a little over two years ago and had to clear the lot after a house fire damaged the existing bungalow beyond repair. They replaced the structure with a large, three-story, modern, angular design.

Zoe held up her sheet for me to take a look—it was a cool house: a mixture of deep-stained wood slats and stucco painted a dark blue with a metal roof that overhung the sides to help shade the house in the summer and keep it cooler. Solar panels lined the entire length and breadth of the roof in back.

Judy and Glenn started noticing strange things here and there after construction was completed a few months ago—things like mail going missing, but only specific types of letters. The couple were politically active and noticed a drop-off in communication once they moved in. The mayor, for example, asked Judy if she received his invitation to a local fundraiser as he usually heard back from her almost immediately—she hadn't. The head of the Travis County Republican Party called and asked why she wasn't sending in responses to surveys or requests for fundraising anymore.

She checked to make sure that they had the right address; they did. She submitted a complaint to the postmaster general to let him know. Finally, after one of Texas' US senators asked her what she thought about of some of the ideas he'd sent her in a series of letters, she came home and started looking around the house for herself. After looking through her desk to see if Glenn had set them there or put them in a drawer, she started looking through garbage cans. Sure enough, she found a campaign fundraising letter for the Republican nominee in one of the open city council spots. She confronted Glenn, who swore he hadn't touched the letters and started talking about some of the strange things he'd been experiencing himself.

It started about six weeks ago, he said, when he got the car back from the paint shop. He woke up early the next morning to drink a coffee and admire his pride and joy, a 1967 Camaro, but instead walked into (what was for him) a horror scene. They had some five-gallon buckets of paint stored in the garage that were left over from the construction in case they needed touch-ups done around the house. He opened the garage door to find almost every one of those buckets off the shelves and scattered around the vehicle, and a mixture of white and gray latex house paint all over his Marina Blue paint job.

What confounded him was that he discovered the incidents with the doors to the garage closed and locked. He sent the car off to be repainted, and since its return two weeks ago, he had walked in periodically to find the tires deflated.

Glenn went on to tell Judy that sometimes when she was working late, he'd be home alone watching a program on his favorite conservative cable news channel when he would start to feel the air cool around him along with what he described as a "hostile energy." Glenn wasn't the type to throw around words like "energy" or "vibe," and he couldn't believe he was using them while he met with Zoe earlier that day. In fact, he couldn't believe he was meeting with Zoe at all. Judy echoed the sentiment and shared her own stories of experiencing the same feelings while watching a morning program on the same channel, or sometimes while she was reading. Finally, and least disturbing, was that historically, neither one of them had been able to keep a plant alive—ever—but their yard and flower beds were thriving, as were two potted succulents they received as housewarming gifts. Those types of aberrations they could live with, though.

The radio on the fridge crackled as I asked, "Did anyone die in the fire that destroyed the previous house?"

Zoe looked up from her sheet and made a finger gun with her left hand.

"Right-o, Jonah, I was getting to that," Zoe said.

She turned over her sheet to show a picture of a couple

in their late sixties or seventies. They were the epitome of the old Austin hippy look—him with a ponytail, beard, and circular-framed glasses wearing an old Hawaiian button-down shirt, and she with long, braided hair and a flowing dress with oversized jewelry around her neck and wrists. They looked into the camera holding one another—comfortable, relaxed, and happy.

"George and Ramona Rodriguez—these are our likely candidates," she said, then continued reading what sounded like a bullet-pointed list. "Met in college, lived in the neighborhood during school, got married, bought the house that used to stand on the lot, and never looked back.

"He was a criminal defense attorney, did a lot of pro bono work for first-time and minor offenders, was active in the community, and represented the neighborhood association in their interactions with the city concerning development of the area. She started an organic community garden in the '70s, started a vegetarian food outreach program for the elderly in the neighborhood using produce from the garden, and had a bit of an arrest history for protests dating back to the late '60s."

"Hope it's them," I said through static. "They seem like people I can work with."

"I hope so too," Zoe replied. "I looked through the house's records and couldn't find any other deaths, missing persons, or even a family that lived in it longer than a few years going back to when it was built in 1935." She surveyed the room. "Alright, any questions?"

"Yeah, why didn't the guy call the police about the Camaro?" Max asked.

"He did," Zoe answered.

"Oh. Did they find anything?" Max replied.

"No. Anyone else?"

She waited—no questions.

"OK, everyone who needs to, hit the restroom. I'm looking at you, Tammy. Stuff's loaded up, let's get going."

The room sprang into action.

"Shotgun!" I yelled over the crackly radio.

Max threw his head back with his hands over his face, wiping them down slowly. I floated behind most of the group as we filed out of the house on a mission. Zoe had stepped up her game, and this group was starting to operate like a well-oiled machine. The van was mostly silent on our twenty-minute drive over to Hyde Park. Around ten minutes in, Max decided to break the silence.

"Jonah," he half-drawled, half-whined.

"Yeah Max," I replied through the speakers.

"Whatcha thinkin' about?" he continued.

I paused, thinking.

"Just how much wood could a woodchuck chuck, if a woodchuck could chuck wood?"

"I'm sorry I said anything."

"I think they actually can chuck wood," I said, "just not enough of it to be considered wood, maybe? Like a twig? Definitely. Tree bark? One hundred percent. Like the size of pieces of mulch in a flower bed."

He leaned up between the driver and passenger bucket seats, switched off the radio, and slowly reclined back into his seat. Everyone in the van exchanged satisfied glances, and we continued on to our client's house in a comfortable silence.

We stopped short, the usual half block's distance from the house, so I could scout ahead. Zoe turned the radio back on.

"Alright, Jonah, you're up. Ready? Jonah?" she said.

The van idled while no one made a sound. The only noises were the crackling of the radio static and the air conditioner on full blast. Zoe looked back in her mirror while the rest of the van looked back at her. A few of the crew adjusted seat belts and fidgeted in their seats.

"Just kidding, I'm ready. Don't ever turn the radio off on me again," I said as I floated up and out of the van.

Chapter 21

I floated toward the house and heard music playing from the backyard as I approached. I decided on the ol' up-and-over routine as I cleared the roof and descended into the backyard. Peals of electric guitar riffs over Mellotron, bass, and drums filled the air.

George and Ramona, I presumed, hopped back and forth in exaggerated gyrations as they danced to psychedelic music coming from—somewhere. They cavorted on decomposed granite in a clearing surrounded by large mountain laurel trees, although "trees" may have been generous; they were really overgrown bushes that stood around ten feet tall or so. Mountain laurels bloom every spring with purple flowers that resemble wisteria and smell like synthetic grape—not in a bad way, but like an amazing grape popsicle or snow cone.

The yard had been xeriscaped to conserve water and probably didn't need a lot of maintenance to continue looking great. Red, purple, orange, and white blooms colored the flower beds from different types of sage and salvia plants.

George noticed me and slowed his dancing as I landed. Ramona took her cue from George and turned around to locate whatever it was he was looking at.

"Hey man," George welcomed me with a laid-back smile and a wave. "You new to the neighborhood? I'm George, and this is my wife, Ramona." George pulled Ramona in toward him, giving her a one-armed hug as he introduced her.

"Hi," she said with a quick wave.

"Hi, I'm Jonah," I said, and then I filled them in on what I'd heard about the current tenants of the house and what I was there to do.

"No," George said, shaking his head, "no man, we're not going anywhere. Those corporate fascists aren't going to come here from *California* and kick us out of our home."

I held up my hands and closed my eyes, trying to calm down the situation.

"No one is trying to kick you out of your home, George. That's not what I'm here to do."

"OK man, sorry, I just get a little riled up sometimes," George said.

"Can I ask why you two didn't move on?" I said.

"This is our neighborhood. We love it here," said Ramona. "We looked for each other when the house caught fire—"

"We died in a house fire," George interjected.

"Yes, thank you, George," Ramona said. "Each of us wanted to make sure the other got out. We found each other—afterward."

George added, "I wasn't going to leave without her." He squeezed her arm, pulling her in tighter and kissing the top of her head.

Ramona continued, "I'm not sure where we would go, or how it could be better than spending this moment with the man I love in the place that I love."

I crooked an eyebrow. "You sure? It could be great."

"Maybe someday," she replied, lovingly wrapping her arm around George's.

"So why are you messing with the people that live here? You two seem like the kind to live and let live."

George's face lit up. "They're the problem with this town now! Come in here with no respect for the past or the culture. Buying up houses and mowing them down. Everything's gotta be new—new house, new car, new suits. It's got no soul, man, no respect."

"Your house burned down," I said. "Also, I'm pretty sure this house has like a four-star green rating, guys. I'm looking at a roof full of solar panels and a backyard that doesn't need watering. That has to count for something, right?"

George nodded his head slowly up and down. "That's true," he said and fidgeted a little, kicking at the granite gravel. "Maybe we just miss our house, man."

"OK, but what about the car? Who did the car?" I asked.

Ramona smiled, and George laughed.

"Yeah, that was way over the line, but it was fun," George said.

Ramona picked up, "I didn't even know I could do that. I walked in to see that outdated, gas-guzzling relic and just pushed out in frustration. I was surprised when the paint fell the way it did. After that, I wanted to show George what I could do, so I dumped the next one."

"Then I wanted to see if I could do it," George chimed in. "So I tried—and I could!"

Ramona said, "One thing led to another, and it ended up a little messy in there. Anyway, serves him right."

"Why, because he has a cool car?" I asked.

"Because cars like that throw off exhaust and fumes with no regard for how it affects the atmosphere!" she replied.

"How often does he drive it? Isn't it just something he takes out every once in a while?" I asked.

"Yes," she replied. "I actually haven't seen it leave the garage."

"It's a cool car, you have to admit," I replied, looking to George for a little backup.

"Oh yeah, the Camaro's a hot car. I always wanted one," he offered up. Ramona shot an elbow to his ghostly ribs, and they shared a laugh.

"So what is it you want? Is there any way you can coexist with these folks?" I asked.

They looked at each other and seemed to share some sort of unspoken communication. Ramona looked to me and sighed. "We just liked things how they were, I guess. Well—not how they were exactly—how we were. We had our little house, our place in the community, and we just want to be useful again—help people."

I had an idea. "Do you two still go out in the neighborhood, or just hang out here all the time?"

George looked down at Ramona. "Oh yeah, we still get out. Like to walk to Shipe Park, stop by and talk to some of the folks from Ramona's old route."

That's what I'd hoped to hear. I reminded them of what I'd been doing and asked if any of the people they checked in on might want to move on. Both their faces lit up at the idea, and I asked them to hang out there while I checked back in with the team in the van.

I could see Max in the passenger seat as I floated back that way—he was obsessed. I phased through the front of the van and right into a conversation about Max's favorite cartoon based on a sponge.

"Check, check," I crackled through the speakers. "Is this thing on? I got a rock mic check on one. I got a hot mic check on two. Teeeessst."

"Is it them?" Max asked. "Is it George and Ramona? Are they moving on? Do these jeans make me look fat?"

The radio crackled. "Yes, it's them. Not exactly, and no—you look fantastic. I think we can find a way for peaceful cohabitation—maaan. Y'all go ahead and get started, but you'll need to improvise. There won't be a neat, tidy ending to this scene tonight. I don't think I'll be back to help you with closure. Change up the format, use the sword, sing—I don't know. You'll figure something out. You're professionals."

Zoe turned back to the rest of the group in the van. "Alright guys, this is a blues riff in B, watch me for the changes, and—uh—try to keep up, OK?"

"OK, Marty," Max said. "Do you like *Back to the Future I* or *II* better? I think the sequel is underrated ..."

Zoe put the van in gear and pulled up in front of the house.

George and Ramona waited for me in their front yard, and we set off to go make a difference—go team ghost. They pointed out houses along the way and shared memories from their time in the neighborhood.

"See that house?" George said. "Our friend Steve lived there in the '70s, along with a series of girlfriends. He had pot-luck dinners there about twice a month, and they were always a real good time. I think he misconstrued the meaning—great brownies though."

He pointed at a two-story contemporary design that took up most of the lot where it sat, leaving just a few feet between the houses next to it.

"Jane Conway used to live there—not in that house, obviously—but she kept a pet goat. Clarence. She kept Clarence fenced in and all, but it was chain-link so you could see through. People were always in her yard taking pictures or would just stop in to look at him on their way to that little bakery on the corner. The city almost made her get rid of it for violating a livestock ordinance, but we were able to get the council to give her a variance." He shook his head. "This town used to be fun. You should have seen it."

There it was, the old "you-shoulda-been-there-when" Austin trope. I decided to let it go. We slowed to a stop at a slat-board bungalow with a decent-sized front porch, complete with a set of rocking chairs. The house hadn't been painted in a while but was a friendly yellow with purple trim. Purple cone flowers, black-eyed Susans, snapdragons, and an array of salvia and sage grew wild in the front yard on either side of a stone-set walkway surrounded by a white picket fence.

"I used to visit Ms. Pirkle here," Ramona began, looking toward the house. "The sweetest woman, but just as shy as she could be. Her husband didn't come back from the war, and she never could bring herself to move out of that house. Worked at the university for thirty-some-odd years until she retired.

"Poor lady didn't have any family, so we helped out by bringing food by every day and always took time with her for a while. She didn't have anyone else to talk to. Toward the end, she didn't like leaving her house, not even to garden.

"The Tompkins moved in after she died, almost twenty years ago, and got her old garden back up and going. They've kept it up quite nicely, I would say. Anyway, George and I were walking by one night, and she was out on that porch, just rocking on one of those chairs. We stop by every once in a while to visit."

We floated up to the front door of the house and Ramona announced us. "Knock, knock, Ms. Pirkle. It's George and Ramona—and we brought a guest."

A sweet voice strained from inside the house, "Y'all come on in. Everyone here just went to sleep a little while ago."

We floated into the house. The walls were painted almost the same color of yellow as the outside and were covered with pictures and eclectic mementos from all over the world. From the look of things, the Tompkins loved to travel. The front door led directly into a living room that was filled with comfortable, overstuffed chairs and a large leather couch. Pictures were displayed on the mantle of a well-used fireplace over which hung an Impressionistic piece of art. Ms. Pirkle sat in a ghosted rocking chair, working needlepoint while she rocked back and forth. She wore a welcoming look on her face, as if she was straight out of central casting for a hot cocoa commercial that needed a grandmother. She wore a purple-flowered dress with a white-lace collar.

"Have you tried our little trick with the music, Ms. Pirkle?" George asked loudly.

"Yes, George, and you don't have to yell anymore. I can hear you perfectly fine. I was just enjoying my quiet and working on my needlepoint. Now, who is this?" Ms. Pirkle asked, setting down her needlepoint.

I introduced myself and told her what I did—and I mean everything: what I did in life, what I do now, where I grew up, my favorite foods—everything. She just drew it out of me with polite nods and smiles.

"That's nice, dear. You sound like a good boy," she responded after what seemed like half an hour of me talking without a break, but was probably only twenty minutes or so.

She went on to tell me about how she met her husband, Harry, how they bought the house together, how he died, and how she carried on afterward.

I asked her why she was still there after all those years, and why she wouldn't move on.

"Oh, I was just scared at first," she said. "That big white light was everywhere, and all I had to do was let it take me. Even though I felt like everything would be OK on the other side of it, I didn't know what to do.

"Then I felt like I didn't deserve it—as if it were too easy. Maybe I didn't trust it. I thought about going up to it every night but always managed to talk myself out of it. *You don't know what's through there, I would think, or, yes, you do know what's through there—and you're just not ready for it.* Before too long, the door stopped showing up."

She stopped her needlepoint but continued to rock back and forth. "That's OK though. Pretty soon, the Tompkins moved in, and I just loved them. I love sitting with them at dinner. They have such good stories and love each other so much. Their kids and grandkids still come by from time to time, and they're such a mess. Especially that little rascal Charlie. They have this grandbaby that comes over here, and he just gets into everything."

She looked up and laughed, then turned her gaze back to her needlepoint with a sad look on her face.

"I miss being around a family like that—I miss my family. Last time I saw any of them was when my niece and her kids came to set up an estate sale."

She looked away from us and gathered herself. "So now, Jonah, you go around, and you can just make these doors appear again for people? They can just move on after all those years?"

"Actually, Ms. Pirkle," I replied, "I'm not sure it's me. I think I'm just reminding them that they have somewhere else they can go—they can see those that they've been missing or just rest."

She nodded, rocking back and forth. "So you can help me move on to see Harry, my old friends, my family again?"

"If you want to. Do you think you're ready?"

She looked to George and Ramona. George's face was set with a soft smile, his eyebrows knit together as he fought back tears. Ramona knelt by her side, took her hand in both of hers, and nodded yes.

Ms. Pirkle set her needlepoint aside, her work fading away as she let go, and slowly stood up from her chair. Her door appeared across the room, illuminating the space with a light so bright it was hard to endure.

"I suppose I've been here long enough," she said as she started a slow shuffle toward the door, her back bent slightly. "I'm sure the Tompkins will be fine without me, although they may miss some of my help with that front yard." She winked at us and stood a little taller as she walked back to hug Ramona and then George.

"I appreciate all you've done for me," she said, looking each of them in the eye, then turned to me. "Thank you too, young man." She patted me on both sides of my face.

Then she turned to walk toward the door, with more purpose in each step, taking on the visage of a young woman in her twenties by the time she reached it and walked through. The light in the room dimmed as the door faded away, leaving the three of us in awe as we floated quietly in the living room.

George managed to speak. "Far out. That was something else, man. Listen, Jonah, do you think we could do something like that? Help more people like her, I mean."

"Of course, that's what I wanted to show you," I said.

"I want to try," Ramona added after a long silence. "I want to do this again. Would you help us learn?"

"You bet," I said. "I'll help if I can."

We exited the house and started back toward George and Ramona's. A couple in matching reflective athletic clothing ran by us as we made our way down the path. It was late, but that meant that it was probably a more comfortable temperature for running than when the sun was shining full-blast in the afternoon. We watched them jog by, and I decided to pick a thread back up from earlier.

"What would it take for you to get along with Judy and Glenn, or at least allow them to live their life in peace?"

"It would help if they would stop supporting corrupt politicians," George replied, starting to get worked up.

"George," Ramona calmed him, "that's not our fight anymore. We can help in other ways now." She stroked his back as we floated along.

"Still wish we had our old house though," he mumbled while he pulled her in close for a side hug.

"What if I could help with that?" I thought out loud.

"You think you can get us our old house back?" George asked, stopping on the sidewalk.

"Yeah, kinda—I think so," I replied, remembering DeeDee and Jeremy. "Let's get you two back home, and I'll see what I can do."

Chapter 22

As luck would have it, we got back in time to see Zoe and the Psy-kicks filing out of the house. I said my goodbyes to George and Ramona and caught up with the group back in the van. Zoe turned on the van with Max in the passenger seat while the Psy-kicks filed in the back of the van, looking a little disgruntled.

"Hey everybody," I crackled through the speakers. "Why does everyone look like they just dropped their puppy off at the vet?"

Max gave Zoe a punchy side-eyed glance. "You want to fill him in?"

She sighed. "I didn't feel like we could take their money yet." She looked back at everyone else in the van. "I'm sorry. I didn't know what was going on with Jonah. I didn't feel right charging them—I made half that stuff up and felt like an idiot."

"You could have at least taken half," Max interjected.

"That's a good idea. I didn't think of that. Dammit, this new business model is throwing me off. Why didn't you pull me aside in there?" she replied.

"Because I just now thought of it. I'm great at coming up with things as soon as it's time to start blaming other people," he said, straightening out and facing forward. "We'll remember it for next time."

"Can we still go eat?" Lin asked. "I'm starving."

"Yeah, we can still go eat," Zoe said, "but first, Jonah, what's the deal?"

"Deal is that George and Ramona have agreed to cool it with Judy and Glenn. We took a tour of the neighborhood and helped out an old friend of theirs. I need to work on something for them, but I think it's safe to send the client an invoice."

The mood in the vehicle brightened. "Good," Zoe said, smiling and putting the van in gear. "Now let's go destroy some pancakes."

I let them know I would meet up with them later and blinked over to Tarrytown to visit my old friends DeeDee and Jeremy—maybe not old friends, but whatever. I floated up to the front of their house and noticed that there was a doorbell, so I gave it a shot, and it worked. After a few seconds, Jeremy answered with an expression that looked like he'd just opened the door to a box of mildewed socks. His nose slightly upturned, he looked down and surveyed me from head to toe.

"Hello, Jonah," he said.

I decided to blink into a tuxedo, which seemed to mildly amuse him. He rolled his eyes and left the door open as he withdrew back into the house.

"DeeDee, Jonah is here," he announced.

I shut the door behind me and followed him into their living room. DeeDee was surveying a tufted leather bench on chrome rectangular legs set just off the glass windows that wasn't there on my last visit. She adjusted its dimensions as she walked around it.

"Hi Jonah," she said, distracted, not looking up from her work. "Do you like this, or this?" she asked as the bench grew a back of tufted leather connected by two chromed supports.

"I like it without the back," Jeremy commented.

"I like them both," I said.

"You're no help," she said, looking up at me and then blinking. "Why are you so dressed up?"

"It's tuxedo day," I replied. "Tuesdays are always tuxedo days."

She nodded. "Tuesdays were always taco nights for us."

"Sounds good, let's taco-bout it," I replied.

"You feel bad about that, don't you, Jonah?" Jeremy responded. "Good, you should feel bad."

"So what brings you by, Jonah?" DeeDee asked, still fussing with the bench that had morphed into an interesting shade of green.

"I wanted to see if I could talk y'all into building something for some friends of mine."

DeeDee looked up. I had her full attention.

"Yeah, maybe. What part of town?"

"Hyde Park," I replied.

DeeDee's face lit up, and she looked to Jeremy, "Something twenty-first-century modern—" she offered.

"Maybe an updated craftsman," he responded.

"Eh. Actually, they kind of just want their old house back," I said.

"OK," she said, assuming a businesslike posture and tone. "I suppose we still owe you one for relocating those gentlemen down the street. I don't suppose you have any pictures or original blueprints we could see?"

"Pictures, yes—blueprints, no," I responded.

"They're probably on file with the city or title company— oh well," she said. "We'll make do with what we have to work with. Let's set an appointment to meet with your friends as soon as possible."

"OK, sounds good. I'll get you access to pictures and in front of George and Ramona as soon as I can," I said.

"Good to see you, Jonah, byyyyyye," Jeremy said.

I guessed it was time for me to leave. *Subtle Jeremy— real subtle.*

I blinked over to the diner, hoping to catch Zoe before the group went their different ways for the night. As luck would have it, they were all there, deep in the same card-based board game from before, but Max, Zoe, and Quinton had joined in. Sweaters and hoodies were pulled close as I entered the room.

"Hi Jonah," Zoe said as she laid down three cards.

Tammy, Max, and Quinton all leaned back in their chairs. Apparently, whatever Zoe laid down had thwarted their plans. A round of "hey Jonah" filtered around the table, but nary an eye moved from the hand of cards in front of them. I watched round after round as the table either erupted in laughter or mock disgust every time a hand was played. Apparently, Lin won, to quiet applause, encouraging fists in the air, and silent cheers from around the table. Except Max. Max sat in his chair with his arms folded—he wasn't the most gracious loser in the world.

Shortly after the bill was paid, the group broke, and I followed them to the van and hovered between Zoe and Max in the front as she turned the key—loud bass and electronic noises booming from the speakers before Zoe turned down the volume and tuned the radio back to static.

"Sorry," she said. "We got a little carried away on the drive over. What's up? Where'd you go?"

I shared my idea and asked Zoe if she could dig up any pictures or plans on George and Ramona's old house.

"Sure," she said. "We'll see what we can dig up tomorrow. We'll even try to see what we can get from the county website or their title company." She looked up and back into the rearview mirror. "Quinton and Lin—you two busy tomorrow?" They shook their heads no. "Good. Quinton—see what you can find with the city. Lin—see what you can find from the title company. I'll shoot you an email with what I find from the county site when I get home tonight. Sound good?" They nodded. "Alright, Jonah, I'll meet you at Max's tomorrow night with whatever we're able to find."

"Cool," I said. "Thanks."

"Anytime," she said, putting the van in gear and backing out of the parking space. We pulled out of the lot and dropped the group off in the regular order. We were deep into a game of "would you rather" as we pulled up in front of our house.

"So yeah, I would rather fight a great-white-shark-sized puppy than a hundred puppy-sized great whites," Zoe concluded as we came to a stop. "Because, presumably, I would be on land to fight the giant puppy and in the ocean or water to fight the sharks—big disadvantage there as I am a land-dwelling mammal. The sharks still have crazy-sharp teeth, and I would be in a piranha-style situation, and I just don't see me winning. I'm in my natural element for the giant puppy, and it's still a puppy—all clumsy and dumb. Who knows—maybe I can befriend it and have a lifelong companion. I would name it Pizza."

"Why would you name it Piz—never mind—I accept your answer and award you seventy imaginary points," Max said with a mystical twinkling of his fingers as he distributed seventy imaginary points into Zoe's account.

We said our goodbyes, Max grabbed a radio that was next to his seat, and we headed toward the house. "That game was bullshit," he said as the door closed behind us and we could hear the van pulling away.

"I don't know. She made some good points—not sure about naming a giant dog Pizza." My voice crackled through the tiny speaker.

"No, the other game—Frebopple," he said. "I was two hands at most from the win—if Quinton and Tammy hadn't worked together against me just so Lin could win. Everyone should just be trying to win for themselves."

"Yeah, that really sucks," I said in mock consolation. "Just like in traffic where that lady cut you off one time, remember?"

"You got no legs, Jonah," he replied.

"What?"

"You are a ghost with no legs. I'm being petty and I just want you to remember you have no legs—or arms. You're a damn ghost, Jonah."

"Yeah, but at least I didn't lose at Frebopple. I still value you as a person though—I just want you to remember that," I said.

Max laughed. "Good night, Jonah."

"Good night, Max."

Chapter 23

"Hey you," said a voice from behind me as I was about to follow Max inside.

It was her, the Cheshire Cat girl. *How does she know where I live?* I didn't really care. I was just glad to see her again.

"Hey yourself," I said.

"I have someplace I need to be, but thought you might like to see it. Do you want to go?"

"Sure," I said.

"Good, come on."

She smiled, casually reached out her hand, and started walking away from the house. I took her hand as I matched her stride. After a few steps we were in another place. A buzz of conversation filled the air, and ghosts were everywhere—and only ghosts. We were outdoors in something reminiscent of a high school keg party or a college football tailgate. Groups of ghosts sprawled out, talking, laughing, and hanging out. It took me a few moments before I realized that we were actually in a graveyard.

"Welcome to the Texas State Cemetery," she said as she gently pulled me farther into the gathering.

"A cemetery," I said, "it's like you know my deepest desires."

"Shut up," she said and laughed.

I noticed various time periods represented by an array of dress. Some spirits wore suits with skinny lapels that you would see from the '60s, some with wide lapels from the '70s, and some from the turn of the twentieth century and before. We passed by a group of cowboys who fell silent as they tracked the two of us with obvious interest … well, they tracked one of us with obvious interest.

"This is the oldest cemetery in Austin," she said. "Stephen F. Austin himself is buried here."

"Is he still around?"

"I don't know, actually. I've never met him."

We weaved our way through the crowd of spirits and gravestones. I could overhear heated conversations seemingly rooted deep in politics, as well as casual conversation about how the town wasn't like it used to be.

"Look up there," she said and pointed ahead.

There, in front of a grand tomb and on top of a makeshift dais sat a group of ghosts, puffed up and self-important, taking great care to look at each other rather than condescend to the gathered masses below. A lectern stood in the middle of the group, and someone was speaking.

"That's the mayor and city council," she whispered as she leaned in to me.

"What? Why? Who elected them?"

"People—corporeal or not—like structure. Electing leadership gives them a sense of control."

"What do they do?"

"Not much, really."

"Sounds about right. Do you have to register to vote?"

"No registration needed, and only a handful of people really vote."

"Did you bring me here to vote?"

"No, I didn't bring you here to vote, but I thought you might like to see this place. I'm actually here to meet someone though. Do you mind if I excuse myself for a bit?"

"Not at all," I said, trying to keep my voice from cracking. *Why did she bring me here if she was just going to leave to talk to someone else?*

"Thank you," she said with a subtle smile and grabbed my shoulder. "Mingle around. People are friendly here."

I looked around the gathering and back to her for a witty departing quip, but she was already gone, which was just as well because I was all out of funny one-liners.

Turning away from the council, I wandered through the crowd. The thought occurred to me that, other than Seph and whatever-her-name-was, I hadn't really met anyone like me in my new life. I scanned groups for friendly faces, and after a few minutes of aimless walking, a cute girl who looked to be in her early twenties looked my way and smiled. I walked over and did my best to casually blend in with her group. Her friends fell silent and looked to me with a range of expressions from open welcome to mild suspicion as they noticed me in their midst.

"Hi," the girl said.

"Hi," I said back with a smile, "I'm Jonah."

"Maude," she replied, then introduced me to her group. I didn't catch all their names … I was a little nervous.

"Hi Maude, hi everybody."

I received a few nods and smiles now.

"So when did you die?" she asked.

The question caught me off guard at first. It seemed so casual, and I guess it was. Death was the one thing we all had in common here and was probably as customary a question as "Where are you from?" or "Where did you go to school?"

"Recently, within the past few months," I said.

"Hey, fresh meat, girls," she replied.

"Cradle robber!" one of her friends said.

Maude's eyes sparkled as she looked me up and down, and the group laughed. I was confused for a moment. She looked and dressed younger than me, but then it all came together. I could dress however I wanted, whenever I wanted. Makes sense that we could look whatever age we wanted as well. So far, the ghosts I'd interacted with were dressed in period outfits because it was either all they knew or because it was how they wanted to dress.

"When did you pass?" I asked.

"Pass? So formal, modern men are so sensitive," said another girl from the group.

More laughter.

"Shut up, Imogene," Maude said. "I passed in the '30s, of old age as we used to say, but probably a cerebral hemorrhage."

"What about you?" another girl asked. "How did you die?"

"Oh, uh … murder," I said.

Hands clapped to mouths simultaneously, and gasps escaped around our little circle.

"Oh my god," Imogene said.

"You poor boy," Maude said.

"Did it hurt?" a girl asked.

"Yeah, I suppose," I said, "but honestly, not that bad. I was so overcome by confusion and the fight for life that I don't really remember the pain."

Based on the slack jaws around the circle, my answer was probably too honest, but before tonight, I hadn't been able to really think through or talk about it with someone aside from Willard. Besides, they were so casual with the question. I didn't think that revealing my cause of death would surprise them.

"So," another girl said, "anyone hear about this guy that's

going around kicking ghosts out of their homes?"

Oh boy.

"Nice change of subject. Deftly done, June," Maude said. "Jonah, have you heard about this?"

"What's that?" I asked, trying to keep my voice from going up a couple notches.

"Apparently someone started chasing people from their homes. Everyone is talking about it," she replied.

"Someone is going around just randomly chasing people out?" I asked.

"I heard they deserve it," a girl said.

"I heard he's a vigilante," June said.

"I heard he's handsome," Maude said.

"I bet it's him," another girl said, looking at me. "Is it you?"

"Oh sure, it's me. Don't I look intimidating? What's your name again?"

"I have a boyfriend," she replied.

"OK, cool. That's cool. I mean, I'm actually here with someone," I said.

Maude cooled, and the group subtly closed the circle, leaving me on the outside.

"They in your pocket? I don't see anyone with you," Maude said.

"Yep, something like that," I said, "nice to meet you, ladies. Have a good night."

I passed by more groups: some hippies in a drum circle, businessmen in cowboy hats and suits, a group of goth teenagers—I did a double take to check and see if they were alive or dead. I was pretty sure they were dead.

Through the crowd I saw a familiar face. Willard Hensch was holding court in the middle of a group of a dozen or so angry men—not that they were angry with him, but that they were angry about something and looking to Willard as though he had the answer to their problems. *Good for him, looks like he's really coming out of his shell.* I eased into the back of their circle and caught Willard's eye.

"Jonah Preston," he said.

"Hi Willard," I replied.

"We were just talking about you," he said.

The group's collective heads whipped around in my direction.

This can't be good.

"No way, it can't be," a voice said.

"Wait—that's him?" asked another voice.

A burly but neatly dressed man stepped through the circle. He puffed himself up and looked down on me.

"Kip Johnson," he said. "Is it true? Did you drive Mr. Hensch from his home? You driving other people from their homes?"

"Uh ... hi Kip. Did Willard happen to mention what happened before that?"

"Answer me."

"Well, no ... actually, I didn't drive *him* out, but there were a few—"

"What gives you the right to decide who stays or leaves?"

"Let's take him in front of the council," a voice piped up from the back of the group.

"Fuck that," said another voice. "Let's take care of him here. Get 'im, Kip!"

Kip looked over his shoulder and back to me, popping his knuckles and rolling his neck.

"Not here, boys," a familiar voice purred. "You know the code here. Arguments are encouraged, but no fighting. This is hallowed ground."

My leather-clad savior returned from her meeting just in time. The tension released from the group as all eyes moved from Kip to Willard. And when I said "all eyes," I meant *all* eyes—we had the attention of everyone in the immediate vicinity.

"Stand down, Mr. Johnson," Willard said. "She is right. His time is coming—don't worry. His time is coming."

I felt a hand gently lead me away from the crowd.

"Nice to meet you, Kip, see you around," I said over my shoulder.

"See you in Hell, Jonah Preston," he replied.

"Good seeing you, Jonah," Willard said over the crowd, his posture striking a new confidence. "I'm sure we'll see each other again very soon."

The Cheshire Cat girl led me through the crowd until people stopped looking and went back to their conversations. We found a little clearing and came to a stop. I tried to play it casual, but my non-corporeal self was electric with fearful energy.

"Thank you for that, but I could have taken him," I said.

"Him, maybe. Everyone? Probably not," she replied.

"How did your meeting go?"

"Better than your mingling."

"Yeah, I have a real way with people."

"I can see."

"Kind of like how we've known each other for a while, and I still don't know your name."

She smiled and looked me up and down. "So you want to know my name," she said.

"Um … yeah, it will come in handy when I try to get your attention."

And maybe for other stuff.

"Did you know that the original name for Austin was Waterloo?"

"Um … yeah, I did actually. What does that have to do with anything?"

She looked at me again with a sideways smile and clicked her tongue. "I have to go," she said.

"What?"

"I have to go," she repeated and pulled me in for a hug.

"I can't tell if you're shady or mysterious."

She looked over her shoulder as she walked away, and then she disappeared behind a young tree. Disappeared. Like the damn Cheshire Cat.

Definitely mysterious.

I wasn't in the mood to mingle anymore. I just wanted to go home. Actually, I wanted to wallow in self-pity, so I decided to take the long way back to the house and have a think along the trip. I floated up high to get a bearing on where I was. The cemetery was located on the east side of the city, so I started floating south and west toward home.

What am I doing here? Why didn't I just take my door? I don't have any friends like me I can talk to, and it seems impossible now that the community thinks I'm some asshole kicking people from their homes. I can't even get a girl's name.

At least not the girl I was interested in.

I floated into my neighborhood and down into my house. It was quiet, Max was asleep, and it just made me feel more alone. I sat on my bed until I faded into morning.

Chapter 24

I faded back in the next night to the sounds of laughter and rapid-fire conversation. I floated through the living room and into the kitchen to find Max, Zoe, Quinton, and Lin around the kitchen table playing another game of Frebopple. There were a few shivers as I entered the room and made my way over to the fridge where they kept the radio tuned to static for me.

"Hey Jonah," Max said.

"Not so fast, you bastard!" Lin exclaimed as she laid down half the cards in her hand.

"Ohhhhh!" yelled Quinton and Zoe.

"I told you that in confidence," Max said. "It's a family secret. Just for that, read these cards and weep amongst the fallen—which may include the father I never knew. Damn you and your indiscretion, Lin."

Max laid down all his cards—to Quinton and Lin's dismay.

"Yes!" Zoe said, pounding on the table. "That's the game. I win!"

Max crooked an eyebrow at Lin, who returned the gesture with an elaborate extension of the middle finger of her right hand.

"Alright losers, clear the game while Zoe and I talk to Jonah about what we were able to dig up today," Max said as he pushed away from the table.

This time, it was Quinton's turn to extend the middle finger of his right hand as he started to gather cards with his left. Zoe pulled her messenger bag into her lap from where it hung from the back of her chair, unlocked some clasps, and opened it, removing a manila folder.

"We were able to find a lot actually," she said, opening the folder and spreading paper out across the table. "We were able to find most of these pictures just through a Google image search of the property, and we were able to get dimensions of the house from Judy and Glenn from their closing packet from the sale of the property. We told them we would need to return and perform another ceremony."

"Good cover," I said, looking at the pictures. "How did you get these of George and Ramona inside the house?"

"Someone made their social media profiles public and turned them into memorials," Lin answered. "There were tons of pictures around anyway. They were super-involved in the community, and there were thousands of pictures to sort through, just from a simple image search."

"What now, Jonah?" Zoe asked.

I tried ghosting copies of the paper, but the imprints of the pictures and words faded as I forgot the content. It was a nice try, but I had a plan B.

"Let's head over to Judy and Glenn's and start whatever ceremony you think it would take to finish up the job. Have someone take this file into the garage and lay out everything on the floor. Keep someone in the van with the radio on so I can communicate our progress and check in periodically."

"Max, think you can handle van duty?" Zoe asked.

"Why do I have to stay in the van?" he replied.

"Because we're on a leaner crew and you look the least mystical," she replied, straight-faced.

"You look mystical," Max mumbled under his breath as the group stood up and Zoe organized the papers back into the folder.

"I'll catch up with you back at their house," I crackled over the radio.

After a couple of, "Bye, Jonahs," I blinked over to DeeDee and Jeremy's.

I walked up and rang the doorbell, and Jeremy answered the door with the look a plate of fine china would give to a slice of congealed fried ham.

"Hello, Jonah," he said. "Come in."

Jeremy left the door open and walked into the living room where DeeDee met us looking highly stylized but professionally dressed. She wore glasses with a perfectly tailored gray blazer over a black dress and chunky heeled boots. Jeremy was outfitted in a tweed jacket, a casual, white cotton button-down, dark-colored jeans, and suede lace-up oxford shoes.

"So," DeeDee began in rapid-fire bursts, "were you able to find anything, do we have a meeting set up with your clients, and if so, how do we plan on getting there?"

"Yes," I replied. "We were able to find a lot: pictures of the outside and inside, and dimensions from the closing docs. As to how we get there, I thought we would just fly over and you can follow me."

"That will take forever though. Doesn't your team have a van? Why aren't they with you?" she replied.

I hadn't considered that they might not be able to fly as fast as I could, and I wondered if they could blink over. I found it interesting that there were such varied talents or abilities in us ghost-types. I wondered if I could just blink us all over at once.

"Let me try something," I said, motioning for DeeDee and Jeremy to come in close. DeeDee was game immediately while Jeremy … wasn't as eager.

"No thanks on the group hug, Jonah," he drawled.

"Just work with me here, Jeremy," I said.

He relented and reached out begrudgingly so I could grab his arm. I blinked over to George and Ramona and checked to see if DeeDee and Jeremy made the trip along with me. The look on DeeDee's face told me she couldn't believe what just happened.

"That is amazing!" she exclaimed. "Can you do this anywhere?"

Jeremy gave me a harrumph of approval, and we walked toward the house.

"I'm not sure about 'anywhere' just yet, but definitely places that I've been to before," I said.

"Dammit, this is one of Peter Fischer's designs," DeeDee cursed as she took in the house in front of us.

"Yes, and it is gorgeous!" Jeremy added. "You never should have let him go off on his own, Deeds. Look at this yard. I bet he did this too—jealous." Jeremy looked to me and explained, "Peter Fischer used to work for us when we started up the firm. He was good, obviously, but wanted to be partner after being on with us for just a few months. DeeDee let him walk, and he started his own design firm. Big mistake."

We heard music from the backyard, so I motioned for DeeDee and Jeremy to follow me up and over the house. DeeDee looked impressed as she inspected the house from a higher vantage point.

"Ugh, that kid is good. Oh well, it's not like we're com-Pete-ing anymore," she said.

Jeremy rolled his eyes. "I've heard that one, Deeds—you're re-Pete-ing yourself."

I laughed. "What's up?" I said, adding my contribution to our little pun parade as we descended upon another psychedelic dance scene between George and Ramona.

"Do you just drop in anytime you hear music playing?" Jeremy said as he descended behind me.

"DeeDee and Jeremy, meet George and Ramona," I said.

The architects hit the ground ready to talk shop and affected a professional manner that was so good it caught me off guard. Jeremy could actually listen to people and add value to conversations without being snarky. DeeDee led George and Ramona through a series of questions that seemed like they rolled off the top of her head but with a specificity such that they could be for no other project but theirs.

We heard the slamming of car doors out front that meant that the Psy-kicks would arrive shortly with her requested materials. She continued with her questions, asking George and Ramona about their favorite memories of the house and the neighborhood, things that initially drew them to the house, and what—if anything—they liked about the current design. I saw cool haircut Quinton exit the back of the house with the manila folder under his arm and walk into the garage.

The lights went on inside, and he was back out and into the house a couple minutes later.

"Let's take a look at what we're trying to achieve," DeeDee said after noticing Quinton return inside. She led us into the garage where we found pictures and plans laid out neatly on the floor. She knelt down and got a good look at a picture of the front of the house and scanned down to pictures of the inside and the overall dimensions. Jeremy's right elbow rested in a perpendicular position atop his left arm as he dabbed the side of his face with his index finger. He focused on DeeDee.

"Now, do you want everything the exact same size?" she asked Ramona.

"Well, actually, maybe it would be nice to have another room—for like art projects, maybe?" Ramona answered.

"Is there anything about the new structure that you want to keep?" she asked, pointing back in the direction of the house.

"Maybe the yard, I like the yard," George replied.

"What about a pool?" Jeremy offered.

"Do you think there's room?" George asked.

"I bet your neighbors wouldn't mind if we borrowed a little land, would they?" Jeremy tempted.

"Oh no, we couldn't do that. That's theirs, man," George replied.

"OK, OK," Jeremy relented. "What if we float it above the yard here—no—what if we had three pools, cascading down like a spiral staircase?"

George thought it over. "I don't know, man, sounds too complicated."

"Yes," Jeremy said, visibly disengaging. "Stairs are complicated."

He cocked his jaw and wandered off to go look at something else now that he felt cut out of the process. DeeDee consulted with them for about twenty minutes more, tweaking some things from the original design to what they would want now that money wasn't an obstacle. She went outside and conferred with Jeremy while we waited inside the garage. I looked around the room awkwardly while George and Ramona whispered excitedly to each other. At least I had a badass 1967 Camaro to look at while we were there. I could just smell the old vinyl and fuel in the garage—except that I couldn't, obviously, because I couldn't smell anything. If you haven't smelled an old car kept in good condition, you should. Not right now though, stay with me for this.

After a few minutes, DeeDee returned to open the door and close it tightly behind her as though she didn't want us to see out the other side. I got a familiar vibe of the big reveal from the many home-improvement shows I'd seen, and I started to get excited.

"George and Ramona, are you ready to see your new house?" DeeDee said on cue.

Damn, that was faster than I expected.

She opened the door and invited them into their new backyard for a big reveal. Ramona's hands went to cover her face in joy, and George doubled over in excitement. I floated up past them to see—a small wood-slatted bungalow painted a bright yellow with lighter purple and white accents along the trim. I looked behind me and no longer saw the garage, but a tasteful little pond to complete the backyard. That must have been Jeremy's contribution.

I couldn't even see Judy and Glenn's house anymore—it was as if it was gone completely. It was like a house-flipping show in reverse—from the huge, cool, modern house, back to the small, old house—and in about the same amount of time. We hadn't even been there an hour. DeeDee motioned to take them on tour, and I decided to check in with Max back at the van.

I floated up and over the house and accidentally ended up inside the second floor of Judy and Glenn's house. Hmm, that was unexpected. I was in a huge bedroom that I would assume was their master bedroom, but we all know what assuming does—saves time.

Quinton sat reading a book in a fuzzy red upholstered chair with his feet propped up on a matching ottoman. Gentle plumes of smoke rose from a bundle of incense in the middle of the room.

I floated out to the other side of the house and down into the driver's seat of the van that was idling out front. Max was watching a video on his phone about various strategies in Frebopple.

Sheesh, Max is competitive.

"Hi Jonah," Max said, his eyes still glued to the screen of his phone.

"How'd you know I was here?" I asked, crackling over the speakers.

"The A/C isn't so great while idling, and you're like, the best air-conditioning."

"That's cool."

"Heh," he replied. "Hold on."

He was getting a call. Nic's smiling face popped up on his screen. I don't think I'd ever seen her smile that way, like an actual person … with human emotions.

Did she always have dimples?

Max put her on speaker.

"Hi Nic," he said.

"Hey Maxim," she replied.

"I'm kinda busy. What's up?"

"Just checking on you."

"Aww, thanks. That's nice."

"Max, I'm worried about you. He was your best friend."

Max looked like he was about to take the call off speaker for a second.

"Thanks, Nic, but you don't have to worry about me. We were so close—it feels like he's still here … like he never left."

"See? That's what I'm worried about. You act like he's still around. Christ, Max, you even bought his house. It's OK to grieve. It's OK to let him—"

"Gotta go."

"Max—"

"Nicole, it's diarrhea. I have to go!"

"Oh jeez, sorry, bye."

We sat for a few moments without saying a word.

"So, it's like magic, right?" I said. "It gets you out of every-thing—"

"Everything, Jonah, everything. So, how are things going with the hippies?"

Crisis averted. We almost shared feelings.

"Good, I think we're about done. I don't think there'll be any more problems for Judy and Glenn."

"Nice," he said, "can I text Zoe and have her wrap things up?"

"Yep. Y'all heading over to the diner after this?"

He typed a message to Zoe. "No, I think everyone has plans."

"You have plans? What are you doing?" I asked.

207

"Yes, Jonah, I have plans. I am a very interesting and eligible young man," he said, trying to locate me, then gave up. "I have a date."

"A date? It's past ten. You don't have dates past ten—you have a hookup. Who is it? Do I know her? Bring up her profile. Let me see!"

"Jonah," Max deadpanned, "I am a gentleman—and a gentleman never tells!"

"OK," I replied. "I'll remember this. It would be a real shame if she came over one night and was—say—*afraid of ghosts!*"

He rolled his eyes. "She's not afraid of ghosts, Jonah."

"Not—yet. Heh, heh, heh." I gave him my best ominous laugh as he resumed his video. "Alright, I need to finish up here. Guess I'll see you back at the house at a reasonable hour since you're such a gentleman."

"Indeed you shall," Max replied without looking up. "I look forward to your presence at such time, good sir."

I floated out of the van, back to the house, and into a small, comfortable living room. The inside of the house was an eclectic design, along the lines of the pictures from the image search but subtly improved with DeeDee's designer eye. The furniture was comfortable and pieced together from different eras: a comfortable leather couch, a yellow wingback chair, what looked like a stool from some far-flung, exotic locale, and a wooden straight-backed Victorian chair. DeeDee had impeccable taste and was able to combine her experience with their past to give them a better version of their home. It looked like she might have talked them into lighter walls with darker wood floors. I followed a tight hallway full of pictures from George and Ramona's life, including their graduation, wedding, vacation photos, and one with Ann Richards in front of the state capital building. I followed voices into a cozy little kitchen to find DeeDee, Jeremy, George, and Ramona around an old wooden table. A gold record hung on the wall behind them. George saw that I noticed.

"Oh, that's not real. I just always wanted one," he said as he stood to welcome me. "Thank you for doing this for us—I mean, thank you, DeeDee and Jeremy—but thank you, Jonah, for putting us together and making this happen." He gave me a big hug.

DeeDee and Jeremy stood. "Yes, thank you, Jonah. This was fun. I haven't been able to stretch my creative muscles like this in a while," DeeDee said with a wide smile.

Jeremy didn't say anything—big surprise. Ramona came over to give me a big hug too.

"Well, we should really get out and try our hand at helping people move on," Ramona said, looking over at George. "I thought we might go visit Mr. Clemmons for our first go."

George nodded, indicating he thought that was a good idea too.

"It was so nice to meet you," DeeDee said, hugging Ramona and shaking George's hand. "Just let me know if you ever want to redesign. Think about some of those options we talked about earlier."

"We will," Ramona said, walking us out.

We stood on the porch for a bit before Jeremy turned to me and said, "So—you want to zap us back now?"

"Yep, sorry," I replied, turning to George and Ramona. "Good to see y'all. I'll check in tomorrow night to see how things went."

I lightly grabbed Jeremy and DeeDee's sleeves as we

blinked back to their house.

"Well, good night," Jeremy said, walking off toward the stairs as soon as we materialized.

DeeDee couldn't wipe the smile off her face and turned to grab me by both arms. "Thank you, Jonah," she said. "I really enjoyed that. I can't believe how much fun I had, and they were so nice! Please do not hesitate to reach out if you need me to do something like that again."

"Thank you," I replied. "You totally hooked me up tonight. I appreciate it. Sorry Jeremy didn't have a good time."

She laughed and gave me a hug. "He had a fine time. That's just Jeremy being Jeremy. He's secretly glad he got to go—trust me."

"Good night, DeeDee," I said.

"Good night, Jonah."

I blinked back home, turned on the home-improvement channel, and watched remodeling shows the rest of the night with a slightly more educated eye.

Chapter 25

Life—or afterlife, whatever—took on the shape of a new normal over the next few weeks. We had a few cases and helped a few more wayward spirits move on. Zoe and Max's business started to take off, and I noticed the group became more focused. A few decided to upgrade their gear with various spiritual accoutrement and higher-quality frayed (this time intentionally) clothing. I listened to a few audio books and went downtown every few nights or so just to get out of the house.

Meanwhile, at home, I noticed a few upgrades around the house. Max bought a new television as well as some VR gear and a new high-performance computer that he placed on a legitimate desk in his room. By "legitimate," I mean a desk that he went out and bought new rather than the one he'd had since Tony Gianfranco left his old one in the dorm after move-out at the end of freshman year.

Max was out more and more, always leaving notes to let me know he was gone, but not saying much about where he was or who he was with—as though that would satisfy my curiosity and not increase it by orders of magnitude.

After fading in one night to the sounds of crying, I naturally assumed it was Max's mysterious girlfriend—I would probably cry too if I were in her shoes. I emerged from my room to discover that I was wrong and that the heaving sobs belonged to a familiar figure that sat hunched over on our living room couch.

Debra was being consoled on either side by Tammy and Lin. Zoe knelt next to Max, who was on the floor of the living room with his arms around his knees. Something was going down, and I needed to know ASAP. I floated into the kitchen where Quinton stood with the other two Psy-kicks—I really ought to know their names by now. Anyway, they were in the kitchen eating what looked like a store-bought pan of cinnamon rolls and drinking coffee.

"What's going on?" I crackled through the radio on top of the fridge.

Quinton sat down his coffee.

"You need to hear this from her," he said, wiping his hands on his pants and grabbing the radio off the fridge.

Whatever it was, the news was important enough for Quinton to forego the usual pleasantries of "good morning," "what's up," or my personal favorite—"hey." The group noticed Quinton's entrance and felt the cooling that came along with my ghostly presence as I entered the room.

Debra looked up with red eyes. "Is that Jonah?" she asked.

"Yeah, Debra, it's me," I crackled back softly through the speaker. "Are you OK? What's wrong?"

"Willard is back," she said, sniffing back tears.

I went on alert and lit off through the house, checking every room once, and then again. I popped up through the roof and surveyed the front and back yards, making a quick check down the street and adjoining properties. I didn't see him or sense his presence, so I floated back down.

"Willard isn't here. He's gone. I think he's staying at another house north of here," I said, trying to comfort her.

She stopped crying, sniffed, and looked at the speaker where my voice was coming from. "Obviously, Jonah. I meant he's back in our lives. He's been coming to me the last few weeks, leaving messages that have become increasingly threatening.

"At first, I noticed the cool spots in the house and the sense that I wasn't alone. Then the messages in the mirror when I got out of the shower: TELL HIM. That just made me paranoid. Tell who? I told Hank the next day about what Janelle from accounting has been saying about his breath to everyone whenever he left the break room—but that wasn't it.

"I brought some friends over with a Ouija board, and that's when we got the details of his message. I tried to ignore him, but the messages kept coming in the mirror: TELL HIM. I called my friends to come over again. We performed a ritual of cleansing, and it worked for that night. They agreed to stay over the next night, and he was back—but this time we weren't strong enough. He took me over—possessed me—again and threatened all of us. If we didn't pass on his message, he would do to me what he did to you, Jonah. I'm sorry. I'm so—so sorry."

"What did he say?" I asked.

"He wants Max gone, out of the house—you too," she said.

"Or what?" I asked, knowing the answer already.

"Or else he'll do to Max what he did to you," she replied.

"Huh," I laughed. "Really? I guess he has a short memory. I would love to see him try something over here again."

Debra dabbed her eyes and nose with a tissue. "He

thought you might say that," she said. "He said to tell you he would be by at midnight tonight to talk."

"Anything else?" I asked.

"No, that's it," she said.

"Fine," I said. "I'm sure we'll have an enlightening conversation here in a couple hours. What do you want to do, Max?"

"Well," Max said as he stared at the floorboards of the living room, "I want to travel to England and catch a game at Stamford Bridge, or have lunch with Dave Chapelle, Hannibal Burress, and Jerry Seinfeld.

"That said, I would settle for a lifestyle where receiving death threats doesn't seem to be part and parcel of my everyday routine." He chewed on the inside of his cheek, thinking through options. "I guess I could rent the place out—maybe do vacation rentals."

"You would never get the neighbors to approve a short-term rental, and no one wants to stay this far south for events," I said, as though we were having a normal conversation that wasn't the result of a supernatural threat to his life.

The right corner of his mouth lifted in a half-smile.

"I don't know, Jonah. Why don't we come up with a plan after you've talked to him? Quinton and Lin brought some pretty killer coffee, so I can stay up as late as we need."

"You have my bow," Zoe offered.

"*And* my *ax*!" Tammy added.

"Thanks," Max and I said at the same time.

"Ha! Jinx, poke, you owe me a Coke!" Max laughed.

"Jinx! Silk! You owe me a milk!" I replied.

"I feel like we're off topic," Zoe said, trying to focus our attention.

"What are we supposed to do until midnight?" I asked.

Max held up his hand and offered as innocently as he could muster, "I propose a couple rounds of Frebopple."

It was an interesting choice in moments, but I guess Max decided it was time to put all that research to good use. Frebopple received universal agreement, and the group moved into the kitchen after grabbing a few chairs from around the house so that the table could accommodate everyone. The mood lifted appreciably for the next few hours, even as Max dominated gameplay. Zoe and Lin managed to squeak out a couple wins, so I guess everyone felt like it was a fair fight.

Around a quarter till midnight, the group decided to put the game on pause and do their best to fire me up. Zoe chose a handful of songs from classic adrenaline-fueled movies from the '80s. "Ghostbusters" (naturally), "Over the Top," and of course, "The Final Countdown." Midnight came, and I psyched myself up to go outside. Max put a hand in the air, indicating that he wanted me to stop just as I was about to head out.

"Wait-wait-wait. Just wait," he said, sniffing in a deep breath for dramatic effect. "Why be on time? It just makes it easy for him. Let's hang out here for a few more minutes."

That would have been a great moment to take an opportunity to teach Max how to rise above pettiness and meet a challenge head-on because it was the right thing to do … but fuck that. I liked his plan better.

"You're right," I said. "Willard is a dick. Let's make him wait."

Max punched in House of Pain's "Jump Around" on his phone, and the room went nuts. Everyone bounced around the kitchen and into the living room to jump on the couch, fell into chairs, and acted like idiots. Smiles were broken, beers were spilled, and a good time was had by all. Max held up his hand again after the song was over, indicating that we weren't yet done. He punched another song into his phone as his shoulders hunched and he extended his neck with his face contorted into a menacing grimace.

A few seconds later, the opening riff of Metallica's "Enter Sandman" started pulsing through the speakers. Max thrashed his head violently as the assembled group went nuts again, playfully pushing each other around in a mock mosh pit.

I shot up above the house as the second line of the chorus hit, hyped with preternatural adrenaline, ready to take Willard head-on.

I saw him as soon as I cleared the roof. He stood on the sidewalk in front of the house, and behind him stood three men who I began to recognize as I floated down to meet the group: three of the four guys from the first Tarrytown house haunting. Willard stood with his arms crossed, wearing a dark-gray tactical rig—pockets everywhere, boots, the whole nine yards.

"Thank you for gracing us with your presence. I hope it wasn't hard to find the place," Willard sneered.

"Oh, no trouble, time just got away from us. We were listening to some music," I replied in my friendliest tone. "So, I hear you have something you want to say to me."

"Oh, I've said what I had to say. I trust your friend Debra passed along my message?"

Wow, we're really dancing around here with the rejoinders. Oh well, why stop now?

"What happens if I don't want to go?"

"Then I do to Max what I did to you—only worse," he shot back. The men behind him smiled and shifted their weight back and forth—they looked ready for a fight.

"Worse? You killed me—not sure how you're going to do much worse. Plus, I'm not sure if you remember, but that didn't exactly work out for you." I looked back at the house. "Do you really want both of us chasing you around this plane forever?"

He smirked. "I will admit, you initially managed to gain the upper hand on me, but I have learned a thing or two since we last met. You're not the only one in this town who's found himself a supernatural advisor."

Willard looked pleased with himself, and the guys behind him laughed.

"One of those guys is training you?" I said, scrunching my face. "Look, man, I'm not here to tell you how to go about getting advice, but you can probably do better than any one of those guys. Especially him." I pointed to the big guy—he seemed to take things personally, and I was kind of pissed off and looking to share the feeling.

Willard blinked. "No—these men are here to assist me." He looked back at them and said, "You don't actually think I would take advice from any of these—"

"No offense, I'm sure, gentlemen," I interjected on Willard's behalf. "Look, it's been great catching up here and all, but I'm a little sick of dealing with you and your threats, Willard. I'm getting a little tired of you three as well. I thought we had a deal."

I gave the guys an exasperated look and held my hands out. I got a couple raised eyebrows and one case of affirmative head nodding.

"Fine then," Willard said.

He bent down and ghosted a small loose piece of concrete or rock from the road and flicked it at me. It grew as it closed the distance between us and was the size of a bowling ball by the time it reached my chest. I was so fascinated by the process that I forgot to try to dodge it. It connected and flung me back against the house where I bounced off it hard and into the flower bed. It hurt—real bad.

I stood up slowly and tried to mask how much pain I was in while wiping myself down, then stopped to realize there was no dirt for me to wipe off—man, I needed to break that habit.

"Neat trick," I winced. "Where'd you learn that?"

"Actually, that one I learned from you." He looked me up and down, taking a beat. "We've been watching you for weeks," he said with a satisfied look on an increasingly punchable face.

"Then you'll just love this."

I yelled through gritted teeth as I grew a comically large fist at least twice the size of my body and threw it against the four figures in front of me in a type of right hook that sent the three goons careening down the street and out of sight, while only knocking Willard a block or so away—not that I should be disappointed with knocking someone down the block.

I picked up the bowling-ball-sized piece of street that Willard hurled at me earlier and sauntered his direction, tossing it back and forth between my hands like it had the weight of a pink rubber bouncy ball. This time it was Willard's turn to get up slowly as I saw three figures running back toward us in the distance.

"Catch," I said as I threw the chunk of rock in a high arc

toward him.

Willard looked up at the chunk as it hit the height of its parabolic momentum and descended toward him. He steadied his body to catch it as it loomed larger and larger the closer it got to him. It overtook him with a cross between a loud clank and a boom as a hilariously large, oversized anvil landed on him and drove him into the ground—or encased him—I'm not sure which actually.

One minute he was there, trying to catch it, and the next he was completely obscured by something I copped straight out of a cartoon. I floated up to get a better view of the scene and saw Willard's goons hightailing it north as though they were one ghostly comet.

Two hands shot up out of the concrete as Willard gracelessly pulled himself from whatever spiritual indentation the anvil had made. He wobbled to his feet and glared at me, swaying.

"I'll be back tomorrow night. This isn't over, Jonah."

"It should be," I shot back before he could blink out to wherever he went.

He was gone, and I guessed we were safe for another night. I floated back down and walked back inside to meet the team and come up with a plan.

Brian Corley

Chapter 26

I phased through the front door to sandalwood-smelling smoke filling the living room as the speakers played Miles Davis' "So What." A Psy-kick was stationed at each of the front windows in the living room, both facing toward the door in such a way that they were half-looking out and half-looking in. Zoe stood about eight feet away from the front door with her peach sword at the ready in case the moment called for her to swing into action. I could tell she saw a figure through the smoke as she crouched into an aggressive stance, the palm of her left hand flat and pushing out as her arm extended, sword in her right arm arcing above her head like a scorpion ready to strike.

I put my arms up, hoping the smoke would outline my surrender.

"Whoa—whoa, it's just me," I said, crackling through the speakers of four small handheld radios distributed around the room.

Zoe relaxed as did the other two Psy-kicks by the windows—I had to get their names, although by now, it was just embarrassing that I didn't know them. Hopefully someone would address them by name sometime soon, and I could learn them. Until then, "hey you" and "aww you" were going to have to do for my interactions with them.

Zoe straightened up and shook out her arms. "It's OK. It's just Jonah—we're fine," she said, turning on her heel and heading toward the kitchen. The rest of the group emerged from different rooms where they'd been keeping watch.

"I'm fine, yes. Thank you for asking," I said as I floated into the kitchen.

"Glad you're OK, buddy," Max said as he walked over to a two-foot-tall travel thermos. He grabbed a mug off the counter, looked it over, and asked, "Is this one mine?"

He looked around the room for some sort of protest. When none came, he unscrewed the lid of the thermos and poured himself a cup. Max leaned against the counter and took a sip.

"It was mine," Tammy exclaimed. "Now we've kissed."

Max rolled his eyes and toasted the air with his mug. "Hope you don't mind the herpes," he mumbled.

The rest of the group filed in and assumed different positions around the kitchen. Lin, Quinton, and Tammy took seats around the table while Debra helped herself to a cinnamon roll. Max pointed at some of the empty mugs and mimed "which one is yours?" with the use of his eyebrows and his free right hand. He poured her a cup as soon as she indicated which one was hers.

Zoe walked over to the dry-erase board on the fridge and pulled down the long sleeve of her shirt over her hand to smudge out the previous items on the "To-Do" checklist. She pulled the black dry-erase pen out of its holster and cleared her throat to get the room's attention.

"So, Jonah, you want to bring us up to speed on what went down out there?" she asked, ceding me the floor.

"Wait, before you fill us in, Jonah," said Max, "I just wanted to say for the record that I don't, in fact, have herpes."

Max looked everyone in the eye individually to make sure they understood.

I filled the room in on what happened with Willard and the three goons—maybe embellishing things a bit to make myself look good—and finished with the thought that even though I was able to handle the four spirits tonight, they would be back tomorrow night—probably with reinforcements.

"OK," Zoe responded as she paced over to the kitchen table, looking up at the ceiling in thought while tapping the dry-erase marker against her leg. Her free hand braced her weight against the back of Quinton's chair at the table. "OK, so here's what we know: we had four spirits here tonight, and Jonah was able to keep them at bay. There is at least one other that is probably stronger than Willard since he mentioned he had a mentor. At a minimum, we're dealing with five spirits tomorrow night, possibly more. Jonah, how many do you think you can handle at one time?"

"I don't know," I said, thinking about it. "Given what I've dealt with so far, I could probably handle two or three more without much of an issue, I guess."

"OK, so let's think through what happens if you're overwhelmed. I propose that you retreat to the house through the front door."

"Why the front door?" I asked.

"One, it will probably be easily accessible given where tonight's confrontation occurred. I believe their M.O. to be one of intimidation, so I don't anticipate any type of sneak attack. Two, spirits need to enter through a threshold of some sort—like a door or a window. We can block the other door and windows by replacing the trim with peach-tree wood. We've been stockpiling some at the shop for something like this … for this or for an add-on sale to ensure spirits stay out of our customer's houses for good—maybe as a prevention method for people that don't have a problem with spirits, but would like some insurance against them."

"That was my idea," Max interjected with a raised hand. "Gotta expand that customer base, you know? There are only so many malevolent spirits out there."

Zoe closed her eyes and motioned with her hands as though she were pushing down energy. "That was Max's idea," she said through slightly clenched teeth as she focused back in. "Quinton has been working on a few other swords in his downtime, so there should be enough to go around tomorrow night. We'll make sure the house is full of incense to try to contain the action to this room as much as we can.

"We'll clear the living room of furniture, set up our spirit-attracting incense bundles in here. Jonah, you'll head to your room, which we'll clear out as well and fill with the attracting-incense bundles. Every other room we'll double down with the repelling bundles to make sure we focus the fight here.

"Jonah, we'll need you to confirm you're safely in your room and we'll position two from the team in front of your door while nailing a piece of peach-wood trim to the top of the doorframe as soon as you're in. From there, we're free to fight back whoever pursues you through the front door. Are there any questions?"

"I don't think the only ways in are through windows and doors. I go up through the roof here all the time. I've also left the Paramount downtown like that as well," I offered.

"That makes sense though. This is your house, and there may be different boundaries in play if you're behind or going into your own threshold. The Paramount downtown is a public space, so it doesn't really have a threshold so to speak," she replied.

"This was Willard's house too though. Wouldn't he be under the same set of rules as I am?"

"I don't think so. I don't think he has a hold on this place anymore since he left. Max is the current owner of the dwelling, and I think your relationship is feeding the threshold now."

"OK, that makes sense," I said.

Debra raised her hand. "Do I get a sword?"

Zoe softened. "Debra, you've been brilliant, but we need you to sit this one out. It could get chaotic tomorrow night, but we've been practicing for this as a group for some time now—well, not for this specific moment, but how to handle ourselves in tight quarters during combat. We may be battling spirits with wooden swords, but believe me—you'll feel it if one of these things connects at full swing."

Zoe shifted her attention to Quinton. "Quinton, can you make sure to set up Debra's house with the peach-wood trim as well?"

Quinton gave her a quick nod, while Debra's lips pursed.

"I just hate to have to sit this out," she said. "I'll at least get my friends together to send some fair fortune your way."

"Thanks, Debra, we appreciate it," I replied. "I ... uh ... I wonder how he managed to find you. He seems to have access to a lot of information."

Debra cleared her throat, gathered her thoughts, and said, "We shared a consciousness—twice now—if only briefly. You come away with certain insights about the other person after that. It's possible that he found me that way."

"Anything you can tell us about him?" I asked.

"He's complex," she started. "He simultaneously thinks he's the greatest guy in the world while also completely worthless. He wants people to respect him, but he doesn't respect himself. I also got a distinct impression that he knows something we don't, and that excites him. He feels like he has the upper hand in this situation."

That made a lot of sense, actually. Hell, I could identify with that. Willard came off to me as someone who was deeply insecure, and his projection of superiority probably fed off the inferiority complex as a coping mechanism. There seemed to be a new sense of confidence tonight though, and that didn't feel like a put-on.

I thought back to the last few times I'd run into him and realized those weren't random, chance encounters—he'd been following me. I wondered if he'd just blink over as soon as he faded in to watch the house, to see where I would go. How much patience did the guy have? There were a lot of nights I just stayed in hanging out with Max or listening to a book. More importantly—who was helping him?

The group sat around brainstorming for a few hours until the coffee ran out. We marked off a battlefield area in front and within the house (specifically the living room), and everyone had a station. Zoe would take lead just inside the front door with Quinton and Lin taking positions by the two front windows. Max and Tammy would be stationed just inside the living room but in front of the door to my room. Tammy was to be the next line of defense should the intruding horde make it past Zoe, Quinton, and Lin while Max was in charge of getting the piece of trim nailed into the doorframe as soon as I made it into my room. The two other Psy-kicks were going to be stationed in the kitchen and Max's room just in case some-one made it past our heavily arbored defenses.

Our battle plan was in place with a few contingencies. Hopefully, I could handle whatever Willard threw my way (yet again), but we were ready in case he managed to throw us for a loop. Feeling confident that we'd thought our way around a myriad of what-if scenarios, Debra decided to call it a night as she had work in the morning while the rest of the team decid-ed on a couple more rounds of Frebopple.

Max walked Debra to her car, and Quinton brewed up one last pot of coffee. Zoe pulled out her phone and snapped a picture of her white-boarded plans while Lin set up the game again. One of the Psy-kicks started shuffling the cards. The group fell in formation around the table as soon as Max returned, and Quinton set fresh cups of coffee in front of each person at the table.

Laughter pealed out, fists beat the table, and snide com-mentary volleyed back and forth round after round.

Everyone had a great night, Max won every game but one, and I let slip that he'd been watching videos online and where the rest of the group could find them. Lin vowed to mine the breadth and depth of the Internet so that they would never again experience a night of such one-sided domination.

She may have been a bit competitive as well.

The group broke for the night, happily intact, and ready to

Brian Corley

get to work the next day, putting up defenses at our house as well as Debra's.

Chapter 27

I faded in ready for action and floated up past the roof to see if Willard was out front waiting for me—he wasn't. *Dammit, did he say he was going to be back the same time tonight, or just back tonight?* I couldn't remember, but I thought he just said "tonight." Whether he meant to or not, it was a great way to get in my head.

I followed the sound of clinking glasses and laughter to the kitchen where Lin was running point on a new board game. This one had an elaborate set of roadways set up across the board. The Psy-kicks sat around the table, each with neat little stacks of fake money in front of them. I could tell Max was putting his best effort into one of his "nice faces," which meant he was losing but trying to look like a good sport. The top of the board was laid neatly between the floor and the wall and depicted a bus moving at a high rate of speed with passengers hanging off the sides and on top of it in varying states of dress. It was called Last Chance for Underpants, and it was apparently even more fun to play than Frebopple—or at least its strategies remained unknown and unmarred among the group.

"Not so fast, Lin," Quinton shouted and threw down a

yellow card. "Go back to Topeka, no Abilene for you!"

The table erupted, as apparently Quinton just delivered a severe burn.

"Friends, Romans, countrymen, lend me your ears!" I crackled through the speakers.

"Wrong radio, Caesar," Max replied.

"Thy evil spirit, Maximus," I said.

"Why comest thou?" he said.

"To tell thee—thou shalt see me at Philippi."

"Well, then I shall see thee again?"

"Ay at Phillippi."

"Alright then, see you at Phillippi," Max said and turned back to the game with a straight face.

The rest of the table looked confused.

"What? Jonah and I were Caesar and Brutus for a play in college." Max relented and let the group in on what we were talking about. By her expression, I felt like Zoe might have been a bit impressed at just how well-rounded we were, but the rest of the group—not so much. Kids today, no respect for the classics.

"Who's next?" Lin asked. Tammy awkwardly raised her hand slightly off the table. "Ah good, go ahead, Tammy. Draw a card."

She drew a great card, won some underpants or something, and the group fell back into the rhythm of the game. I floated back and forth around the house and vacillated between trying to figure out the game and checking to see if Willard was outside yet. Around ten o'clock I decided to ask if everyone had everything they needed, and Zoe put a pause on the game.

She walked me through the work they'd done on the trim around the doors. It was clean work; I couldn't even notice the difference as they painted the peach wood the same color as the original trim pieces.

"We thought about staining them—peach wood has a unique grain that you don't get to see often—but decided it would just be easier to paint them. We were a little pressed for time today," Zoe offered as part of the tour.

There was a big, military-surplus, olive-green rucksack in the middle of the living room floor. Zoe unzipped the bag and pulled out a fleece-wrapped bundle. She unwrapped it to reveal a peach-wood sword. "Lin," she announced, holding the sword by the blade and waiting for Lin to pick up her weapon for the night. "Tammy," she said and went through the rest of the group one by one. She handed Max his sword last, and I kicked myself for zoning out. It would have been the perfect time to learn those last two Psy-kick's names. *Dammit, Jonah*!

Zoe continued, "Keep these with you at all times tonight. I don't care if you're at the table or in the bathrooms. These weapons do not leave your side."

She surveyed the room, making eye contact with each individual to make sure they understood her direction.

"Good. Now, everyone reach in here and make sure you have enough incense to keep your station smoky. If we have leftovers in the bag, that means you didn't get enough. We light this place up as soon as Jonah lets us know they're here. Everyone got it?" Heads nodded in the affirmative around the room. "Alright, go make your stations ready, and let's kick on some good-quality jams."

Lin punched in a playlist on her phone, and the group went to work moving furniture to the sides of the rooms and setting up their individual stations as "Bring 'Em Out" by T.I. blared through the speakers. After a few songs, I decided to float up and get a good lay of the land. My head barely cleared the shingles of the roof before I saw him on the sidewalk in front of the house. Just Willard, standing there with his arms crossed and a look of determination set on his face. I floated back down and let Zoe know he was out front—alone. Zoe motioned for Lin to kill the music.

"Hmm," Zoe thought aloud. "I don't like it."

"Yeah," I said. "I feel the same way."

"Think he's here to offer up a deal or apologize?"

"I don't think so. He looks kinda pissed."

"Be aware of your surroundings, Jonah. Don't let him draw you out just to flank you. You cannot let anyone between you and the door," she said, pointing to it. "We need them to follow you through that front door. Do not forget, Jonah. Where do we need you?"

"Now!" I said and raised my right arm up in a cheer. She couldn't see it, but I heard Max laugh, and that's all I needed.

"Through the front door, Jonah. Say it with me," she said.

"Through the front door," I mumbled.

"Alright, go get 'em, Jonah," she said.

"Yeaaaah, put 'em in a body baaag, Jonah!" Max yelled from behind me.

Tammy laughed. "*Karate Kid*! I love that movie!"

Yeah, Tammy, we all know it was from Karate Kid. I steeled myself and phased through the front door.

Willard took notice and stood a little straighter, offering no commentary this time as I approached.

"Willard," I said, nodding in his direction.

"Jonah," he said, nodding back.

"So what are we doing tonight? Want me to step on a giant, rocket-powered skate while you chase me around town all night only to have me escape through a hole you painted on the side of a canyon wall while you smash into it?"

What started as a blank face slowly twisted as Willard began to comprehend my dumb reference.

"No, I want you to meet a friend of mine," he said through gritted teeth.

232

A form obscured the light around us as a large winged beast descended behind Willard. It landed softly, elegantly for something its size, into what looked like a gracious bow. His head rose, a pointy mass of darkness with glowing red eyes that morphed into a handsome, angular human face as he joined us on the street. His wings folded in behind him as he took on a humanoid form, seven feet tall, not entirely masculine, and dangerous like nothing I'd ever seen.

A strange presence accompanied him—not a darkness, per se, as I could still see—an empty light that cast a shadow of dread and hopelessness, like an inverse but watered-down version of what I felt when Seph revealed his true self. There was no mistaking what stood before me. This must be the demon from my conversation with the angel in my living room.

I thought back to my previous encounter in the garage over in Tarrytown and began to draw power to myself as discreetly as possible.

"Hello, Jonah," he said with a smile and a low bow. "I am Masephson."

His voice was smooth, with an English accent, and as he spoke, the feeling of darkness and dread fell away, almost like the feeling when you've been out of a pool for a while, walking around with water in your ear, and then suddenly it's gone. He reached his hand out for me to shake, and I took it.

Am I really shaking this thing's hand? Eh, seems like the polite thing to do.

I racked my brain for a witty response and came up with a good one, "Hi."

"We've been watching you, Jonah. We've been watching you," he said as he gracefully paced the street in front of the house. "Well, actually, we started with this one here, but he told us so much about you—we just had to find out more." A fallen branch caught his attention on the street.

"I swear to God, if you pick that up and start singing and twirling it around, I'm just going to go back inside," I said to an incredibly powerful being of timeless origin and unknown power.

He snorted out a laugh. "You're an interesting one, Mr. Preston. Oh, you certainly have our attention—the talk of the town!" he exclaimed, flinging his arms wide.

He wore a dark suit that could have been pulled straight from wardrobe on a Tim Burton movie: high collar, skinny sleeves with long, lacy cuffs spilling through. His animated voice dropped down to a dulcet tone. "You've done good work around here, Jonah, helped a lot of people. You should be proud."

"Thanks," I said.

"And you can fight!" he exclaimed, raising his fists up on either side of his face in theatrical fashion. "One at a time, two, four? You take them all on. It's very impressive."

"Where are you going with this?" I asked.

"We like fighters, Jonah," he said, beaming at me. His face dropped its mask as he gave Willard a sideways look. "We like winners, Jonah," he continued, and I watched Willard deflate as he took that last comment personally. "I've come here with an offer, Mr. Preston, a chance to belong to a cause bigger than yourself—bigger than this town—bigger than any of us. Do you want to join the team, Jonah?"

"Nope," I said, shaking my head, "I'm already on a team— I'm good."

He smiled a wide, gleaming grin—charming, but with a hint of menace. Perfect teeth, with points just a little sharper than normal.

"Yes, Jonah, you're on a team, but with such limitations— such small victories and with such fragile teammates." His eyes took on an inspired sparkle. "Maybe they too can join us one day."

"What the hell?" I wondered out loud.

"Yes! Jonah, thank you for bringing me to the question! What the hell?" he said, shouting out into the night. "But maybe more importantly, why the hell? Why should there be a Hell at all, Jonah? Why should there be such a place to throw the soul of someone who saved millions with a vaccine alongside brutal murderers just because they didn't believe in a God they couldn't see?

"That doesn't make any sense. Why should a kind old man in the middle of a jungle in South America be punished eternally because he hasn't been exposed to the existence of God?

"He sensed something, like his father before him, and his father before him, and so on and so forth back through a thousand generations. They sensed something and decided it was a sun-sized god that brought the morning on the back of a jaguar, and left to go home at night. A loving god that gave them life—food, shelter, a family. Thrown into a lake of fire because they didn't know the actual story. Is that fair, Jonah?"

"Yeah, that would suck," I responded.

"So join the cause, Jonah. Help us save them! We can liberate them along with the believers—everyone in Hades and Sheol—wherever they rest. We will liberate them as well."

He concluded with a flourish of his hand and a pose as though he'd just finished a dance.

"I'm not sure if you're just going through the motions here, or if you actually thought that would work," I said.

His face shifted from a vulpine-like grin to a foppish pursing of the lips.

"That might have convinced me," I continued, "if it was the end of, like, a multi-hour, deep conversation over a long dinner with plenty of cocktails. However, seeing as you dropped in as the form of some sort of gargoyle throwing off an energy to inspire at best the creeps, and at worst the strongest case of heebie-jeebies I've ever encountered—I'm going to stick with the feathery-winged side whose light is so bright that it terrifies me. I'm scared either way. I may as well side with the good guys."

His faced dropped. "We all think we're the good guys, Jonah. Well," he looked to Willard, "most of us."

Masephson turned on his heel to face him. "Alright, we had a deal. You feed us information about the boy here, and we train you up and get you your house back. I suppose it's time we deliver our end."

He turned back to me with perfect posture while straightening the hair along his face, and I had the feeling that I was about to have my ass handed to me in a very quirky Victorian method.

I held my hands out in front of me. "Hold on now. I believe we have one more night here."

"Is that true, boy?" he looked back at Willard.

"Yes, I gave them three nights," he replied.

"Well," Masephson said, grooming himself once again, "you shouldn't have said that."

Now was the time to release all the energy I'd been taking in during the course of the conversation.

"Hadouken!" I yelled.

A ball of energy shot out of my hands and into the breadbasket of my demonic adversary, blowing him back about five feet.

Dammit. I just hit him with more power than I could imagine throwing, exactly where I threw it, and he barely moved. Just last night I punched four guys out of reflex and sent three into another neighborhood and the fourth a block away, and I was only able to move this guy five feet.

He did wince, though, so I had that going for me.

I ghosted my hand into a left cross that made my arm look like it was eight feet long and sent Willard flying down the street. Good, that felt better.

That feeling wouldn't last long …

Chapter 28

Claw-like hands grabbed me by the shoulders and sent me flying up and over the house toward the backyard.

Masephson was behind me in no time, grabbing me in midair with his feet—which had now transformed into something like a giant eagle's talons with an additional digit—and lifting me higher like a bird of prey.

It hurt, and I screamed as his claws dug into my shoulders.

His wings emerged again as he tossed me higher in the air and soared up to grab me again. He was toying with me—great.

I pulled hard, trying to loosen a talon without any luck. Masephson was stronger than I could handle.

"He is actually powerful, that one—Willard Hensch," he commented as we ascended farther into the sky. "He managed to kill you with an earthly tool, and that is just not done—it's not permitted." He tossed me again and laughed. "We can do a lot with him, but he's just not—ambitious. Lacks drive, creativity, and more importantly—style."

His talons gripped harder. Higher and higher we climbed, Masephson reveling in the disparity of power between us.

He adjusted his feet, and it felt like he was going to rip me in two. We continued to a height reserved for experimental aircraft and weather balloons, miles away from anyone, then came to a stop.

As we hovered, his wings pumping huge gusts of air, he transferred me from his taloned feet to his clawed hands and pulled me in close. His eyes blazed red like coals in a well-fanned fire.

"You dropped an anvil on his head?" he asked.

Oh no.

"Um … yes," I said.

A growl rumbled deep from within, like a cross between a bear and a V8 engine. The sound choked into sputters.

"That's hilarious!"

The deep growl transitioned to an airy laugh, which was fairly endearing for an otherworldly being that probably inspired countless terrifying stories and nightmares.

"Very creative. We could train you, you know—give you power. You could join the others we've amassed over the millennia."

He released me, and we hovered together.

"You could do such great things," he said.

"What is happening right now?"

"I'm recruiting you, young man. Aren't you listening?"

"Yeah, but I already said no."

I guess I blacked out temporarily after he slapped me and came to as the sound of wind filled my head. Once coherent, I was able to slow myself to a stop just above the clouds.

Did he really just slap me? Damn, we were high.

Masephson floated next to me, back in his quirky, angular, humanoid form. He was flattening his hair to his face again and pulling on his cuffs.

"Sorry about that, Jonah, but it was an unacceptable answer."

"No … sir?" I asked.

His lips straightened, with only the corners of his mouth slightly upturned.

"Better, but still unacceptable. Let's try this again, old boy. Are you ready?"

I nodded.

"I need a leader for my army, Jonah. I want you to command my legion. Will you consider it?"

"Sure."

"There's a chap."

"No … sir."

"What's that now?"

"I thought it was more respectful this time."

"How do you mean? What are you talking about, boy?"

"I mean, I considered your offer, but the answer is still no. Sir."

"Oh. I see … well, sorry about this then."

He hit me with a hard, downward punch that whipsawed my neck. I shouldn't have felt my neck considering I didn't have a body, but the pain somehow found a way. I woke up on the descent again but didn't have long to get my bearings.

Before I knew it, I found myself at least ten feet below the earth, and I was in pain—a lot of it. Being underground hurt, the soil burned, and I wanted out of it.

If I had bones, they would have been shattered and scattered across and inside the lawn. Thankfully I didn't, so I just had to manage unimaginable suffering without permanent disfigurement. I found that I couldn't just phase up through the earth like I could through everything else I'd tried so far, and I struggled inch by inch for what seemed like an hour before I made it topside again.

I dusted off my pants and shirt out of a humiliating habit and realized, once again, that I didn't need to, so I stopped. The demon had resumed his gargoyle form and was there to meet me as I rose. He wasted no time, punching me square in the chest and sending me back toward the house and, as luck would have it, through my front door. The room was filled with smoke that curled in a tunnel-like formation as I cut through the living room like a missile and hit hard against the kitchen wall. I picked myself up and flew to my room as fast as I could.

"I'm in," I yelled as soon as I crossed the doorway.

Max flew into motion, grabbing the piece of trim from the floor and biting down on three nails as he held the wood in place above my bedroom doorjamb. He reached down to pick up a hammer as Willard flew through the front door. Zoe swung her sword like a baseball bat and connected with Willard, the momentum flinging him to her left and against the wall closest to Quinton.

Quinton was able to see the outline of Willard's body through the smoke, so he knelt down beside him and held him in place by jabbing his sword into Willard's chest. Max started hammering the trim into place as an enormous figure filled the living room, displacing the smoke.

"What is that?!" Tammy exclaimed, her voice wavering as the fear and dread that accompanied Masephson overtook the room.

Zoe sprang into action with a double-handed lunge straight toward the demon that just came through the front door. He was still in the process of unfurling himself after shrinking down to fit through. A rift of confusion channeled through his confident face as Zoe's sword made contact and drove him back. It looked as though she actually hurt the beast.

Something shone across his chest as his hand snatched at the source of his pain. He felt his wound and looked down to examine his now-bloodied hand. He roared as Zoe expertly swung high and down, catching him where his neck met his shoulder. The room shook and eyes widened as everyone could now see what stood in our midst—an injured monster.

Masephson flicked Quinton aside with the back of his hand, grabbed Willard, and flew backward out the front door. Zoe leapt forward and set her peach sword into two brackets that had been mounted above the threshold. Her feet planted firmly with eyes glued to the door, Zoe held out her right hand, motioning for Lin to relinquish her sword. Lin sprang into action, gave up her sword, and made a beeline to my room to join me behind my peach-wood-enhanced threshold … although, if they were able to make it back through that door, we were all in a lot of trouble.

Zoe resumed her sentry duty in a defensive position with a look of unintimidated determination screwed tightly on her face.

"What—the—fuuck?!" Max said.

"What-the-fuck-was-that?" Lin added.

"What-the-fuuck-was-that!" said Quinton.

"Shhh!" Zoe said. Her left hand reached out low behind her, palm flat, to silence the room.

Rather than cower in my room helplessly, I rose up through the ceiling and poked my head above the shingles of the roof and scanned for Willard and Masephson. I couldn't see them, so I floated a little higher, turning in a complete circle and looking for any place they might be hiding. There really weren't many options as most of the neighbors kept tidy yards. They could be behind one of the houses, so I did a fast sweep of the streets on the block, checking behind and around every house. I got to the end of our street and rose high above the neighborhood—still nothing. I felt comfortable that they decided to retreat for the night as Masephson didn't strike me as the type to hide and ambush. He was more than likely reporting back on everything that just went down.

I flew back to the house, up to the front door, and bounced right off it. Hmm … should have seen that coming, I guess. I floated above and down through the roof into the living room where everyone maintained their positions.

Chapter 29

"They're gone," I said, my voice crackling through the speakers in the room.

The room seemed to exhale all at once, and the Psy-kicks relaxed their posture, some shaking out their arms and legs just as they would after any sparring match or competition.

"What was that?" Max asked.

"That was Willard and his mentor—" I started. Dammit, what was his name? "It was Willard and a demon."

Zoe smiled, admiring Lin's sword, flipping it from hand to hand, then giving it a twirl.

"Quinton, great work. These saved us tonight," she said.

Quinton smiled, admiring his own sword as he ran his fingers over the carvings. "Thanks," he said. "I can't believe I was able to just hold him down like that."

"Great job tonight, y'all. Everyone kicked ass!" Zoe exclaimed.

A collective whoop filled the house followed by a couple high fives and hugs. Tammy slapped Max on the ass. "Good game," she said as she went on to high five Lin. After a few minutes, Zoe held her hands up to settle down the room.

"Alright, alright—grab a seat," she said, bringing the room to attention. The group settled in and took positions on the couch, the one chair, and the floor. I hovered next to Zoe as she kicked off her post-battle speech. "OK, so again, good job tonight. That was scary, but you all hung in, and I'm proud of you." She scanned the room making eye contact with every person there. "No one panicked, no one ran—you stuck to your training, and it paid off."

The room filled with a mutual pride as eyes lit up and humble smiles emerged on the faces in the semicircle.

"This was a new one for us—we faced down an actual demon tonight. I want you to know that during my time with Kevin Yang, we saw clients who were possessed—or alleged to be possessed. We came in and chased them out—or in some cases, discovered the issue wasn't spiritual, but chemical. We never saw what you witnessed here. I've never seen that. There is no mistaking what we did tonight—we faced down a demon and won."

The group clapped, and there were a couple of whoops. Zoe smiled, then held up her hands to quiet down the room again.

"Celebrate this. Know what you're capable of, believe in yourself, but don't think this is over. Jonah, we need you to tell us everything that happened out there and don't leave out a thing. Every detail you can give us is critical."

The speakers came to life in the room as I gave them the whole story, without embellishment this time. I was lucky to make it out at all.

I'm not sure what would have happened to me exactly ... I just knew I was scared. When I was alive, death was the overriding fear. I buckled my seat belt because I didn't want to die in a car wreck—among other things. I was afraid of the ocean because I was afraid of being eaten by a shark. OK, that one was a good fear to have, but exaggerated.

My mom let me watch Jaws when I was in second grade. Couple that with the old James Bond movie *Thunderball*, where they trap him in a pool with a shark, and I was set up with a complex for life. Seriously, I thought a shark would attack me in a pool. Who lets elementary schoolkids watch those types of movies? Answer—my mom.

Anyway, now that I was dead, I didn't know exactly what I should fear, but I had a similar type of mortal terror overwhelm me in those moments with Masephson. I wasn't sure what it was he could do to me, but I was certain it was bad.

After I ran through the play-by-play of the altercation, Zoe had me go through it again a couple more times. After the third retelling, the room went silent, and she went to the kitchen to collect the whiteboard off the fridge. She came back without a word spoken among the group.

"OK," she started, "let's brainstorm. Last night, Willard arrived at midnight with three other spirits. Tonight, he arrived at the same time with a demon. Tomorrow, we should expect some combination of the two, or worse. Let's hear some ideas." Zoe looked at the group expectantly and waited.

"Alamo," said Lin, right out of the gate.

"Great idea! Jonah, pop down to San Antonio and bring back Bowie, Travis, and Davy Crockett," Max drawled.

"Not helpful, Max, we're brainstorming here. We need ideas," Zoe rebuked Max with a stare that would freeze molten steel.

"Actually, I like the Alamo idea," I offered. "We don't know what or who they're bringing with them tomorrow night, but we do know the wards work. They can't get through, and if they do, we'll hit them with the swords. I say we double down on defense and utilize every resource we can between now and then."

"Aren't we all overlooking the fact that we lost the Alamo?" Max said.

"Shut up, Max. Thanks, Jonah. I think you're on the right track," Zoe said, nodding her head. "OK, what else can we use that we haven't thought of already?"

One of the Psy-kicks whose name I didn't know spoke up. She had a streak of purple in her hair tonight—looked cool. "My mom used to hang evil eyes around the house and at the front door. I could grab some tomorrow."

"Good," Zoe said, rolling her hand to encourage further responses. "What else?"

"We could bring Debra and her friends in, or have them set up a ritual or something," Quinton offered.

"Yes! Good, Quinton." Zoe rolled her hand more excitedly. "What else?"

"Let's reach out to Father Chandler at St. Raphael's," I said through the speakers. "He seemed like he wanted to help out with Willard, but couldn't because he could only perform exorcisms with demons. Well, now we have a demon problem."

Tammy shifted awkwardly, but Zoe snapped her fingers. "Good, I'll reach out to him tomorrow."

"The Alamo is a good idea," I offered, "but what if they couldn't see us at all? Maybe I can get DeeDee and Jeremy over here to make it look like Max leveled the place out of spite. If there's no house, maybe Willard moves on from his obsession with this place. If they figure it out, we still have our defenses—this would just give us another layer."

"A cloaking device—I love it!" Max clapped and pointed in no particular direction. "See? All those years of sci-fi and video games are finally paying off, despite everything Mr. Gunderson said!"

"Mr. Gunderson?" I asked. "What the—that struck deep. Let's explore this."

"Let's not," Zoe said, putting her foot down.

Zoe mapped out a plan and assigned everyone a task, whether it was picking up supplies, making a phone call, or both. My task was to reach out to DeeDee and Jeremy immediately.

I blinked over to Tarrytown and floated up the front walk to their house. I could hear Jeremy from behind the door. "Deeds, it's Jonah."

She answered the door a few seconds later. "Hi Jonah," she said with a smile. "Come on in." DeeDee was outfitted in a green-and-white patterned wrap dress with green heels, while Jeremy reclined in a navy wool cardigan over a gray-and-red checked shirt with tan pants and slippers.

"How did you know it was me?" I asked, walking in.

"No one else comes over to visit—ever. Who else would it be?" Jeremy replied from the couch without turning his head or making any effort to get up. DeeDee shot Jeremy a look.

"What?" he said. "Seriously, he's the only one that ever comes by."

Jazz was playing through the house although I couldn't quite place who it was, not that I was some expert in jazz anyway. To be honest, a lot of it sounds the same to me.

"What are you up to?" she asked.

"I need your help."

"Shocking," Jeremy replied.

"Jeremy," DeeDee said.

"Fine," Jeremy said, "how can we help you, Jonah?"

I relayed the night's events as well as the background on Willard.

"Jesus," Jeremy said in such a way that—to my surprise—made it sound like he was interested. "What do you need from us?"

I went on to tell them about our plans for the next night.

"Yeah, we can do that, I suppose," Jeremy said after taking in the plan.

"Really?" I asked. That seemed too easy.

"Yes, really, but if you want this done, we need to do it now. I'm sure as hell not showing up tomorrow night to do it. I'm not risking running into that crowd—oh no, no thank you."

Now that sounded about right for Jeremy, and hey, at least he was willing to help this time. Maybe we were becoming friends.

"Thank you," I said, relieved. "You're really helping me out of a tight spot here."

"I know," he said as he got up from the couch and walked toward me and DeeDee.

"Alright, Jonah," DeeDee said, "let's go."

They positioned themselves close to me, and I blinked them back over to my house, which DeeDee and Jeremy surveyed from the street.

"This is your house?" Jeremy asked.

"Yep," I replied.

"I don't get it. Everything you've described over—this?"

He stood in the street with his right elbow resting in his left hand while the fingers of his right hand supported his chin with his palm to his Adam's apple. He waved his hand into the air and said, "I would just move."

"Jeremy!" DeeDee exclaimed. "So rude." She turned to me. "Sorry, Jonah."

"No offense, Jonah," Jeremy said.

"Yeah, no offense taken—how could I be offended by that?" I trailed off.

Jeremy rolled his eyes and went to work slamming a huge garbage receptacle full of construction debris into the front yard. He warped one side of the house into the appearance of a large pile of dirt.

Taking a cue from his work, DeeDee set about her work on the other side of the house, obscuring it into a massive pile of dirt, and so on and so on until the house was no longer visible. The two architects floated back and surveyed their work from the street, conferring and commenting on each other's efforts.

Jeremy created a bulldozer, and DeeDee created a backhoe set on opposite ends of the property. After a couple more private conferences, they laid down some tracks in the dirt and made a huge scar through the front of the yard as the main access point from the street. They rose up one at a time to check and recheck, then invited me up to see what I thought.

"Well," Jeremy drawled, "how's this?"

I looked down on what appeared to be the remnants of a demolished house. Just piles of dirt, debris, and an overflowing dumpster—it was convincing enough for me. I made careful note of the debris that now marked the front door and the top of the house so that I could get back in later.

"Looks great," I replied. "Just like a construction site. Willard is going to be pissed."

"Well then, our work here is done. Deeds?"

"Happy to help out, Jonah. Anything else we can do?"

DeeDee asked.

"Nope, I think that does it for me. I really appreciate it," I replied.

I took them both by the arm and blinked us back to their house. Once back in their ultra-modern showpiece of a home, Jeremy pulled something from his sweater and handed it to me. It was a white, oversized envelope.

"What's this?" I asked.

"Your invoice," he said through a yawn.

I opened the envelope, and sure enough, it was an invoice for $25,000. I floated over to their coffee table and material-ized a briefcase.

"Great. Do you take cash?" I asked as I opened the brief-case revealing stacks of $100 bills. "You don't have to count it in front of me. I left you a little something extra for your trouble."

That actually got a bit of a laugh out of Jeremy, and I felt like I was starting to win him over.

DeeDee laughed and turned to Jeremy with wide eyes. "Jeremy, we're rich! We're rich! Our money problems are over. I'm going to buy a giraffe with all this."

"Bye, Jonah," Jeremy said as he halfheartedly jumped up and down with DeeDee. She was turning him in circles with a huge sarcastically playful smile on her face.

"Bye, Jonah," she said, laughing. "Thanks for all the mon-ey!"

I smiled, waved, and blinked back home. The house was dark, and Max was asleep, so I decided to wind my night down with some home-improvement television. I turned on the TV to find that—coincidentally—it was demo day. Nice. I watched an excited host hand out helmets and awkwardly cajole two property owners into smashing up their old kitchen, and eventually I faded out.

Chapter 30

I faded in the next night to a quiet house, which was surprising, considering what was to come. Wary that something may be up, I phased my head just a few inches through my door. I could tell the house was darker than normal, but not completely dark. The living room was lit by what appeared to be a little over a dozen candles. The furniture remained to the sides of the room to allow for a clear, open space. The Psy-kicks sat cross-legged, meditating in a circle on the floor.

Relieved, I phased through the door to my room and joined the circle. I could feel an energy around them as I drew closer and watched the candle flicker violently as I came near. The group looked up almost as one as they sensed me join them, and I received a flurry of zenned out "Hi Jonahs."

"Hey, everybody," my voice crackled through several speakers in the room.

Zoe smiled, closed her eyes, and led them through a few breathing and stretching exercises to close out their meditation before breaking the group. I could feel a slight release of energy as the group got up and spread out around the house—some to the kitchen, some to the bathroom—while Zoe and

Max stayed behind to bring me up-to-date on what they were able to accomplish that day.

Father Chandler was away for a conference in Chicago but promised to have the attendees pray for us as well as a small prayer group he led in Austin.

"Which is a huge help," Max said sarcastically.

"Hey, you'd be surprised. He's helped me before," I said, remembering my introduction to Seph. "Why so cynical? We're dealing with an actual demon. This kind of thing helps," I said.

"I think I was just hoping for a guy with a cross and some holy water, and to be honest, I feel let down," Max said.

"Moving on from that," Zoe jumped in. "Talked to Kevin, and he's out with a group at Enchanted Rock and can't make it back."

Enchanted Rock is a huge granite dome outside Llano, Texas, where people go to hike, camp, and take pictures for their various social media sites.

"I'm starting not to like Kevin," I said.

"Maybe now you can see why I struck out on my own. Anyway, he has a new group of college dropouts and PhD candidates to train now, but he let us raid his store of incense and candles, so that was nice," Zoe replied.

"That was nice," I added.

"You told me you just took them out of spite," Max said and laughed. "Jonah, this is like skyscraper levels of spite. The back of the van was full when she got here. Floor to ceiling, three-quarters of the van full."

Zoe shrugged. "Well … we need a lot to smoke out the yard."

"Alright," I said, "we have spiritual help from Father Chandler, things to light on fire from Kevin, and—wait—we're smoking out the yard?"

"Yeah," Zoe said. "Kevin had these three-foot incense sticks like the kind you can buy to keep mosquitos away when you're outside—except these actually work. We set them up around the house and lit them right before we started our meditation. Should be good through two o'clock or so, at which point we'll go stake some more out if we need to."

"Nice," I said. "I was able to get Jeremy and DeeDee to cloak the house last night. It will look like a demolition zone when they show up. Were y'all able to come up with anything else that we didn't think of last night?"

"Yep," Zoe said, "these."

She lifted the cuff of what looked like pants made from olive-green ballistics material to reveal a neon-pink heel-cut sock on one foot and a fluorescent-yellow sock on the other. She was wearing white canvas shoes, but I was pretty sure she was talking about the socks.

"Those don't even match," I said.

"Heyyy," she replied. "We have history. These are my lucky socks." She bobbed up and down on her heels, further displaying them. "One of my old roommates used to buy these socks—in matching pairs. Somehow these ended up in my sock drawer, and I never wanted to give them back. Four years on, I think they're officially mine."

Max smiled, admiring the socks. "Oh, on that note, I'm wearing one of my original Willards."

He gestured with his hands in a display worthy of any game show from the '80s to present the original Willard meme on the front of his shirt.

"Sounds like we're ready then," I said.

Max snapped his fingers. "Oh, also, Debra got her friends together tonight, and she said to tell you hi."

"Great," I said. "That's great. So—what now?"

"I think Lin brought over a new game," Max said and then raised his voice. "Lin! Did you set up the game?"

"Yes, relax!" she replied from the kitchen. "We're waiting on you two—three—sorry, Jonah!"

"Shall we?" Zoe made a theatrical bow and waved her arm toward the kitchen.

"Yeah, uh-huh," Max said, cracking his knuckles as he strode into the kitchen and threw himself onto one of the old chrome, diner-style chairs.

The group once again pulled several chairs from around the house to help accommodate everyone at the table. Lin was leading the game, and everyone had a handful of small dice in front of them or in their hand.

The game moved fast, and the wins were pretty evenly distributed over the next few hours until Zoe put everything on hold around eleven thirty.

"Alright," she said as she pushed back from the table. "Everyone make sure your station is ready. Same plan as last night if they actually make it in past the front door. Luckily for us, this guy is a creature of habit, so we can expect him to be here at midnight—be ready."

The group broke, and people spread out in different directions. Max and Quinton collected coffee cups that were scattered around the kitchen and put them in the sink, while some of the other Psy-kicks headed off to the bathroom or directly to their station. Zoe went into the living room to distribute the swords from her huge canvas bag to the person or at their station if they weren't there. Everyone took their position, either bouncing around or stretching, all preparing themselves for whatever happened next.

Around midnight, I could hear Willard's screams from outside but couldn't make out just what was being said. It sounded like he was talking to someone, but I couldn't hear the other side of the conversation. The speakers started to pick up his voice as he apparently came closer.

"… gone! They knocked it down! What do you mean? Look at it!"

I decided to peek my head up over the roof to see what was going on. Willard was apoplectic, zigzagging across the lot in furious fits of speed while yelling at the gargoyled version of Masephson between bouts of coughs.

"Calm down, Mr. Hensch," he said, coughing into his arm. "It's here—just look."

"I can't even stand to be here—it's making me sick!" Willard exclaimed.

"It's a trick—it's smoke and mirrors—almost quite literally," he replied.

Willard kicked a part of the house disguised as debris. "We had a deal, Masephson. I want my house back!"

"Relax," Masephson replied. "We'll get you your house back—trust me. Just go back there with everyone else and let me handle this."

The plan worked. Willard was beside himself, but I forgot that angels could see through the various planes—guess that meant demons could too. Masephson wasn't fooled.

Willard retreated to the street in front of the house to join about a dozen menacing-looking spirits. I couldn't tell from here if they were ghosts or demons, but I would venture to guess that the group was a mix of both. They calmly bobbed up and down, floating just above the pavement and glaring toward the house.

"I see you, Jonah," Masephson said, spinning into his humanoid form and looking up at me. "Why don't you join us outside for a little talk?"

"Hard pass," I replied.

"We can come in anytime we like, Jonah. You may as well make this easier on everyone inside."

I thought about it for at least a half a Mississippi count before replying, "No, you can't."

He materialized a lacy handkerchief from his waistcoat, coughed politely, pounded a fist against the front door, then laughed.

"Clever. Same as the weapon that injured me last night. The Demon Tree, the Tree of Mount Tu Shou, the Tree of Life—all derivations of a simple peach tree."

He held the palm of his hand just off the door, feeling the energy, and disappeared the handkerchief back inside his waistcoat.

"Good sample, good ceremony—well done. My compliments to the young lady and her team. These trees stand sentry at almost all the gateways to the other plane—Hades, Sheol, Abaddon, Tartarus." He waved his hand in front of his face to help displace some of the smoke. "Whatever you want to call it. They can't get out—we can't get in. Very clever, but it will not save your friends this night." He floated in perfect posture until he was eye level, fifteen feet away from me. "That is," he continued, "unless you decide to come with me."

"Hollow threat, you're not getting in here tonight, and you can't lay a finger on my friends," I replied.

He smiled as his feet floated up, turning him on his side so he faced me as though he were lying down. "Oh, I see—you're confused. Not those friends," he said and clapped his hands.

Two hideous, greasy, winged reptilian creatures emerged from the darkness and floated about thirty feet above the assembled group on the street. Each creature held one side of a pole stuck through a large cage, which looked to be about ten feet by ten feet by ten feet. Within the cage, clinging together and scared, were George and Ramona Rodriguez, both doing their best to put on a defiant face.

"Why do they look like that?" I asked.

"Who? The two in the cage or the ones holding it?" he replied.

I rolled my eyes. "Holding it."

"Scarier—wouldn't you say?" He straightened his collar and pulled on his white sleeves underneath his jacket. "Look, boy, we've spent millennia cultivating an image. Just admit that you're impressed or at least a little terrified and let's get on with this."

He looked back toward the floating cage, then focused on me again with a smile somewhere between genuine and condescension.

"Now, they both said they don't know you, but I think you know them—am I correct?"

"Yeah, I know them."

"Good, I didn't want to have to tell you that we were the ones running by you that night in Hyde Park—although I suppose I just did." He twirled into an upright position. "Yes, Jonah, you've made some enemies, and you've made some friends. I'm happy to use both against you if that's what it takes—and it's easy—believe me.

"Now, I'll give you a few moments to say goodbye to your friends back inside. I expect you to repeat Mr. Hensch's wishes again to your roommate, and then we'll meet you back here.

"Oh, and I suppose we should compensate him for the property. I could come by tomorrow afternoon with an agreement and a check," he added, looking back at me as he moved back toward the group on the street. "I won't—but I could."

Masephson rejoined the group, and I sank back inside like

a slowly deflating balloon.

"We heard most of it," Zoe started solemnly, sensing the change in temperature to the room. "We could hear him outside, and you were coming through the speakers."

"Don't go back out there, Jonah," Max said. "You can't trust that guy, and we know they can't get in here."

"They have George and Ramona in a cage, Max," I said. "I have to go back out there."

"In a cage—damn. That's messed up," Max replied. "Still, I don't want you to go."

"I know. I don't want to go … I think I need to though," I replied, thinking through what I was about to say next.

I thought about showing up to college without knowing a soul, waiting in line to register, and turning around to strike up a conversation with someone I'd spend most of my time with for the rest of my life. Late-night taco runs, all-night studying at various diners, road trips, holidays—I even stayed with his family for a summer. Now I was about to say goodbye for possibly the last time.

"Goodbye, Max," I said.

"Bye, Jonah," Max replied, looking up with tears in his eyes.

I floated up through the ceiling and over the roof where I hovered for a moment.

"Let 'em go," I said.

Masephson strutted forward, now outfitted with a jaunty, crystal-handled cane. He had style—I had to give him that—*a* style anyway. He threw his right hand above his head so far that it bent backward.

"Release them," he said in a loud, projected voice.

One of the greasy, winged, reptilian demons kicked the side of the cage, causing the bottom to drop out like a trap door.

"Jonah, don't do this," Ramona said. "This isn't our first time behind bars."

"It's cool, man," George said. "We're old pros at this."

I smiled at the sentiment, but Masephson cut through our moment.

"Goodbye, George. Goodbye, Ramona—be on your way." He made a shooing motion with his hands. "The bargain has been struck. The deal is done."

"And neither you nor any of your associates bring any harm to any of my other friends after this. You steer clear of them forever?" I asked, making sure I understood the deal.

"Sure. Yes, of course. Come, Jonah. Your chariot awaits." He smiled wide and motioned toward the cage.

Both demons holding the cage rose up, leaving George and Ramona behind, and flew toward me. In an effort to retain some semblance of control, I decided to meet them halfway. They lowered the cage over me while Masephson walked underneath and swung the bottom of the cage shut with his cane.

There I was, stuck in a cage. The bars were made of wood, peach—tree of life wood—the whole bit from before. I tried to blink out and head downtown, but no luck. I was in.

"Are you comfortable, Jonah?" Masephson asked.

I didn't feel like talking, and I couldn't think of a witty reply, so I said nothing.

"Don't worry. We'll take care of you, at least for the next half hour to hour. Cheer up." He smiled back at the group and got a little murmur of approval. Masephson sucked in air through his wolf-like teeth. "Fine. Not my best work. Let's go."

My two captors rose at once, as did Masephson. I looked down at the group below and could make out some familiar shapes. Willard sunk to his knees in defeat; in his eyes, the house was gone. He could have phased through a door or window if he were lucky enough to guess where they were through the disguise, but those entrances were blocked with the Psy-kicks' wards. I could recognize the three goons from last night, and they seemed to be reveling in Willard's bad fortune.

As we rose higher, I noticed the figure of the man from the diner and the Electric Fern concert just behind a neighbor's tree across the street. I knew it—he was with them all along.

Chapter 31

We rose high enough so that the rest of the group became outlines against the landscape as we headed northeast. We flew over I-35, which cut just east of downtown with north- and southbound traffic. I-35 (or just "thirty-five" as it's known to locals) through Austin is feared throughout Texas for its gridlock. Go ahead and add twenty to thirty minutes per mile if you need to take it for any reason between the hours of 6:00 a.m. and 10:00 p.m. (excluding holidays—they're worse). The interstate diverges into upper and lower decks just east of campus, and the two demons holding my cage dove toward the lower deck and down through it.

Down, down, impossibly down at a rate of speed that I could hardly comprehend. I imagined I was experiencing a feeling similar to what the families on the out-of-control boat ride felt in the Gene Wilder version of Willy Wonka as we continued on with no signs of stopping.

But then we did stop abruptly, which is to say—immedi- ately. No reduction in momentum, no warning, just an end. We stood stock-still in a gray, imageless, colorless space, a void without sound or feeling. I guess there was a feeling, but it was hard to describe. Internally I felt fuzzy—like the inside of your mouth after drinking tea that has steeped too long.

A passageway yawned open in the void somehow without spilling forth any light. Inside, oranges and yellows danced against limestone walls that curved out of sight. We moved slowly and steadily forward in silence, gliding past the entrance and into a tunnel that curved to the right, and then up, over, and through an Escher-like maze my captors seemed to know by heart. I looked down through tunnels as we passed by, some filled with a similar lighting scheme: orange, yellow, and red dancing across the walls as if lit by fire. Some were brilliantly lit by a bright-white light, some with a dappled-blue hue, as though a light were bouncing off water, while some were completely dark. We entered a clearing, or maybe just a large room lit in a warm, brownish-orange light. I guessed the dimensions to be somewhere in the range of a fifty-foot ceiling, a football field in length, and a basketball court in width. Gnarled stalactites hung down from the ceiling with sharp stalagmites rising to meet them like the pointed teeth of a viperfish.

My wooden cage settled to the floor with a solid thunk, and I heard a rush of wing beats as my captors ascended to the ceiling of the cave. The sounds of their wings faded as they reached the top, and I watched as they hooked their claws in and dropped to dangle down headfirst like two enormous bats.

"So, are you reptiles or bats?" I said, looking up. "Pick a classification and stick with it."

One of them ignored me; the other hissed out a laugh. "Bats are mammals, but I get what you're saying."

"What?" I shot back, confused.

"You said pick a classification—bats are mammals. You

chose a classification—reptile, and an order—bats," he hissed back.

"Oh yeah, I guess I did. Order, huh? Wouldn't bats be in like a family or genus?" I replied. I was genuinely interested; I didn't expect this discussion.

"Oh, you might think," he started and waggled a finger. "But it's an order—Chiroptera, second-largest order behind rodents—Rodentia. Bats make up about twenty percent of all mammalian species—they're actually quite fascinating."

"Hey, thanks," I said, "I genuinely learned something today. You're really smart."

He made a shooing motion with his hand. "Naaaah, I just have a lot of free time on my hands," he hissed and then shrugged with two open palms.

"Did you just say that because you're hanging by your feet and you wanted to make a pun on how your hands were free?" I asked.

"Yes," he said, blinking at me with big, frog-like eyes. OK, so frogs aren't reptiles. Horned frogs are though.

"Mister Preston." A voice interrupted my internal dialogue and reverberated around the limestone cavern.

"Please call me Jonah. My dad—forget it. Hey, Masephson," I drawled, turning to try to locate the voice of the slinky, overly theatrical demon.

He was practically dancing into the room in his humanoid form. "How was your flight? Did you enjoy the view of downtown lit up at night? I do hope so, because I'll hazard to guess that's the last time you'll be seeing it for quite some time," the demon said, almost singing the words as he twisted and twirled his way into the room. "Welll?" he prodded.

"Oh, I just assumed those were rhetorical questions."

"We know what assuming does, Jonah," he said as he rounded my cage like a shark with two legs.

"Yeah, yeah, it saves time," I shot back.

"Humph," he laughed. "You're probably wondering what you're doing here." Masephson held his arms wide and slowly twirled as he held his head back to look at the ceiling.

"Not really, I was thinking about horned frogs," I replied. "Did you know they're not really frogs?"

Masephson's expression changed mainly because his face changed, and his face changed because his body changed as he raged into his gargoyle-like form, grabbed two bars of my cage, and ripped it in half. Wood splintered, and the walls echoed with two large cracks followed by various diminishing crashes as the sides of the cage hit the walls on opposite ends of the open space.

Slowly and menacingly, he moved closer until he was just a few inches from my face, inhaling and exhaling huge gusts of air as he tried to bring himself back under control. I took that moment to reflect on how grateful I was not to have the sense of smell at that moment as his breath would have been heaved into my face in two-second intervals.

"Focus, Jonah," he said.

He took a deep breath, exhaled, and straightened himself up. His wings folded behind him and morphed back into his humanoid form.

"Let's start over," Masephson offered. "Do you know where you are?"

He floated up with one arm set over the other, like you would normally cross your arms, but he wasn't—kind of like a genie.

"Is this Hell?" I asked.

"That's the spirit, no! You're not in Hell. Hell doesn't exist—not yet, anyway—and it won't if we can help it. No, this isn't Hell, but we've done our best to create a version of what people's concept of it would be. For starters, we set it underground, created bits based on Dante's descriptions, borrowed a little from this movie, that movie, a TV show here and there. Personally, I enjoy a good stalagmite, so I had this room created as my own little holding area."

"And you set it under I-35. Nice touch," I said.

"Yes, that wasn't my idea, but I must say I rather like it. Traffic is a torture even we could not envision, but you humans always surprise us with your creativity."

"Thanks," I said and gave him two finger guns.

He laughed.

"Shall I take you on a tour?" he asked.

"Sure," I said.

"Brilliant, then follow me," he said as he turned back toward the opening.

We flew down the limestone hall and made a sharp right, past openings large and small, lit and dark, until Masephson pulled to a stop and hovered in midair. He held his left arm out, leading me to a large room filled with spirits.

"Do you like ping-pong," he asked.

"Um, not really," I replied.

Masephson straightened his lapel with the flat of his palm as he looked over the room. Hundreds of ghosts huddled around tables in various states of play and observation. The room was peppered with demons watching and officiating different games. The game was almost something else entirely when the players could float and fly.

"Shame, it is quite popular here," he said.

A mixture of groans and cheers rose up from one of the more crowded tables, and I focused in on the action. It was clear that someone just scored a decisive victory as one ghost's arm was held aloft by a grinning demon, earning the smiles and admiration of his gathered friends and colleagues. The other was escorted away, head down, by another demon smiling just as wide. His friends dispersed without making eye contact.

"What's going on there?" I asked.

Masephson took a few seconds to evaluate the scene after he turned in the direction I was pointing.

"Ah, yes, looks like those two put stakes on the game. Happens all the time."

"Stakes?" I asked.

"Yes, we're big on punishment and reward here. We love winners—we need winners. So we encourage winning."

"What does he get?"

"Depends on what he risked. Could be first choice of opponent on Fight Night, better seats for Fight Night, time with one of the demons, etcetera, etcetera."

"What about the other guy?"

"Based on who's leading him away, I'd say mucking out latrines."

"Latrines? We don't need them. I don't understand."

"You're right—you don't need them. We don't need them either, but we have the ability to take physical form, and will happily do so when the occasion arises."

Gross. I thought about how long it took Willard to move the knife across the house to bump me off and shivered to think how long it would take to clean up a demon latrine. I decided against asking more questions on the subject.

"Ready to see more?" Masephson asked.

"Sure," I said.

Masephson waved to the largest demon on duty, and I watched the demon snap to attention and return a salute. We floated back into the hall and picked up speed, Masephson indicating rooms as we passed—general quarters there, another rec room, an improv theater—until we slowed to a stop.

We floated into a beautifully lit room of blues and golds bouncing across the ceiling of a large open space the size of a city park. A crystal-clear pool of water shimmered below us with demons and ghosts floating, splashing, and having a good time.

We floated back out and down the hall a few hundred yards into another room of similar size, but with a giant sign that read "No Swimming." The room had a natural beach with the same gorgeous, crystal-clear water, but no one was in it. The beach was large and accommodated beach towels, bocce ball, and meticulously ornate sand sculptures. A new group of spirits wandered in below us, and Masephson's posture changed. A smile cracked across his sharp face, and he leaned forward, eyes flitting from the group to the water.

Most of the group observed the sign and veered off toward the other activities, but two ghosts ventured out on their own into the water. One spirit, who appeared to be in his early twenties, leapt into the water, went under, and emerged to splash his young lady friend on the beach. She playfully recoiled and laughed, rising off the beach to either avoid the splashing or make a bigger one herself. Her faced transformed from joy to horror as she hovered over the water. I followed her eyeline to a massive shadow materializing from the blue.

My mind jumped to various documentaries and shows

about sea life I'd seen before, to the shots of the ocean floor that look simply like rocks and sand until the sand shifts and a predator emerges to grasp an unsuspecting fish. I shared the young lady's terror as her partner was caught unaware and pulled under with terrible speed and unforgiving brutality by the massive, hulking shadow.

He was gone within fractions of a second as she screamed out in terror. It all happened so fast, she couldn't warn him. Some ghosts noticed her distress and flew to her aid; some turned around to watch. A cheer emerged from some. Demons rose above the water to observe the creature recede back to the deeper, darker parts of the pool, settle to the bottom, and become practically invisible again.

This was a game to them, a common occurrence, probably like clockwork when they received new recruits. Masephson chuckled.

"Always read the sign," he said as he turned to me.

"What happens now?" I asked.

"Well, we can continue the tour, or I can take you back."

"No, I mean, what happens to him?"

"Ah, yes, of course. The creature below is a leviathan—ancient and pseudo-spiritual, as though a demon mated with a shark."

"Did it?"

"Jonah. Surely, you wouldn't believe such an abominable act could take place … maybe."

"So, what happens now? Did he die?"

"I think you meant to ask, was he destroyed? He was already dead, but no, he was not destroyed. The creature below can feed off his energy for as long as we allow, potentially until the end of time if we'd like … or if she'd like."

"What do you mean, as long as you allow?" I asked.

"Periodically, we'll arrange for her to spit them back up. She can be very specific, regurgitating certain spirits as we call for them. It is quite amusing. It's an annual event we all look forward to."

"So he's stuck in there for a year?!"

"No, no, just a few months. The purge is coming soon."

"But why? That guy trusted you, and you need spirits for your army."

"We need discipline, Jonah. We need recruits that will follow orders. This is a simple test, and a lesson they won't soon forget."

"Does it hurt?"

"Oh yes. Not only is she leeching energy, but it's quite a confined space—not the cavernous stomach from the *Pinocchio* movie or even the story of your namesake. Although they're all trapped with others, they tend to keep to themselves with the occasional whimper or cry of pain and frustration. It would be very boring if not for the constant electrical burning sensation."

I nodded and looked down at the beach. The young woman had been escorted from the room, and life had returned to normal. A sculptor put finishing touches on a large, detailed, cartoon-like dinosaur invading a stereotypical Tudor-styled castle. Bocce balls hit sand, and laughter echoed throughout the enormous cavern.

Masephson looked down and waved to a scaly demon of authority who quickly snapped to attention and returned a disciplined salute. He began to float out of the room and motioned for me to follow.

Brian Corley

Chapter 32

We picked up speed down the hall and passed room after room. Masephson looked over his shoulder, then rolled his body so that he was floating on his back, slightly inclined toward me.

"That's one our movie theaters," he said with an arm outstretched, "stocked with the latest projectors and releases."

"How?"

"You know how churches have long feared that the entertainment industry is fueled by Satan and his armies?"

"Yes."

"It's much worse than they ever could have imagined."

"Really?"

"No," he said, then laughed. "No, I'm joking. We pay for them. We practically invented money. We have quite a lot of it."

"What's showing tonight?"

"'Today, I think you mean," he replied.

"What?"

He pulled a pocket watch from his waistcoat, flicked it open, snapped it closed, and returned it.

"My boy, it's four o'clock in the afternoon."

"But, how?"

"How do you mean?"

"I thought, with some exceptions, we ceased to exist during the day. I always just kind of fade away as the sun comes up," I said.

Masephson came to a stop and hovered, and I did as well.

"You see, up there," he pointed, "during the day, the atmosphere is constantly being bombarded by radiation from the sun. When the solar radiation hits the atmosphere, atoms lose their electrons and become ions. Follow me?"

Oh god, no, I didn't.

"Yeah, sure, go on," I said.

"Now, there is a particular level in the atmosphere called the ionosphere that actually restricts electrical activity while being bombarded with radiation during the day."

"OK."

"Are you old enough to have ever used the radio, Jonah? Not satellite or Wi-Fi mind you, but AM/FM radio?"

"Of course."

"Did you ever experience dialing in a signal at night that gave you a perfectly clear sound, only to find it fuzzy and cluttered the next day, or vice versa?" he asked.

I knew exactly what he meant. Growing up, we liked to leave the radio on for our dogs when we left the house. I liked to dial in classical music for them when I'd go to swim practice in the morning while it was still dark outside. It was always static-y when I got back later on when the sun was up.

"Yeah, I know what you're talking about," I said.

"Same principle. Solar radiation stimulates the ionosphere during the day and relaxes it at night, allowing you to come to form."

"So how am I here at four o'clock in the afternoon?"

"How familiar are you with the Faraday cage?"

"Doesn't it block electricity, or redirect it?"

"Yes. Smart boy, Jonah, smart boy. A Faraday cage is a mesh-like structure that keeps external electric fields from interfering with what's inside it."

"So this place has a Faraday cage around it? But wouldn't it further restrict the electricity like the ionosphere?" I asked.

"Maybe, if we set it up without a power source of our own to offset it. Down here, we've created our own, stable environment. Also, I should point out that we exploit something like a Faraday cage. It's actually something I discovered long ago."

"Nice. So, now I'm curious. What's the power source keeping us here twenty-four hours a day?" I asked.

"Ah, have to keep some of my own secrets, I'm afraid. Besides, who doesn't love a bit of mystery?"

"OK, cool, I guess … so what's showing right now?"

"I don't know. I think Guardians of the Galaxy or Casino Royale. I forget."

"Those aren't new releases," I said.

"Yeah, but they're good, and we have the prints, so we might as well show them. Have you ever seen Bedazzled?"

"That old Brendan Fraser movie?" I asked.

"Oh no, no, no. The Dudley Moore version," he said.

"Who's Dudley Moore?"

Masephson sighed.

"It's showing later. You should go—it's quite good. A local favorite here," he said.

He floated on again, and I followed. Picking up speed, the rooms flew by faster and faster, blurring until I could no longer see individual entrances. I felt a hand on my shoulder and an immediate stop in momentum. We were in a large clearing the size of ten football fields with a cavern-like ceiling ten stories tall. It reminded me of one of the Death Star scenes from Star Wars where hundreds, if not thousands, of stormtroopers stood in formation among a handful of parked starships.

There were thousands of spirits in the room in front of me, some in precise military drills, free from the construct of gravity. Hundreds of ghost soldiers in precise, geometrical patterns that were changing shape through the air to the call of a scaly demon commander shouting orders from a riser on the ground below.

Large groups practiced fighting mechanics in unison with what looked like large spears. There were circles of spirits on the ground with two combatants in the middle, fighting each other to the cheers of their comrades in arms. I looked down to the circle closest to us and recognized a figure standing head and shoulders above the other soldiers in his squad.

"Is that Kip Johnson?" I yelled loud enough to be heard in the room.

The tall, burly figure turned toward me, eyes squinting to try to distinguish who was calling him. They widened and slacked, along with whatever other tension that was held from the shoulders up.

"Is that … is that Jonah Preston?" he yelled back.

"It sure as hell is, Kip. Good to see you."

"I told you I would," he said with a broad smile.

"Friend of yours?" Masephson asked, arching an eyebrow.

"Eh, not really," I replied.

"Eyes on, soldier!" Masephson shouted down to Kip.

Kip wheeled back to the action within his circle, and Masephson turned to me.

"I wanted you to see this." He floated farther out into the room, arms wide. "All of it could be yours, Jonah. A legion to command."

"I don't want a legion to command," I replied.

He nodded, floating back toward me.

"Some of the greats said the same thing."

I looked out over the assembly without saying a word. It was awe-inspiring. The precision of the drills, the discipline in the ranks. I could lead … maybe I could even be great. It was still a demon horde though, and I couldn't do it.

I didn't need to say anything; Masephson could read me. His head bowed and shoulders slumped for a fraction of a second. A momentary drop in his mask revealing defeat, but it was only a moment. He mustered his glorious form back with a pointy smile and led me away from the room. We began to float back down the hallway.

"Jonah, Jonah, Jonah. Look around you—that room, the tunnels we took to get here, the channels that you saw leading off to other rooms, tunnels that lead to other chambers and so on, and so forth, etcetera. All were created by spirits just like you. Do you understand?"

"No," I replied.

"We recruit talented individuals such as yourself for several reasons. One, to build. We …" he looked up and rotated his hand as if searching for a word, "demons, as you would say, we're creative, but we're not builders. In fact, it was only a few thousand years ago that we noticed the spirits of humans creating copies of the world they'd left behind—usually with improvements. It was quite the breakthrough as it developed a new reality in this plane as you've already experienced for yourself, no doubt.

"I must say that it was a particularly ingenious idea to deconstruct your house, by the way. Poor Mr. Hensch. Your friends, the architects, do outstanding work.

"I am a great admirer of theirs. Ms. Kunkel, in particular, is quite talented. Mr. Randolph shows great promise, but is a bit overindulgent for my taste."

"OK, so why am I here? You know I can't build things—or haven't yet," I replied.

"Haven't yet—see?! That's one of the reasons we're interested in you, Mr. Preston. That enthusiasm. We need you to join us, Jonah, join our ranks. You could someday command my legions with your talents and leadership abilities. Just think of what you've done so far!"

"I had help," I countered.

"Of course, and you'll have more, much more!"

We picked up speed. I stopped trying to keep up with directions as we took hard lefts and rights, zigzagging through tunnel after tunnel.

"Mr. Hensch is quite a strong spirit, Jonah, as we've discussed, and yet you were able to overcome him your first night in this plane of existence. That shows a tremendous amount of natural ability. Just think what you can become once we hone those natural reactions into well-practiced skills. You would learn from some of our best from over the millennia, travel the world! Have you ever been to Rome, Mr. Preston?"

"No."

"It is beautiful—you would love it. Although, now that I think of it, you may enjoy Vienna just a bit more," he said as we slowed to reenter the large room from before, parts of my cage still scattered about.

"I like it here—well, not here at the moment, but I like Austin," I said.

"As you should. It is quite a delightful little town, isn't it? Well then, what is it you want to do, Jonah?"

"I want to keep helping people. I want to spend time with my friends, and make new ones."

"Yes. Good. Well, I suppose I could help you spend more time with your friends," he said, then clapped his hands twice and boomed, "Bring them here!"

I could hear a noise in the distance, the soft sound of wings beating against air. The sound grew louder until I saw two more reptilian demons enter the room carrying a cage identical to the one in which I was previously held. They came to a stop and slowly descended to set down George and Ramona Rodriguez.

Masephson strutted over to the cage, released a latch toward the bottom of the cage with his foot, and signaled for the creatures to exit the room. They slowly ascended as the lower part of the cage fell open to release George and Ramona into the room with us.

"Welcome!" he beamed. "Welcome, welcome, George and Ramona!"

"We had a deal Masephson!" I exclaimed.

"We had a deal that I would let them go and would not harm your friends. As you will recall, I let them go, and as you can see, they are no worse for wear. Besides, we simply cannot allow you or them to continue to deplete our resources by moving them on to the next plane. We were concerned that this trend may continue, and it would just not do to have the practice expand. Thus, you see the decision before me, and here we are."

"That wasn't the deal, Masephson," I proclaimed.

"It was the deal. It was!" He smiled his vulpine smile. "You were not specific enough. You should always know what you're getting into when dealing with the Devil."

I rolled my eyes. "You're not the Devil."

"Indeed, I am not, Mr. Preston. Indeed I am not. Merely a devil, I'm afraid. Now I'll leave you three to talk amongst yourselves. Consider my offer, Mr. Preston. Ta-ra!" Masephson waved as he disappeared behind a stalagmite.

"I wondered if that would happen," George mused.

"Those bastards," Ramona said.

"Are you two OK?" I asked.

They looked at each other and back to me, nodding.

"Not that I blame you, Ramona," George started, "but it probably didn't help that you walked up and smacked that guy as soon as they took off with Jonah."

Ramona covered her mouth as she laughed. "It felt good though. At least I got a shot in before they locked us back up."

George laughed, looked at me, and shrugged. "Well, now what?" he asked.

"I don't know," I replied. "Want to play cards?"

"Sure," George and Ramona said almost at once.

We went to work setting up an extravagant green-felted, dark-stained oaken table. I opted to create a chrome-legged stool to sit on, while George and Ramona went with taller wooden chairs stained the same color as the table.

I created a deck of cards and asked, "What should we play?"

"How about poker?" George offered, and Ramona shrugged in the affirmative.

"Works for me," I replied.

I dealt the cards out one per player in a clockwise distribution, marveling at how they slid perfectly across the felt to George and then Ramona. I was never able to deal like this in life. We each created twenty-five chips of the same value and began to bet.

I drew an incredible hand—a royal flush, ten of spades through the ace. Ramona started us off with two chips in the middle of the table, followed by a call and a raise by George. I didn't want to tip my hand early, so I just called. Ramona put in four chips this time, and George raised again. I couldn't have a better hand and pushed in all my chips.

"All in," I declared with a smirk.

Without hesitation, Ramona pushed in all her chips and looked to George. He raised an eyebrow and breathed out a sigh.

"Wow," he said, "this game got brutal early."

"Alright," I said, "let's see what you have."

"Sorry, boys, better luck next time," Ramona said as she fanned out her cards—a royal flush, ten through ace of hearts.

"Not so fast, honey, full house!" George said, slamming down his cards.

"George, for the last time, a full house doesn't beat a royal flush," Ramona chastised him.

"Royal flush," I said, sheepishly laying down my cards.

"George, you thought a full house beat a royal flush?"

"He always thought it was the best hand," Ramona interjected.

"Ugh," I said. "These cards are just going to be whatever we want them to be. We need to figure out another game."

George cracked up, and Ramona scrunched her face. We went on to try Battleship and found our hit screens full without actually ever hitting one another's ships. We tried Monopoly but were able to roll whatever number we needed.

We finally settled on a paper-scissors-rock tournament. Ramona annihilated us during the first hour, and neither George nor I were able to recover. We got bored after a while and figured out we could set up a checkers or chess board and play that as long as we had a third party looking on, although it was hard for me to keep up with what pieces went where during George and Ramona's game.

"Hey you," chimed a familiar accented voice as the Cheshire Cat girl in the motorcycle jacket appeared from behind Ramona, circling the distance between us and putting a hand on my shoulder. She cocked her head and gave me a small half-smile. "Want to take a walk?"

"Will they be OK if I leave?" I asked.

"Yes," she said, "of course."

"Are you OK for me to go?" I asked Ramona and George.

"Oh, I'm sure we'll find a way to manage, Jonah," Ramona said, "somehow."

"Alright, let's go for a walk," I said as I rose from my chair.

Chapter 33

I heard a gust of wind and a voice that said, "I can't let you do that." One of my reptilian guards swooped down from the ceiling to land between us.

"Says who?" replied Cheshire Cat girl.

"You know," he replied.

She blew hair out of her face as she rolled her eyes. "Fine. You can follow behind us. Will that work for you?"

"Yeah, that works," he replied, then turned to me with an outstretched hand. "Name's Busquamet. Sorry we didn't get a chance to exchange pleasantries earlier."

"Jonah," I said and shook his hand. "Now, the million-dollar question, who are you?" I asked, turning to Cheshire Cat girl.

"Did you know Kurt Russell's first role in a movie had him kicking Elvis in the shin?" she replied.

"What?"

"What did you hear me say?"

"Something about Kurt Russell and Elvis."

"That's what I thought—well, not exactly. Apparently, you cannot know my name, Jonah," she said.

"Fine," I said, recalling my earlier conversation with Seph. "I'll just call you Cat."

She smiled as she touched my shoulder, gently nudging me forward for a walk through the halls.

"I've been briefed on Masephson's actions tonight. He is—theatrical. Look, this isn't how I wanted this to happen, but he had leverage with Hensch and thought he could recruit you both this way. I find his methods to be—a little overindulgent for my taste."

"Yeah, he should've tried the ol' show-up-at-random-places-and-befriend-Jonah trick. I never see those coming."

She gave me a playful punch in the arm that lightly shoved me away as she looked off to her right. We exited the room and were now walking down a tunnel lit by openings every fifteen feet or so that looked out to a much larger chamber from what I could tell.

"So, you know what I am," she said softly while fidgeting with her hands.

"Yes."

"How does that make you feel about me?"

"That it makes sense a demon would try to hide what they were, get me to like them, and mislead me over the course of a summer." I smiled, looking off at nothing.

"It's not like that. I couldn't just say, 'Hello, Jonah. I literally cannot tell you my name. I am a demon. Want to go out some time?'"

"It's certainly not as good as my fineapple line," I mumbled.

She laughed, then stopped to face me.

"I want to tell you my version of the history you know. It may give you a different perspective."

"Sure," I said. "Why not?"

She nodded, ignoring the bite to my comment, and started with her story.

"You're familiar with the tradition that Lucifer was arrogant enough to think he could overthrow God, that he split Heaven in half and started a civil war?" she asked.

I nodded.

"There was no war, Jonah. It wasn't even an attempt at a coup," she said.

"What?" I asked.

"I know," she said.

"What do you mean there wasn't a war?" I asked.

"It's not as though there were always two sides, angels and demons. We spent billions of years together as one cohesive unit. We traveled between worlds, reported back, ate together, sang together, trained together. To be quite honest, I'm not sure why we had so much combat training, but the military structure in place worked quite well. Heaven is a … um … tricky concept."

She paused, looking up to gather her thoughts. "In some people's minds, a version of it exists today. In others', it does not. Meaning, some see Heaven as the home in which God dwells today, and that place truly exists. Sometimes it's referred to as Paradise. Heaven, the new Heaven, will exist in the future—here—on Earth. So, in short, Heaven is wherever God is really—Paradise today, Earth in the future. Follow me so far?"

"Kind of," I replied, "go on."

"OK, good," she said, looking down at her shoes as we walked farther down the tunnel. "After eons of living harmoniously together in Paradise, flitting back and forth between

His creation—or what you would think of as different worlds or planets—word began to spread about a new project. He decided to build a world for a class of creature that would bear His likeness."

Busquamet cleared his throat behind us. "Species."

"What?" Cat stopped and turned on her heel, cocking her head sideways toward our guard.

"You said 'class of creature' when referring to humans. They're a species," the frog-eyed reptilian demon continued.

"Oh. Oh, yes, I suppose you're right—good catch," she said.

"Thanks, it's kind of my thing," the demon responded.

"It's definitely his thing," I agreed. "That guy knows his stuff."

The demon shot me his own set of finger guns as Cat turned back around to continue our conversation.

"Where was I?" she wondered aloud. "Oh yes … news spread that God decided to create a *species*—" she turned to acknowledge Busquamet, then continued her focus down the hallway, "in His own image. Now, that means more than just the two-armed, two-legged, eyes, ears symmetrically proportional bit of anatomy.

"Word began to spread that the creatures would be able to function in such a way that they could *create* using the resources around them, communicate using original ideas—have original thoughts on their own—outside the evolutionary survival process. Of all the worlds circling all the suns or stars in the infinite universe, there had never been such a concept.

"I've heard humans talk about the concept of free will as though it is unique to them, which is obviously a flawed hypothesis disproven in the opening chapters of the Bible. Everyone focuses on Eve choosing to eat from the Tree of

Knowledge, but there was someone tempting her to do so, having already fallen based on their previous choice. I'm sorry. I'm getting ahead of myself. Creativity combined with free will is what sets you and your species apart. Do you understand?"

"So far," I replied.

"My kind—angels, although my faction are now referred to as demons in order to distinguish sides—were comprised of many different forms and functions, all for different purposes—a traditional humanoid shape with wings as we're depicted in modern society, but so many other variations. There are those comprised mainly of eyes or ears so they can see or hear everything that happens in a particular place. Some of us are multi-winged, some of us are mighty, some of us less so—we all have our place. The one thing in which we are not adept— the one thing we lack—is the ability to create.

"Oh, we're spectacular when it comes to the refinement of an idea. There are those of us who are quite eloquent and clever. However, the concept of creation remains foreign to us to this day."

"How is that possible?" I asked. "It seems to me that you're creating something just by having a conversation. You're choosing words to make a point. I mean, you have to be creative to even refine an idea."

"I see your point," she said. "Maybe it's in our core structure like a governor on a car engine or something. Did you ever read *I, Robot*?"

"Yeah, of course," I replied. "Are you saying your version of following the three laws is that you just can't create?"

"Yes, basically, with a few other caveats." She seemed to think out loud. "He made us the way we are. Maybe we would be too powerful if we could create things—even small things, like the table you and your friends came up with back there."

We walked in silence for a while before she continued.

"Lucifer saw this project as a threat to everything we held dear—our ecosystem, our relationship with God. What if He could not control this creation? What if they were able to rise up? What if they were able to influence and hold dominion over His other creations? What would happen to us then?"

"Do you mean what would happen if we were able to travel to other planets?" I asked.

"Yes. Why put everything we've ever known at risk for this one little world—an atom within a cell, within a molecule of water, within a vast ocean? It wasn't just Lucifer's concern; it was a growing concern among us all. As God's favorite and grandest creation, we called on him to speak to our Lord—beseech Him to abandon this perilous endeavor. So, he did."

"You think we're going to be able to travel to different planets?"

"Jonah, please."

"What? I'm curious."

"Yes, I think someday, humans could travel to other planets."

"Huh. Cool."

"May I continue?"

"Sorry."

"For days, Lucifer implored Him to put an end to the project until it was time. God set a new universe in motion with an explosion that sent stars flying. Planets coagulated from chunks of debris, orbits were set, and life was seeded by the passing of comets whose dust trails combined with the existing elements of the new planet set just the right distance from what you know as the sun.

"We began to meet in secret. Hordes of angels, thousands upon thousands gathered to listen to news from Lucifer in his conversation with our Lord. He remained unmoved by Lucifer's pleas. On Earth, the ocean began to teem with life as single-celled organisms became creatures who swam the depth and breadth of the newly created world. Lucifer implored God to leave it as such and rethink His plan, but He would not hear him.

"Land emerged, more and more of it as the ocean receded, and new formations occurred as magma spewed forth through volcanoes. Life began on the newly formed shores, and Lucifer beseeched Him again to be satisfied with this new world and go no further. Again, He would not be swayed.

"Enormous creatures came forth to roam about the Earth and swim through its oceans. Surely, he said, this is sufficient, my Lord. He begged Him to stop there, but it was too much—he pushed too hard. Our Lord turned His attention upon all of us.

"He would not abide insubordination. He would not allow us to question His authority. He confronted Lucifer as we met in what we thought a secret meeting. The great battle that is described in earthly literature was an argument, an epic debate that thundered on for ages, until finally, He cast us all out.

"Expelled from our home, Lucifer rallied us to inhabit the very catalyst of our ouster. He was certain he could prove to God what a mistake He had made. We all came, but for different reasons. Some believed, along with Lucifer, that they could show God He was wrong—that the humans He created were dangerous abominations. Some of the strongest came to Earth to protect the creations they had overseen for billions of years. They could not bear the idea of their cultures and ecosystems thrown into chaos by the unholy creatures of Earth should they decide to one day leave their planet and explore other worlds. Some came purely out of spite. Having been cast out, they saw no hope and relished the idea of tormenting a species so dear to our Lord.

"We found that God still allowed Lucifer to return to His halls from time to time to discuss His creation and continue their disagreement. We formed new ranks in our new home. As new leaders emerged, all reported up to Lucifer.

"Before humans finally came to be on this world, Lucifer either convinced God of the potential danger or God indulged His favorite creation with a bargain—He would set His experiment in motion with a caveat. Should the humans become unsatisfied with their environment, they would be castigated—much as we were out of Paradise—to endure a harsh existence without His light upon us."

"Well, we all know how that turned out," I said.

"Jonah."

"Sorry."

"So, human life began in a trouble-free environment—a lush, soft land populated with beautiful, delicious flora and docile beasts. They knew no danger, wanted for nothing, and from time to time dwelled in the presence of God Himself. Adam and Eve were a construct to a story, a family among thousands that existed in an area not much larger than the city you live in. Tasting the fruit of the Tree of Knowledge existed as the one boundary that could not be crossed.

"Lucifer was satisfied with the arrangement. The danger was contained in an environment that seemingly left all parties satisfied. There were others, however, who were not comforted by this détente, who still longed for retribution.

"The majority of our kind were forbidden inside the boundaries of the garden, but there were those that were powerful enough to breach its borders and find ways to interact with the humans. It is believed by most of us that it was one of those, not Lucifer, that finally convinced Eve to seek the fruit of the Tree of Knowledge."

"So you're saying Lucifer isn't the monster we've been led to believe he is?"

"Not with that hair," she mused.

"Really? The hair? That's twice I've heard about it. Must look fantastic."

"Mm-hmm. Anyway, we all have our suspicions as to who actually tricked Eve into eating the fruit, but it wasn't him."

"Interesting."

"So. God was furious and cast out the humans from their carefully cultivated environment into a world of hardship. Lucifer was held responsible for the decision, regardless of who really tempted the humans, and we were subject to a harsher punishment to be administered at the time when God decides to remake this place. Lucifer continued to petition our Father to rethink His position toward humans and this world, but we all accepted the inevitable once he sent His Son.

"Since that time, he relented to the demands of his generals to recruit an army of gifted spirits like yourself—extremely useful as spies, artisans, and craftsman today, but formidable soldiers in the war that is to come. We're spiraling toward a real battle against an impossible foe, but man's ability to create combined with our power may give us an edge in the time to come."

We approached a sharp bend in the tunnel where she stopped to face me.

"That's why we need you, Jonah."

"Need me to be one of the millions of collected spirits? Lead a battalion? I don't get it," I replied.

"No," she replied, "you don't. You are unique, Jonah."

She played to my pride, but I wasn't that easy.

"Not really," I replied, "I watched Willard do a lot of what I can do, and I have friends that can build a house in like an hour. There are plenty of people that can do what I do."

"I watched Masephson train Willard Hensch. He could not do in training what he did in front of you. Your friends, the architects, it took them months to get their house right. We watched them take weeks on the outside then work their way in, coming back out to add detail, create a landscape. Yet, you called on them to help your friends, and they created the Rodriguezes' house within an hour."

"So, if I'm an inspiration, what do I inspire you to do?" I asked as I lay down on the gravelly floor of the tunnel, leaning over on my side. "Paint me like your French girls, Cat."

She rolled her eyes and playfully kicked gravel toward me.

"You're an amplifier," she said and offered her hand to help me up, which I took. "Not only do you have the ability to create copies of nearby items, but you can also quickly improvise once they're in hand or create them whole from nothing.

"What sets you apart from anyone else we've encountered is that you enhance the natural abilities of those around you as well. When Mr. Hensch came to us with his story about what he did to you, we were excited. It is extremely rare to have someone come to us with an ability to utilize actual artifacts from the other plane like he did to eliminate you."

"Except he didn't—eliminate me," I butted in.

"Exactly. After monitoring Hensch in training, I began to

have my doubts about his story, so I personally investigated its veracity. I watched for some time as you discovered the new world around you, helping those around you—living or dead. I saw an individual with not only a tremendous talent but someone that was kind, loyal, and had a good heart—all attributes I like to see in a recruit."

"Of course," I responded, "if there is one thing we all know, it's how loyal, kind, and true demons are. Story after story tells us so."

A sad smile softly stretched across her face. I think that hurt. I may have gone a tad too far.

"You're right, of course. There are monsters among us, but I hope you heard what I had to say earlier. We're not all bad …" She paused, looking up like there were words on the ceiling. "Like your Republicans."

I breathed out a laugh. "Uh-huh, just like them—nice analogy, coming from a demon."

"Maybe I should have said all politicians, mea culpa," she said, holding up her hands and kicking at the dirt. "Jonah, I am going to ask you something, and I need an answer before we turn this corner."

She nodded to a curve in the tunnel ahead.

"Let me train you. I will oversee you personally, place you under my command. You will train with the elite I have assembled over thousands of years. Good people—noble, honorable."

"Why would I do that? Look, Cat, I like you—really—but all I want to do is get George and Ramona and leave. That's it. I don't want to pick a side. I just want out."

She sighed, and her shoulders slumped. I got the feeling that the sad look on her face wasn't an act.

"The only way you will leave this place is among our ranks. When we turn the corner, you will be offered another way to join our organization—one you will not enjoy."

"Ah, so we're threatening now. That sounds more like it," I shot back.

"I'm not threatening—I'm trying to help you!"

"But you're saying if I don't join up with you, there's going to be trouble around the corner."

She nodded.

"So two demons here versus innumerable around the corner."

She nodded again, and I amassed energy for a devastating right cross. I swung and immediately found myself on the ground. Cat stood above me with her right arm extended casually, the flat of her palm pinning me in place.

"I watched you fight the halfling. You were courageous, creative, and strong. We need you in our ranks, but you are no rival for someone like me—not even with the proper tools."

The pressure of whatever she was doing was enormous, but I managed to get a few words out. "See? You don't even need me."

She released whatever hold she had and offered me a hand—I took it.

"Don't feel bad. There aren't many in the host that are a match for me."

She pulled me up.

"I guess humility isn't one of those things you value," I said, dusting myself off again. Maybe one day I'd learn that I can't get dusty.

"Humility is a nice to have, but again, I value honesty. Just wanted you to know." She raised an eyebrow. "I can train you to take on some level of angels with the right tools, and with the aid of an army, you'll have the ability to overcome by sheer numbers. I want to help you, Jonah, but I need an answer."

I took a moment to think. My instincts told me I could trust Cat. I didn't believe she took me on a stroll to obfuscate the truth. This was her truth, and she made some interesting points. Literature is full of stories of man's creation gone terribly wrong, from *Frankenstein* to the entire *Terminator* series.

Even today, we face a serious ethical dilemma of how far to go with artificial intelligence. We know we can create programs that learn and distribute information orders of magnitude faster than we could ever imagine, and we can connect that technology into our lives—be it through shopping, travel (cars, planes, etc.), running our house, and maybe even our military. What happens when we're finally able to add the ability for that programming to make its own decisions. What will it do?

I understood their fear of us as a creation. I understood the jealousy that stemmed from being supplanted as the former favorite of that Creator. I even understood how our behavior over time reinforced that concern. Moreover, I understood the desire to stop a punishment that lumped good people—or angels—into the same yolk as the bad. The terrible. The unimaginably evil.

Still, even with this new information, with everything I'd read or learned, my experience with Seph, my experience with Masephson, even my experience with Cat informed me of what my choice should be. All the evidence was there.

"I'm sorry, Cat. The answer is no—whatever the consequence."

"No, I'm sorry, Jonah—truly," she said.

Brian Corley

Chapter 34

We stepped through an enormous open maw of a door into a buzz of excited chatter similar to any that would be heard in a full stadium waiting for action—minus the frenetic, over-the-top, adrenaline-pumping beats.

I went to the Superdome in New Orleans once in college, and I would describe the space in front of me as a combination of that and the Roman Colosseum with stalactites instead of steel girders across the ceiling. The arena was lit by a soft yellowish-orange light, as if illuminated by a giant torch rather than the bright-white lights of a football game. Various spirits sat, stood, and hovered just above the seating provided in the stands.

Masephson posed before us in the middle of the arena, decked out in a red top hat and tails befitting a circus ring-master while holding the same walking cane he had with him in front of my house. His eyes sparkled as he watched Cat and I enter the arena.

"And now, for our main event …" He began speaking into the end of the cane with an amplified voice that filled the stadium. "Are you ready, Fight Night?"

The crowd cheered with one voice and applauded.

"I said, are you ready, Fight Night?"

The crowd roared, and competing chants broke out in

different sections around the stadium.

"Well done, well done. Settle now, settle." Masephson milked the moment. "Up first, from Lyon, France, with a record of nine hundred ninety-nine wins and two losses, the fast, the frenzied, the very French—RE-NEE—LA-CA-ZETTE!"

A howl of approval went up through the crowd as a slight, young-looking man burst forth from the opposite side of the stadium with his hands above his head, pointing and shouting into the stands, then staring over and pointing to me. Masephson waved his arms down in a motion to hush the crowd, and they did. "And here, accompanied by [Cat]."

I'm not actually sure what name he used, but my ears chose to hear the name "Cat."

"A local boy made good, from Austin, Texas, recently deceased. No doubt, some of you have heard of him already—the young—the resourceful—the formidable—JO-NAH—PRESTON!" Masephson's hands went wide and above his head as he said my name. He twirled for theatrical effect to the audience at large. The response was loud, although not near the response for Renee Lacazette.

I leaned in and whispered out the side of my mouth to Cat, "What the hell is this?"

"This is the hard way," she responded.

"So I can fight my way out of this?" I asked.

"You'll see," she said.

Masephson left his feet and circled into the air.

"Tonight," he began, "should Monsieur Lacazette secure his thousandth win, he shall be awarded the rank of lieutenant commandant in the esteemed Legion Cinquante Cinquième. Bonne chance a toi, Monsieur Lacazette." Masephson gave a polite nod of the head to Lacazette, and they exchanged words the rest of us could not hear.

"He's very good, Lacazette," Cat said in my ear. "This will be a unique challenge for you, taking on one of the best from the ranks of the unproven. You can beat him, I think, but I'm curious to see how you adapt to his fighting style."

"Unproven?" I winced. "He's basically gone unbeaten for a thousand fights."

"I see," she said. "That still sounds like a lot to you."

"Why didn't you just tell me this was what I would be facing?"

She dismissed me with a wave of her hand. "It is as though you do not know the first rule of this sort of thing."

Did she really just make a Fight Club *reference?*

Masephson calmed the crowd once again and, once he felt he had their attention, began to speak.

"Mr. Preston will be fighting for something else entirely." His face cracked in a sinister grin. "Lower the cage!" he rumbled with glee.

The assembled throng looked up to see a trap door open in the ceiling as two reptilian demons lowered a cage containing George and Ramona.

"You said they would be OK!" I turned on my heel and shouted at Cat.

"They are," she responded flatly. "I tried to stop it. I gave you a chance. We could have avoided this—and still can, if you join my ranks right now."

"Tonight," Masephson boomed, "Jonah Preston will fight for his friends. If he wins, they will continue to dwell with us here. If he loses, they will face a generation of torment within the Pit of Khepri!"

A massive shape—at least eight feet tall, with dark, chiseled features and the head of a scarab beetle—ascended from beneath the floor of the arena with a large staff in his right hand. Khepri raised the staff above his head to a deafening roar.

"Still a no. What happens in the Pit of Khepri?" I leaned in and asked Cat.

"Your friends will be bound and thrown into a pit full of beetles that will burrow in and out of their bodies for the duration of one generation on Earth—about sixty-four years. They will suffer the unending torment and frustration of restrained captivity compounded with the pain of tens of thousands of insects nesting within their bodies."

"Yeesh," I replied. "I thought a generation was like twenty years or something."

"We measure it differently."

"OK. Well, any words of advice for me?"

"Don't let him know you're scared," Cat said. "Don't look overconfident. Trust your instincts."

"Anything else?" I asked.

"Don't lose," she said solemnly then retreated into the shadows of the arena.

Masephson pointed at Lacazette and shouted, "Are you ready?"

Lacazette nodded, rolled his neck, and punched the air.

Masephson then turned to me. "Are you ready?"

I nodded, zeroed in on Renee Lacazette, and tried to put on a neutral mask to disguise my fear and keep from pissing him off by throwing off an arrogant air.

We jogged toward each other in the middle of the ring, circling and sizing each other up. I had about five inches in height on him but knew better than to think that would be an advantage in this type of fight, or on this plane. He got in close enough where he was in my striking distance, but I was still outside his. I jabbed hard with my left, setting myself up for a hard right hook. I connected with my left, but he disappeared by the time I started the motion for my hook. In a fraction of a second, he was gone, and I felt a blow to the back of my head.

I staggered as I felt another blow to the side of my head, then saw him materialize in front of me for an uppercut that landed just underneath my jaw and sent me flying about twenty feet in the air. I felt a blow to my chest and went screaming back down to solid ground.

My head was spinning. My hands reached out to feel for earth like a pilot might use an altimeter. I'd completely lost my bearings. I looked up to see him dancing in front of me with his hands stretched high, playing to the crowd. They loved every second of it.

It took me a few seconds to realize that he was teleporting all around me as he rained down hit after hit.

I could probably do the same thing by blinking around the room like I did between home and downtown.

I had a thought. *Why haven't I tried to blink home?* So I tried—no luck.

I tried to blink to the other side of the ring—success.

The corners of Lacazette's mouth bent down, and he nodded his head as though impressed. He teleported behind me and started throwing me around the half-dome. My energy faded as his repeated blows and throws began to take their toll on me. He could tell and milked the moment. He would grab me by the shoulders and throw me across the ring only to catch me. The crowd started singing a song about Lacazette like we were in a Champions League match.

My mind clicked back to an old multiplayer game Max and I used to play together. There was a weapon called a "sticky bomb" that you would throw at an opponent. If it hit, they would keep on running, sometimes completely unaware, and then blow up a few seconds later. It was always fun to stick an opponent with one as they ran into a cave to meet up with the rest of their team that we were previously unable to target from the outside and take them out for us.

Maybe that was my way out of this. I imagined two sleeves full of sticky bombs running down the length of my arms, from my shoulders to my wrists. It wasn't too long before Lacazette grabbed me to throw again, only this time, I teleported to the top of the half-dome and watched as he tried to shake the sticky bombs from his hands.

They exploded, and pieces of Renee went flying to every

nook and cranny of the arena—either hilarious or a horror show, depending on your point of view. My particular emotion was relief. Masephson appeared at my side and raised my arm in the air as I watched Lacazette's arm inchworm across the gravel-dusted floor toward another piece of his body.

"Your winner—JO-NAH—PRESSSS-TON! Let's hear it for Jonah, folks, a perfect one and oh start. What did I tell ya? This kid is resourceful! Better luck next time, Renee."

Masephson looked down, smiling, and Lacazette began to retake shape as pieces found each other from across the stadium. A few smaller demons appeared to collect the pieces and speed along the reassembly. I could only imagine Lacazette's fate, given the stakes put on ping-pong games.

Masephson looked up at the cage. "You can release George Rodriguez. Let's hear it for George, everyone! George, do you have anything you want to say?"

One of the reptilian demons unlocked the cage and yanked George out by his left leg. George tried to fight him off with no luck, ignoring Masephson and flying back up to hold Ramona through the bars of the cage.

"Nothing, George?" Masephson chided. "OK, well, Jonah—that was an excellent fight. Do you want to know who you're going to face to free Ramona?"

"I was under the impression that was supposed to free them both," I said into the microphone cane.

The audience roared with laughter.

"Isn't he just precious?" Masephson mocked, shooting a fist underneath my chin. "Just great—thank you, Jonah. Why don't you go back to your holding area over there with [Cat]."

He flew to the middle of the dome with a flamboyant twirl. "Now for the second leg of our main event. Are you ready?"

Chapter 35

The crowd erupted with their approval.

"Woof. This next lad, quite a brutal chap. All the way from jolly ol' England." He milked the crowd. "A not-so-jolly heap of former humanity. You know him. You fear him. No qualities to endear him—Monster Nigel Monhollon!"

The crowd responded with tremendous enthusiasm as the embodiment of every warty, troll-like monster entered the arena. A muscles-on-muscles, hulking behemoth emerged, his eyes fully focused on me. No regard for the spirits in the stands, he seemed happy to have the opportunity to fight and was eager to get his hands on me. Masephson motioned for him to float up to talk, but he merely acknowledged his presence then focused back on me. Masephson floated down for a prefight interview.

"Now, Nigel," he started, "you came to us almost two hundred years or so after some grizzly business with your shop, isn't that right …"

Cat emerged next to me as Masephson continued a very one-sided interview. "That was creative, if not anticlimactic," she said, putting a hand on my shoulder.

"Come on, it wasn't that bad. What's the story with this guy?" I asked.

"He obviously augmented his appearance—although

somewhat unintentionally, I think, over time," she replied. "I am surprised Masephson recruited him for this. It will be an excellent test of your ability to adapt your fighting style. He is cruel, loves to fight, and will want to inflict as much damage as possible from the outset. Don't let him get hold of you."

"Any weaknesses?"

"Yes, he's even dumber than he looks."

"OK, anything else?"

"If you get the chance, you may want to play to the crowd on this one. It may benefit you to have them on your side down the road."

The crowd grew restless, and Masephson wrapped things up with Nigel.

"Riveting stuff, Nigel. Nigel Monhollon, everyone." He shot back up to the middle-middle of the arena.

"Mr. Preston, are you ready?"

I nodded.

"Mr. Monhollon, are you ready?"

He nodded.

"Mr. Khepri, is your pit ready?"

Khepri raised his staff above his nodding head, and the crowd went ballistic.

"Let the fight begin!"

Nigel shot toward me with his arms out, ready to grapple. I had a couple choices in front of me—I could fight him heads-up, mano a mano, or I could take a page from my previous opponent. As I watched the massive Nigel Monhollon loom larger and larger as he closed the distance between us, I chose to adopt the latter fighting style.

I blinked behind Nigel, produced an absurdly large hammer, and bashed him over the head with barely a result. I blinked up higher and out of reach and threw the hammer into the stands, letting it dissolve before hitting anyone.

Nigel looked up at me in consternation. Apparently, he wasn't able to play a vertical game. I mentally salivated at the options and started dropping down ghostly firecrackers to annoy him. The crowd loved it—Nigel, not so much.

After a few, he decided to stand still and started taking the tiny explosions in a show of strength. Naturally, I took the opportunity to drop a comically large, cube-shaped black weight on top of him with "1 Ton" hand-painted on its side in white.

It took a few seconds, but Nigel emerged from underneath it, picked it up, and threw it at me. I should have dodged rather than watched, and ended up crushed between it and the ceiling, narrowly missing a limestone stalactite in the process.

Dazed, I fell back to the floor of the arena alongside the weight. Nigel was on me at once with a grip I could not escape. I couldn't blink out. I couldn't move. He held me face-down to the floor with a heavy boot on my back, then grabbed me by the wrists and pulled. I could feel my arms beginning to separate.

Inspiration struck, and I elongated my arms like two cords released. Nigel went flying back with the slack and wound up ass over tea kettle about a hundred feet away. Unfortunately for me, he still had a firm grip on both of my wrists.

The stadium filled with laughter and a couple jeers as I shot up across the arena in the opposite direction of Nigel until I stretched the limit of my elongated limbs, and looked back and down at the grinning maw of Nigel Monhollon.

"Aww, all stretched out little guy?" he asked.

The thought occurred to me that maybe rubber bands had not yet been invented while Nigel was alive, so he must not have ever fallen prey to a friend or sibling tricking him into grabbing for one while they fought him for it only to let it go to sting the hell out of his hand.

Unfortunate, that, as I was now one giant rubber band pulled to its absolute limits. I turned my potential energy into kinetic and screamed back toward Nigel, pulling in my arms as I closed the space between us.

He was driven back and down into the ground as my feet connected satisfyingly with his face. He released my arms, and I was free—free to tumble gracelessly across the floor of the arena. Laughter erupted from the stands as I stood dusting off my pants. I'd figure it out one of these days.

Nigel's feet stuck out of the ground, and I remembered the pain from the altercation in my front yard, the burning of the dirt and rock. Apparently, I was much nimbler than my foe. His feet were moving, but he wasn't making any headway extricating himself from the floor of the stadium.

Masephson hovered over him to see if he could continue, but the crowd started to turn. Sensing their waning interest, his face erupted in a broad smile, and he spoke into his cane microphone.

"Looks like we have a knockout!"

The crowd erupted in a mix of cheers and laughter as Masephson mugged for the audience. "Better luck next time, Nigel, and congratulations, Jonah, on another hard-fought victory. How 'bout this guy, folks?"

Some sparse cheers sprung from the audience along with a smattering of applause. More clean-up demons appeared to try to pry Nigel from the gravel floor. I couldn't imagine a punishment fit for an abomination like that. Maybe customer service.

"Release Ramona Rodriguez, please!" Masephson said.

A reptilian demon kicked open the bottom of the cage and left Ramona floating next to George as the guards ascended through a trap door in the ceiling.

"Congratulations, you two, feel free to take a seat wherever you'd like. Make them feel welcome!"

They floated over to where I retreated at the far side of the arena. Cat was back at my side.

"Now for the twist, I think," she muttered close to my ear.

Ignoring Cat for the moment, I addressed George and Ramona, "You two alright?"

They nodded in sync.

"Thank you, Jonah," George said. "Good job out there."

"What happened? When did they take you?" I asked when they got close enough.

"As soon as you left with her." Ramona glared at Cat.

I turned to Cat, "You said they would be safe."

"They were. The outcome would have been the same. I've told you. I tried to help. It was all I could offer in this scenario."

"That's bullshit, Cat, and you know it."

"Jonah, I'm sorry. I'm trying to help."

"Fine, tell me how to get out of here," I said, hoping I could spark some sort of sympathy from the demon.

"I told you—join me. You and your friends. We need you, Jonah," she said.

And there it was—they needed me. I wasn't getting out of this situation. Why shouldn't I just make the best of it and join a team that needed me, where I could make a difference and potentially save millions more people in the process if we won at the end?

Brian Corley

Chapter 36

Because in the process I would be helping literal and figurative monsters.

"Still a no, Cat," I said.

Masephson rose to the middle-middle of the arena again and addressed the crowd, "Is everyone having a good time tonight?" He reared his head back and spun in midair as he basked in the response from the crowd. "Good! We have one more match for you tonight, folks. I think you're going to just love it. A fight between two rivals—a killer and a thriller!"

He leaned back to an impossible proportion as he basked in the roar of the crowd, then he shot down to Khepri for an impromptu interview.

"Mr. Khepri, tonight has just not been your night, has it?" Masephson asked before pulling an exaggerated frown for the crowd. The crowd showered down boos with a few spirits standing up to give the double thumbs-down as is appropriate on these occasions as well as professional wrestling.

Khepri spoke, "It has been an unsatisfying night, Masephson. I demand you deliver what you promised me."

The crowd went wild with excitement, demanding grist for

Khepri's mill. Masephson smiled wide and calmed the crowd down.

"Calm down now, everyone, calm," Masephson said. "Mr. Khepri, you shall have what was promised. You shall have it."

He floated back up to the middle-middle of the arena and shouted into his microphone-topped cane, "This bout shall satisfy a score and promote a leader to the fore. Tonight's winner shall command this area's army as my general, while the loser shall be Khepri's for a total of one generation.

"One generation bound up as food and shelter for his skittering horde of beetles. Mr. Khepri, does this satisfy you?"

Khepri raised his staff above his head, and the crowd responded with a thunderous chorus of cheers and applause.

Cat grabbed my arm and leaned in with urgency. "Jonah, I can stop this if you join me. Please."

I shook my head no. "I'll figure a way out of this. There's no way I'm fighting for either one of you."

Masephson boomed, "We've marveled at the ingenuity, strength, and stamina of Mr. Preston tonight with one more round to demonstrate his mettle. Have you enjoyed him, folks?"

The crowd actually cheered, so I gave a sheepish wave.

"Good luck to you, Jonah!" He held for an applause break.

"His opponent tonight, another hometown boy, one that pulls no punches. Ruthless, methodical, smart as a whip! No doubt some of you have seen him train. You've seen him fight. Entering the ring with a respectable record of thirty-four and one—MIS-TER—WILL-ARD—HEEEEEENSCH!"

If there were a decibel reader in the stadium, it would have barely registered as Willard Hensch shot into the arena. The crowd was not on his side. He flew straight toward Masephson to grab control of his cane-handled microphone. Masephson allowed it, but feigned shock and surprise.

Willard immediately began speaking with no flair for the dramatic. He wasn't playing to the crowd, but it was clearly a moment he'd been waiting for.

"I've been waiting for this, Jonah," he declared, pointing a finger at me. "For weeks I endured you and your infantile friend as you chattered on incessantly, defacing my home, and treating me with a complete lack of respect. For months, I've witnessed people walking around Austin with *my face* on their shirts in various sorts of compromising positions. I've endured the humiliation as I've seen my visage on posters and screen savers—made a laughing stock—a mockery.

"Tonight, not only will I vanquish you, I will give you ample time to think about your impudence and dwell on your defeat. Tonight, Jonah Preston, we bring our conflict to an end."

Willard handed Masephson back his cane, and he received it with a sickening grin.

"Well said, Mr. Hensch, well said!" he boomed through the mic. "Mr. Preston, anything you would like to say in response?"

I blinked into one of Max's Willard meme T-shirts. The crowd seemed to enjoy it.

"Nicely played, Jonah, nicely played. A man of few words," he responded. "Are you ready, Mr. Hensch?"

Willard's eyebrows knitted together, his face in a sneer. He nodded his head yes.

"Are you ready, Mr. Preston?"

I nodded my head yes.

"Then begin!"

I floated up cautiously to meet Willard. I got the sense

that he may have been holding back the last time we met. Why else would he be so eager to come at me now? We began to circle each other. When I got within twenty feet of him, we were each looking for an opening. Willard shot toward me, and I blinked out of the way and behind him, delivering a blow to the back of his head.

He adapted quickly and blinked away as he responded in kind. Smarting from the hit, I teleported to a far corner of the arena to regroup, but he was right behind me, relentless. I blinked around, in seemingly random patterns around the stadium, with Willard fast behind me, until something wrapped around me and dragged me to the floor of the arena. It took me a moment to realize that I was entangled in a weighted net.

The crowd erupted in cheers as Willard pounced, raining down blow after blow while I was disoriented. I managed to blink my way out of the netting and up toward the ceiling of the stadium, looking down on Willard. His head was on a swivel, and he shrieked as he zeroed in on my location.

"Coward!" he shouted. "Face me!"

Willard's eyes burned, and his face twisted with rage. He shot up toward me, swinging wildly and missed, cursing something undiscernible as he flew by. His anger was short-circuiting his ability to think through a strategy to win.

We circled each other as Willard feinted, then dove for me, connecting with a foot to the side of my head that drove me down toward the ground. He followed fast in pursuit, and I countered with an uppercut that sent him reeling toward Masephson and the stands.

Masephson caught Willard and steadied him while whispering something into his ear. Willard sunk down into the stands without breaking eye contact with me then disappeared into the crowd. I scanned the area, trying to distinguish his face from the many others with no luck.

I felt a solid crack along the back of my head and plummeted to the floor. I'd not felt anything like that before and was completely disoriented. My head pulsed in throbs of pain, and it felt as though my muscles had been replaced by soggy sponges—even though I obviously didn't have muscles as a spirit.

I got another crack to my back as I stood and another to my chest, throwing me back onto the floor of the arena. My incorporeal body screamed in pain, and it took everything I had to push the pain aside and focus on the moment.

I blinked to the upper reaches of the stadium and Willard followed. I blinked above the stands on the opposite side, and he was upon me in moments.

I blinked to the floor, back high, over and around the arena, with Willard in close pursuit. I looked for an opening and tried to get behind him, but he moved just as fast.

He blinked to a position in the middle of the stadium and stirred up the crowd.

They roared with approval.

I blinked behind him, and unfortunately, it was just what he wanted. He outmaneuvered me, and I felt a blow to the back of my head and dropped to the floor of the arena.

It was as though I had a nervous system again and could feel each individual nerve ending cry out in agony. But my nervous system wasn't enough for the torment—it wanted more. It felt like it created more nerves outside my body to grow the pain. It was almost unbearable. *How was he doing this?*

I had to focus or he would have me, and so would Khepri.

I watched Willard descend toward me with victory written across his face, a familiar implement in his hand. He circled me as he brandished a peach sword.

"How is that fair?" I asked.

"Fair? Do you see any carousels around here?" he responded. He smirked as he raised his sword in the air and started playing to the crowd.

Years of watching professional wrestling taught me this was a big mistake, and I had an idea.

I blinked up to what basically looked like a full-frontal body hug with Willard. I imagined teleporting to the far side of the arena with just him, leaving the sword behind.

It worked.

Willard's face went wild with surprise as we watched the sword fall to the ground and almost simultaneously blinked to the exact spot where it landed. Our hands reached the sword at the same time, grasping it in different places, his on the blade, mine on the hilt.

We wrestled each other for control, then Willard tackled me, taking a page from my earlier strategy and teleporting us across the arena. Just like before, we blinked back at almost the exact same time; however, this time I was able to get there a fraction of a second earlier. I snatched the sword and swung before he could blink out of range. My nerves still crackled with electric pain, and I could feel the power in the weapon.

Willard flew hard to the gravelly floor, and I pinned him to the ground with the tip of the sword just like Quinton had done at the house.

The crowd erupted and rose above their seats for a better view of the impending finale. Willard looked up at me with wide, searching eyes, eyes that welled with tears—tears of frustration, tears of rage, tears that retold the story of a misunderstood kid under constant siege from the world around him. A kid that never felt in his element unless he was alone. A kid that had no one. A kid that grew into a man that continued to face the same struggles—the spirit beneath me.

I reached down, gripped his arm, and blinked over to the corner where George and Ramona stood watching.

"It doesn't have to be like this," I panted as I held him down. "We both still have an option out."

"What are you talking about?" he whimpered. "Just take your victory and leave me to my fate."

"We can both take our doors," I offered. "Conscripted to lead Masephson's army is almost as bad as becoming a human beetle farm for me. I'm going to try to open mine here. If yours won't show, just come with me."

"I don't understand," he said. "Why would you help me, after all that I've done?"

"I don't know," I replied. "You're kind of a dick, but I understand where you come from, and I think I know what life will be like for you if you continue on here. I want to help, Willard. I'm taking this way out. Come with me."

I thought back to my conversation with Angela, the first spirit I helped move on, and tried to remember what we were talking about that brought her door back to her. I remembered Seph saying that I gave her hope. I thought back to the life I led, the people I'd known, the people I'd lost—my dad. I thought about seeing him again. I released Willard and helped him up.

An angry chorus of indignation filled the stadium.

A bright rectangle of light appeared on the floor of the

arena, blinding the first few rows of spectators with its sudden appearance. I looked over to see familiar silhouettes waiting to welcome me just on the other side of my door.

Another light erupted inside the arena, and I looked over to see Willard gazing toward his own door. He looked to me with a small smile and a nod.

I nodded in return, and he started floating toward his portal to the next plane.

I shot a look to George and Ramona and waved them over.

"Come on," I said. "This is our only way out."

They looked at each other, steeled themselves, and floated toward me.

"We had to go sometime, Jonah. Now is as good a time as any," George yelled over the chorus of boos and shouts of outrage that began to fill the arena. Ramona hugged him tightly as we hurried toward the other side.

A seven-foot shadow descended to prevent Willard's departure. Masephson stepped forward, taking shape as he moved toward us and away from the light.

"Not so fast, Mr. Hensch. I will not allow you to leave here tonight."

He stretched out large and looming as he took on his grotesque gargoyle form. Darkness, despair, and feelings of hopelessness bore down on Willard and seeped into my consciousness as Masephson stretched his demonic muscles.

"I have plans for you," he said.

"I can't allow you to go either, Jonah," Cat said, stopping us in our tracks with her right hand raised to impede our progress to the door. "We need you here. I'm sorry. I'll help you understand over time."

I exchanged apologetic glances with Willard. All hope was lost.

Chapter 37.

I tried to rally and gave myself a pep talk. I thought through other ways to get us out of the situation. Maybe I could open a door at another time when they locked us up like they did earlier, although I had to admit they probably would learn from this particular tactic. Maybe I could convince them that I was actually on their side to the point that they would allow me the latitude to go off on my own in a couple thousand years—I could do it then. Ah, the long con.

A new light burst forth into the arena from the stands. The crowd in the immediate vicinity flew in different directions as though it were some sort of explosion. It wasn't.

A light arced from the stands onto the floor of the arena. Landing about ten feet away was the face I'd seen for weeks—at the diner, the concert, and the house as I was flying away. Before, I was convinced he worked for Masephson, but now I could see that all along he'd been working for Seph.

In a few more seconds I realized that he was the angel that reached out to me in my dream that night I met Zoe and the Psy-kicks for the first time.

"That's enough, Masephson," he boomed.

We were thrown to the floor and held there as though we were in the depths of the ocean with miles of water pressing down upon us. Masephson squinted and shielded his eyes like someone stepping out of a movie theater in the middle of a sunny day.

"You and [Cat]," he continued, "have exceeded what we allowed in our conference."

"You have no authority here," seethed Masephson. "We will do as we please in our home. Be gone, before you suffer the same fate as Mr. Hensch."

Khepri appeared from below the floor between Masephson and Cat. He pounded his staff on the ground and flexed in a show of strength. The floor rumbled beneath us.

"You are outnumbered, friend," Cat said calmly. "Whatever overreach you think may have occurred can be discussed in counsel at another time. Leave in peace now."

A brighter light than I thought imaginable filled the entire arena as a battle-armored Seph appeared before Cat. Spirits fled in terror, dispersing from the room in a chaotic array, until the three demons were left on their own to face Seph in his angelic form.

"Maseph," she acknowledged.

"Father," Masephson said.

Seph acknowledged them both as well as Khepri.

"I've been informed of a breach of our agreement. I'm here to collect the subjects of our arrangement and take them back to their homes. We will discuss the implications of your betrayal at another time and place." The impact of Seph's angelic voice felt like it was going to rip my mind into little tiny pieces and scatter them into the air.

"We will not—you shall not come into my home and take what is mine," Masephson said.

"Silence, child," Cat interjected in a soothing voice while grabbing him by the arm. "You are no match for his sentry, let alone your father. We have been undone. We must go."

Khepri opened up a passage in the ground and hopped through as Cat pulled Masephson along.

"This isn't over, Father. We will meet again!" he said as he disappeared through the floor.

The light in the arena dimmed as Seph and the other angel resumed their human forms. Seph chuckled as he gave his sentry a pat on the back and then looked over to me.

"Sounds like you had a hell of a night—no pun intended."

I rolled my eyes. "I had them right where I wanted them."

"Oh, I'm sorry. I can probably call them back—" Seph walked as though he were going after them.

"Whoa, whoa—that would just be anticlimactic. We can let them go for now, I guess," I replied.

"Everyone OK?" Seph asked. "George, Ramona—Willard?"

Ramona and George responded with smiles and nods. Willard responded with a cautious, "Yes, thank you."

"Good, good—that's good," Seph replied. "Jonah, have you met [Bob]?" Seph asked, using a name that entered my ears as "Bob."

"Not officially," I said, then sheepishly offered my hand and half-whispered, "Hi, I'm Jonah."

"I know," Bob replied. "I'm [Bob], pleased to officially meet you, Jonah."

Seph continued, "[Bob] was the guy that was supposed to step in the night you were killed, but he got held up by something, didn't you [Bob]? You want to tell Jonah what it was, [Bob]?"

Bob looked to the ground sheepishly. "Not really," he responded.

"OK," Seph replied. "Maybe another time then." He leaned close and whispered, "It's hilarious. Remind me to tell you later."

"Please don't," Bob said.

"I've had [Bob] assigned strictly to you since that night he flubbed Father Chandler's request. He got a little extra juice from his recent requests as well. They didn't even notice him during the confrontation in front of your house. He just flew back with them."

"Shoddy security," Bob deflected.

"Gee, [Bob], it's almost as though you had some extra help," Seph sarcastically reminded him. "Welp," Seph continued, clapping his hands and rubbing them together, "what say we get out of here?"

"Works for me," I replied. "I'm a little over the Morlock chic look of this place."

"It may be a little tricky getting out of here," Seph said. "Stay close though. We'll figure it out."

"What do you mean, 'tricky getting out'? How did you get in?" I asked.

"I could locate where [Bob] was, but now that I'm here, things are a little dicey," Seph replied.

"I think I can help," Willard sheepishly offered. "They gave us these talismans to help us get in and out of this place." Willard produced something that looked like a key from one of the many pockets in his tactical gear kit. "As long as this is on you, you only see the tunnel system that takes you where you want to go. Follow me."

Seph gave me a look as if to ask if we should trust him,

and I gave him a nod in the affirmative. We took off through the door I came in with Cat, through the same tunnel we walked down, into the room where they held us, through a series of tunnels that took us to a dead end.

Willard floated up to the solid limestone wall, and it began to slowly open to the deep, dark void. We entered the chamber and shot straight up as fast as we could and out past I-35, straight up until we stopped about five hundred feet in the air, the Austin skyline beneath us.

Freedom met me like air to desperate lungs. Seph and Bob floated without expression, while George and Ramona held each other, Ramona's face buried in George's chest. Willard looked sad and a little lost.

"What's next for you, Willard?" Seph asked.

"I—I don't know," he said.

"I do," I interjected. "You're going home."

"It's not home for me anymore," he said.

"Not with that attitude it isn't," I replied. "Look, I know you can't step in the same river twice, but that is your home. I'm happy to share it with you. I know we can figure something out."

"I think I would like that," he said with a flat smile.

I'd take that flat smile; it was about as positive an emotion as Willard could produce. Guys like him didn't allow themselves to be happy too often, but maybe I could help. My mind then turned to something else that had been bothering me for the last half hour or so.

"So Seph—Maseph. What was the story back there? He's your kid?" I asked.

Seph shook his head and exhaled like a smoker taking the last drag off their cigarette.

"Yeah, he's my kid."

"I don't know why I never thought about angels having kids before. Is Cat his mother?" I asked.

"Who is Cat?" he asked.

"You know … the hot one … dresses in all black …"

"Oh," he laughed, "no, [Cat] isn't his mother—she's just an old friend. Without going too far into it, there was a time after everyone was cast out of the garden where we may have gotten a little too familiar with some of the people."

"Too familiar? What do you mean?" I asked.

"You really want to know, huh?"

"Seph, I just found out I've been the target of your son since the moment I died. Yes, I want to know."

"OK. Alright. I guess I owe you that much. See, we thought the grand experiment was over, you know, God's pet project? I have a feeling [Cat] talked to you about that, right?"

"Yeah."

"Yeah, I'd probably walk you through the same thing if I were her. So, some of us revealed ourselves to them since we didn't think we were watchers any longer. They were interesting to us, given what they were modeled after, and we wanted to get to know them. Anyway, I fell in love with a woman after a couple hundred years—there wasn't a specific rule against it, mind you. It was considered acceptable behavior. Well, one thing led to another, and the next thing you know she's having a kid.

"Now, it turns out the fallen had been doing the same thing, but for different reasons. They started this race of semi-divine beings that were bigger, faster, and stronger than the rest of the population. Some even had superhuman abilities. Next thing I knew, the hammer came down all at once.

"As punishments were meted out, the other side pointed to me as one who engaged in the same behavior and zeroed in on me for punishment as well. So, I was bound for sixty-four generations and thrown into a dark pit."

"With the beetles?" I asked.

"No, I wish. That would have at least given me something to focus my attention on—pain, the creepy, crawling, chittering sounds. Instead, I was unable to move, and all I had were my thoughts. Sixty-four generations to think about that stupid mistake—or if it was a mistake at all. Sixty-four generations removed from everyone I knew or loved. Separated from the light I didn't know I needed so much until plunged into darkness. At least I can be thankful that life spans tanked after the first few generations of humans. People used to live like a thousand years back then."

"That sounds horrible," Ramona said. "Did you ever get to see your son?"

Seph shifted to look Ramona in the eye. "Not until much later. After a few thousand years, with a little time off for good behavior, I was released and demoted. I spent some time in Northern Africa learning about our new structure and how we watched over people.

"I was taken aback at how far they'd progressed. I couldn't believe how they went from little huts made of grass, mud, and sticks to the buildings I saw before me—the pyramids. It was hard for me to wrap my mind around.

"I was shown spirits that for one reason or another chose to stay on Earth rather than move on to the places of rest that were created for them to stay until the Earth was remade. I was assigned to Scandinavia when my son found me. He started showing up to make requests on behalf of the fallen—quite the public speaker, that kid. I learned that he was among the first, if not the first, to discover that they did not have to move on after they passed. His nature made him quite powerful on this plane, and the other side valued him as an advocate as well as an organizer. He revealed who he was one day during a motion to petition, unveiling his lineage, singling me out in front of my battalion, and adopting the moniker that he uses to this day. He resents me because I was not there for him or his mother and has managed to find me wherever I've been assigned."

"What about Cat?" I asked. "You two were friends?"

"We've known each other a long time—billions of years," he said as he looked off into the night sky. "I don't know that I was surprised when I heard she was part of the group that was exposed. She was always naturally curious, and maybe even skeptical. Still, it's hard to be cut off from someone you know like that."

"How could you have been friends with a demon?" Ramona asked with a look of shock.

Seph took a deep inhale and replied, "Eh, they're not all bad. Some of them just had questions. Don't get me wrong—there are some mean, twisted, dark souls in that number, only made worse by the separation and sentence. That said, they're kind of like Republicans—mostly well-meaning with a handful of real motherfuckers."

Seph was speaking George and Ramona's language, and they nodded in unison. George found the metaphor particularly amusing.

"That's funny, but I wouldn't expect that type of language from an angel," he said.

"Don't tell anyone," Seph said and winked. "Well, it was nice seeing everyone tonight. Let's hope next time we meet it's amid less dire circumstances."

"Wait," I interrupted. "What happens now? Aren't they just going to come after us again?"

"Oh no, thanks for reminding me," Seph replied, snapping his fingers. "No, they successfully petitioned for something I can't share with you, but I'm sure you can figure out for yourselves. They overstepped in a few places tonight but were way out of bounds when they prevented you from moving on. That was the egregious behavior we needed in order to intervene. After what they pulled, they can't influence you directly in any way ever again." He almost laughed. "Big mistake."

"So, that's it then," George said. "We just go back to our normal lives?"

Seph nodded his head. "I might use the word 'routine,' given your current state, but yes."

"Works for me," George replied with a hearty laugh.

"[Bob]," Seph said, "why don't you go ahead and escort George and Ramona, and I'll see these two safely back home."

Ramona floated over and gave me a hug, with George close behind her for another. She looked to Willard and gave him one as well.

"I hope things work out for you, young man," she said. "You let us know if you ever need anything, OK?"

Willard was visibly taken aback and gave them a nod yes. "Thank you," he replied. "I certainly will. Likewise, OK?"

Ramona smiled and put her arm around George as they headed west with Bob back to Hyde Park. We started floating south, taking our time as we admired the view.

"Can I ask you a question, Willard?" Seph asked.

"Yes."

"Why did you open your door back there?"

"What do you mean? I wasn't interested in being food for insects."

"Nah, that's not the only reason, is it?"

"No."

"Come on, you can tell us."

Willard fidgeted with his fingers. "I trusted them. I liked belonging to a group again, but then I saw how quickly they were willing to break their word and toss me away. I decided to face down whatever punishment met me on the other side—at least I would be able to find peace and rest for a few hundred years."

Seph and I chewed on Willard's words and allowed for silence as we floated south.

"I'll tell you what I told Jonah the first time we met— things you do here matter. Your ledger is still open until you choose to move on, so make your time here count."

We floated along Ben White, and Seph remained quiet for a bit before he asked, "What are your plans with this second chance?"

"All I can think about is how hard it is going to be to live in the same house with Jonah and Max again, but I'm going to do my best to be a good roommate. Maybe we could make some house rules to start."

I smiled as his control issues eclipsed his efforts to turn over a new leaf. Oh well, at least he was willing to try.

"Have you given any thought to doing something like George and Ramona are doing in their neighborhood?" Seph asked.

"Like Jonah and his friends?" Willard asked.

"No, they're charging for it, and I'm still on the fence as to whether that's slightly unethical, or entertaining. Look, I just think you might be able to reach some spirits that may not respond to Jonah, George, or Ramona."

"I don't know," he said. "I've never been very good with people."

"I know," Seph responded. "That's alright. Believe it or not, there are a lot of people like you out there. Just consider it, OK?"

"I will," Willard said as though it were a solemn oath.

We were back in the neighborhood before long, and I was more than a little relieved to see the pecan trees over the roof-tops indicating we were almost home. Willard pulled back to a stop about a street away.

"I'm sorry, Jonah. I just want you to know that I am truly sorry for everything. I don't know why I let myself become what I did, continuing to fall prey to every negative feeling that crossed my mind—jealousy, selfishness, rage ... murder. I hate what I've become. I want to be better. I just—I'm sorry."

"Willard," I replied, "I accept your apology." And I meant it.

I accepted the apology of the man who killed me in cold blood. The man that went on to threaten my friends and delivered me into the clutches of a freaking demon army. I was of two minds—I couldn't believe that I was actually accepting his apology, and I thought it would be harder for me to do.

On the other hand, I could let go of a constant source of conflict in my life—routine, whatever we're calling this. Anyway, I preferred to have him as a friend than an enemy. After all, my death may have been the best thing about my life so far.

I was practically a superhero.

I gave Willard a hug. "It's OK," I said, "really."

"Thank you," he replied, and we floated down to the house—our house.

Chapter 38

We hovered over where the front walk used to be, or still was … Willard and I just couldn't see it.

"So, I guess I'll leave you to it," Seph said.

"Wait—one more question before you go," I said.

"Yeah, what's that?" Seph replied.

"Why does your son have an English accent? He's thousands of years old and probably isn't from there."

Seph smiled and shrugged. "I don't know, probably thinks it makes him sound smarter."

"Makes sense, it kinda works," I said.

"Yeah, I guess," he replied.

He smiled and looked away like he didn't want me to see his eyes. I'd been thinking of Masephson as some ancient monster the past few days, and maybe he was, but he was also his son.

Seph turned to Willard and spoke gently, "Remember what we talked about—everything counts. There's a good guy in there, Willard, but there's an asshole in you too. Ignore what I just said—you're a good guy, Willard. Focus on being a good guy. Try to help some people while you can, alright?"

Willard nodded, and Seph clapped him on the shoulder.

"Be good, boys," he said. "I'll see you around."

Seph took off and was out of sight within a fraction of a second. The house was still disguised as a vacant lot with piles of dirt, a dumpster, and two big pieces of equipment, but I knew the pile that marked the front door.

I invited Willard to be the first into the house.

He bounced off the front door, and I felt bad. It was funny, but I felt bad.

"Oh, right," I muttered. "Let's try another way. Follow me."

I took him by the arm and blinked into the house. We could hear Max's one-sided Xbox conversation.

"That's right, Timmy. That's what you get for camping there every damn time! What's that? No. No, it's not weird that I play these games as an adult. It's weird that you're so bad at them. What's that, Timmy? No, your mom is here … yeah, she is … she's dirty, Timmy … she's so dirty."

"Max, why are you always so rough on that kid?" I crackled through the speakers.

"Gotta go, Timmy. Stay in school! What's that? Oh damn, that was a good one. See, you're learning—stay in school. What's that? Yeah, I said stay in school—stay in school, Timmy! I said stay in school! Oh dammit, I see what you did there. Bye!" Max threw off his headset.

"Jonah, thank God!" He stood up and held his arms out wide like he was looking for a hug. I went ahead and mimed a ghostly embrace.

"I'm ghost-hugging you right now," I said.

"This is a ghost hug," Max repeated. "We're having a ghost hug."

Zoe padded in from the other room.

"Did I just hear Jonah?" she asked.

"Yes! He's back. Quinton! Lin!" Max replied and called for the two Psy-kicks.

"Did Max say he was getting a ghost hug?" Zoe asked.

"Yeah, you want one?" I replied.

"Well … *yeah*," she said.

"This is a ghost hug," I crackled through the speakers. "You're getting a ghost hug."

"It's kind of cold," she said. "How are you? Where've you been?"

Quinton and Lin joined us from the kitchen, and I filled them in on what went down over the past few days. Zoe and the Psy-kicks had been staying with Max since I'd left to protect him and to see if I'd come back. Max had come to his wit's end and decided to put the house on the market.

"Max, why are you selling the house?" I asked.

"To clarify—you're asking me why I'm selling the house where my best friend died, came back, and was attacked by a ghost and a demon? Why would I want to leave such a place? Is that your question, Jonah? Huh? Is it?"

"Yes."

"Well, because of all that, *and* I'm making a butt load of money. Time to upgrade," he said, prancing around the room in a weird high-kneed walk with his arms outstretched, palms down. "Meme in my Coffee is straight *killin'* it—no offense, Jonah. The door business has taken off. We're making money hand over fist with the Psy-kicks—everything I touch turns to money!"

"I need to talk to you about the Willard memes, Max," I said and immediately felt an electric shock branch throughout my body. I was still wearing the Willard meme'd shirt I'd blinked into during our battle. I changed into a regular navy T-shirt and prayed Willard wasn't thinking about it. "I need you to stop—please, for me?" I asked.

"Willard memes? Oh yeah, Willard memes are over—no problem. We're diversifying! Politicians as cats doing crazy things? Check. Vultures invading basketball clips whenever someone is fouled hard on a dunk? Check. Clips of football players tripped up by hermit crabs as they fall in an open field? Check.

"We have a new face to the company—Captain Trash. He's a grackle. We just add him onto any hot meme, and boom—gold. People love him. They buy T-shirts, mugs—everything. Oh, and the peach-wood door thing has really taken off too. People love them. We're seeing orders outside the Psykicks business just because they look great. We're trending, Jonah!"

"Good, Max, good," I replied.

"Good? Great! Jonah, I'll probably sell this house the same day I put it on the market for forty percent more than I paid for it. Real estate is insane right now."

"Cool, cool," I said. "Max, I have Willard with me. Say hi, Willard."

"Hi, Max," Willard responded.

"The fuck—you have who now?" Max replied, bewildered. "You brought who into my house?"

"Jonah … why?" Zoe said.

"Easy buddy," I said. "You're starting to sound like the old Willard—or Gollum."

"My precious," he wheezed, "my precious."

It was an old trick. We both loved *The Lord of the Rings* movies, and *The Hobbit* was one of our favorite books. I was always able to distract him with a reference.

"Seriously though, why is Willard here?" Quinton asked.

"Look, I know it probably seems weird, but he and I have been through a lot now, and I invited him back—it was his house too."

"I just want you to know that I'm sorry for everything I did," Willard interjected, crackling through the speakers. "I'll leave if you want me to."

"No, no," Max said, "if Jonah says you're OK, I'll trust him. I'm not going to be here much longer anyway."

Willard looked to me with his eyes wide.

I looked back at him.

"Will you tell him I'm OK?" Willard asked.

Max started to say, "I didn't mean literally—"

"He's OK, Max. Willard is OK," I said.

Willard looked relieved for a moment, then tensed.

"What?" I asked. "What's wrong?"

"I'm worried about who moves in next. What if they're even louder than both of you? What if they're the type to be on trend?"

"What if you actually like them?" Max interjected.

"I have an idea," I said. "Wait here. Max, bond with Willard. Tell him the story about that barista who called you out in front of the entire coffee shop. Oh, and can you take that peach sword down over the front door? Would be nice to come and go that way if we need to."

"Oooh, I want to hear a barista story," said Zoe.

"I love a good public-shaming tale," said Lin.

"I'm going to go … do something else," said Quinton as he walked away, looking at his phone.

Max walked over and reached above the front door to grab

the sword, twirled it in his hand admiring it, then jumped over the back of the couch and fell into a reclined position.

"He doesn't want to hear about that. Will, can I call you Will?"

"No, it's Willard."

"OK, so I was at this coffee shop by campus—"

I blinked over to Tarrytown to pay a visit to my favorite architects. Their front lawn was now a veritable maze of raised steel retaining walls with plantings hanging over. Looked like Jeremy had been busy landscaping. I floated up the front walk, rang the doorbell, and knocked twice for good measure.

"Coming," I heard Jeremy say from behind the door. He opened it wide with a welcoming smile that dropped as soon as he saw it was me. "Oh, hi, Jonah."

"Hi Jeremy," I replied. "Wait, I thought I was the only one that came over."

"You used to be, but word started getting out that we build and remodel, and now we have people showing up here all the time," he replied, then shouted up to the second floor. "Deeds? Jonah's here!" He looked back at me with a flat expression. "What have you been up to? How did everything work out with you and the demon?"

"Oh, I lead Satan's army now, thank you for asking. I've come to collect both your souls." I paused, sizing up Jeremy. "Maybe just DeeDee's."

"Come up to the office," I heard DeeDee yell from upstairs.

"Glad you found a hobby, Jonah. Come back anytime," he said and floated away to his favorite spot on the couch.

I floated up to her office where she sat, dressed in business attire complete with dark-framed glasses, in front of a drafting board.

"Jonah, hi, so good to see you!" she said, floating to meet me with a big ghostly hug. "We were so worried when we didn't hear back from you."

"Jeremy was worried?" I asked.

"I was so worried when I didn't hear back from you." She laughed.

"What's this?" I asked, hinting toward the drafting board that was holding an incomplete design.

"Oh, we started taking on clients," she said. "I told Jeremy that people found us, but I've been spreading the word. It feels good to work, although, it has been taking more time to build again for some reason. I really thought I figured out a process that sped things along—anyway," she waved her hand. "I'm working on a design for a cute couple over on West Campus. What can I do for you?"

"Well, I need your help—again. I wanted to do something with my house."

"Oh, of course, you're probably tired of the deconstruction-meets-piles-of-dirt vibe. What would you like to see?"

"It's not exactly for me …"

I filled her in on everything that had gone on between now and the last time I'd seen her.

"That's so funny that one guy was so interested in taxonomic rank," she said.

"Isn't it though?" I replied.

"Also, you really need to have a talk with Max about what

he says to kids," she added. "Well, let's get Jeremy and head back over to your place."

She grabbed a sketchbook and pen off her desk opposite the drafting board, and we floated back down the stairs to find Jeremy in his regular place on the couch. He looked up as though the very motion was a task of Sisyphean proportion.

"What now?" he said.

"Oh, come on, cheer up. We have work to do."

Jeremy jumped off the couch with the speed of a young sloth assigned the task of cleaning his room. We met in the middle like the world's worst basketball team and put our hands together to blink back to the house.

We returned to Max wrapping up the coffee-shop story—damn, he really made a meal out of that one.

"So, she like broadcasts to the entire place—*selfish Max, selfish Max*—your pretzel is ready."

"Oh my god, you're an idiot," said Lin.

"Ha, dumb," Zoe said.

Willard surprisingly cracked up and couldn't stop laughing. We gave him a few seconds to collect himself before he noticed we were there.

"Willard," I crackled through the speakers as well as clearly through the ghostly plane, "I'd like you to meet DeeDee and Jeremy. DeeDee and Jeremy, this is Willard."

They exchanged pleasantries, and the living among us took that as a cue to head out. They didn't say it, and they wouldn't, but they were all exhausted after the last few days and were probably ready to go home.

"Jonah, so glad you're alright. Willard, watch yourself. We're here a lot," Zoe said as she heaved her oversized canvas bag over her shoulder.

"Bye, Jonah. Bye, Max," Lin said as she opened the door for Zoe. "Quinton! Let's go."

"Bye, y'all," Quinton said on his way out.

"Thanks, everyone, I appreciate it. Be at the dojo first thing, Quinton. We have a shipment coming in," Max said.

"Bye, Max," said Zoe, giving him a hug. "Bye, Jonah."

Max closed the door behind them and locked it.

"Well, I'm off to bed. Hi and bye, DeeDee and Jeremy. Good night, Jonah and Willard. Jonah, let's catch up tomorrow night."

Max received a round of good nights from the group through the speakers, and he waved over his head as he ambled off toward his room.

DeeDee set to work acquainting herself with Willard, asking him about what he liked about the house, things he didn't like, what he could change now that he didn't have to worry about a budget.

Willard's face beamed over the course of the conversation, and he lit up in excited chatter, frantically using his hands to describe his perfect house.

"—and I won't be able to see or hear them, and vice versa?" he finally asked.

"Yes, you will be completely separated," DeeDee confirmed.

"Now about the yard, I was thinking—" Jeremy continued.

Once plans were agreed upon, DeeDee and Jeremy exited the house to work on the exterior, coming back in after an hour or so and asking us to close our eyes while they finished up the living room as the final piece. Both DeeDee and Jeremy remarked at how much faster they were able to work again that night, but I decided to keep quiet.

"OK, Willard, are you ready to see your house?" she asked in a fashion worthy of a show on the home-improvement channel.

Willard and I opened our eyes to a black-and-white-velvet wallpapered, wood-floored Victorian sitting room. Round-framed, curved-glass portraits and photographs hung around the room. A settee and two sitting chairs were placed in a semicircle in the middle facing a lit fireplace. Willard floated around the furniture, running a hand across the upholstery, smiling with his eyes closed. A large clearing opened up on the far side of the room along with a sturdy, steel spiral stair-case. DeeDee took us upstairs, through a wood-lined hallway, and showed us a candle-lit bedroom with lush, deep-red velvet curtains, a four-post bed, and a small writing desk next to another fireplace.

She took us to a reading room that led to a library, which led to another staircase that spiraled up to an observatory complete with a large brass telescope. We floated out of the observatory and down to the street in front of the house to take in the view.

Jeremy had landscaped the front yard in the Victorian style as well with several sections of flower gardens coming together to make one large design. Outside, the house itself was a gorgeous black Victorian masterpiece—macabre, but not creepy, kind of like the house from *The Munsters* or *The Addams Family.*

Willard hugged his arms close and bit down on his bottom lip.

"I love it," he said over and over. "I love it. Thank you so much. I've never had anyone do something like this for me—do anything this nice for me—ever." He turned to me. "Jonah, I promise, I am going to turn things around. I want to help people. I want them to feel like this, or move on. I want to start to make a difference."

"OK," I said. "Good. I'm glad." I awkwardly patted him on the back and gave him a hug. *Damn, I sucked at these types of things.*

"Thank you," he said, choking back ghostly tears as he hugged DeeDee and then Jeremy.

Jeremy hugged him back. *Jeremy hugged him back. What just happened?*

"You know, I've wanted to take on a project like this since my first trip to Disneyland," Jeremy said, then told a long, boring story. He was doing me a huge favor though, so I endured it.

DeeDee explained that she left part of the house unfinished so that I could still communicate with Max and the team and have my old room to sleep in. She told Willard she would come by and finish things up after we moved out, and he agreed that was for the best.

We called it a night, and I blinked DeeDee and Jeremy back home and came back to find Willard on his new settee staring at the fire.

"Good night, Willard," I said.

"Good night, Jonah," he replied.

I floated off to my room and settled onto my bed. I found the remote in the same place I normally kept it and turned on the television to veg out on cartoons until the sun came up.

"You did good, Jonah," I thought to myself. "You did well."

"Can you turn that thing down? I'm trying to have a moment," Willard called out from the other room.

"OK, buddy, OK."

Chapter 39

Willard and I spent the next couple weeks scouring the neighborhood for spirits to help move on, and he even joined the Psy-kicks for a couple jobs. Seph was right. Willard's bedside manner wasn't for everyone, but there was at least one spirit we met that I couldn't reach, and who wouldn't have moved on if not for Willard.

Max and I moved up to the Zilker neighborhood and into a brand-new white Scandinavian farmhouse with a black roof. Maybe not the best choice of roof color for Texas, but the house was a stunner. Inside, the house was stark but well-appointed. Beautiful mesquite floors, white walls, concrete counters in the kitchen and bathrooms along with white subway tile. The toilets were a Japanese model with a heated seat and an auto-bidet system.

"I had those installed myself," Max said, pointing at the toilet as though he'd just invented the breakthrough for faster-than-light travel through space.

"That's amazing, Max," my voice crackled through a softly buzzing speaker system that had been wired into every room in the house. "You're going to have the cleanest butt in the neighborhood—maybe all of Austin."

"Yep, that's the idea," he replied. "Alright then, I have a date. I'm heading out."

"Yeah, I've been meaning to ask you—who have you been seeing? I noticed you and Zoe seem to be getting pretty close."

"Zoe? No. I don't think I'm her type," he said, taking a deep breath, visibly steeling himself for what he was about to say next. "I've been seeing Laura from marketing."

"What?! Noooooooooo! Why? Of all the people in this town, whyyyyy?" I lamented.

"Because she's hot. We talked outside after your funeral, but it took me weeks to track her down after that. Thanks, buddy."

A blood-curdling howl screamed across the night sky outside, followed by an eerie cackle.

"Did you hear that?" I asked Max.

"No, hear what?" he said.

"Probably nothing," I replied, "have fun tonight."

So Max went out on a date with the girl of my dreams, and I went out to track down a nightmare. Not sure which was scarier.

Did you enjoy the book?
Please rate it wherever you
can and tell your friends!

We indie authors need all the
help we can get…

Acknowledgements

I had a lot of fun writing this book, and I couldn't have done it without the help of a lot of great people. Thanks to Jonathan Isaacs for encouraging me to write this story and being brave enough to read it before it ever saw an editor.

Thanks to Michael Rowley, Sharon Honeycutt, Emily Mullen, Crystal Watanabe and Jessica Reed for their guidance and support throughout the process. You were all amazing to work with.

Of course, special thanks to my family and friends for all their help along the way as well, I couldn't have done it without you.

Printed in Great Britain
by Amazon

16506015R00200